G[...]
rage, [...]
attenti[...]
and Distrust and destroying him in turn. Several more
dead guards stood just beyond the gate, and they rushed
to meet him as Gren stomped through. These were of a
kind with the first, and Gren let his anger and his light
wash over them as well.

The first guard to reach him swung his sword at
neck-height, but Gren blocked it, knocked the blade
aside, stabbed his own sword through the creature's
stomach, and then sliced upward, pulling his blade free
as it exited alongside the neck. The creature collapsed, its
torso sliced in twain, and Gren let his anima consume it
as he stepped over the body. The next guard tried a
downward stroke, sword held in both hands, but Gren
simply moved inside the blow. He used his shoulder to
shove the creature back, and then spun and removed its
head with a backhanded blow. The third creature advanced, sword at the ready, but Gren knocked the blade
aside and cut him diagonally across the chest, putting so
much force into the blow that the creature literally fell
apart as it dropped. He didn't give the next guard a
chance to swing, but simply stabbed it and then ripped it
open before getting close enough for the guard's shorter
sword to reach him. Each body disappeared in a white
flash as it dropped, leaving only ashes around him.

Gren continued on toward the palace, sword at the
ready, still letting his rage control him. All thought of
strategy was gone, as was any sense. All he knew was
that he was going to have his revenge, for his friends and
for the people the Sower had killed...

Exalted Fiction
from White Wolf

Current Series

The Trilogy of the Second Age

For all these titles and more, visit
www.white-wolf.com/fiction

THE CARNELIAN FLAME

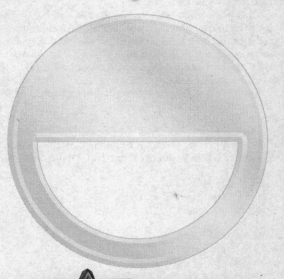

AARON ROSENBERG

ISBN 1-58846-882-8
First Edition: November 2005
Printed in Canada

White Wolf Publishing
1554 Litton Drive
Stone Mountain, GA 30083
www.white-wolf.com/fiction

IT IS THE SECOND AGE OF MAN

Long ago, in the First Age, mortals became Exalted by the Unconquered Sun and the other celestial gods. These demigods were Princes of the Earth and presided over a golden age of unparalleled wonder. But like all utopias, the age ended in tears and bloodshed.

The official histories say that the Solar Exalted went mad and had to be put down lest they destroy all of Creation. Those who had been enlightened rulers became despots and anathema. Some whisper that the Sun-Children were betrayed by the very companions and lieutenants they had loved: the less powerful Exalts who traced their lineage to the Five Elemental Dragons. With that betrayal, the First Age ended and gave way to an era of chaos and warfare, when the civilized world faced invasion by the mad Fair Folk and the devastation of the Great Contagion. This harsh time ended only with the rise of the Scarlet Empress, a powerful Dragon-Blood who fought back all enemies and founded a great empire.

For a time, all was well—at least those who toed the Empress's line.

But times are changing again. The Scarlet Empress has retreated into seclusion. The dark forces of the undead and the Fair Folk are stirring again. And most cataclysmic of all, the Solar Exalted have returned. Across Creation, men and women find themselves imbued with the power of the Unconquered Sun and awaken to memories from a long-ago golden age. The Sun-Children, the Anathema, have been reborn.

Now, those who are Chosen must stand up for the cause of righteousness and find a place for themselves in this time of tumult.

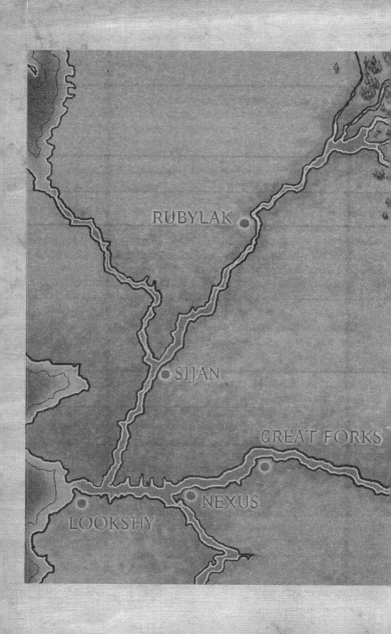

RUBYLAK

SIJAN

GREAT FORKS

NEXUS

LOOKSHY

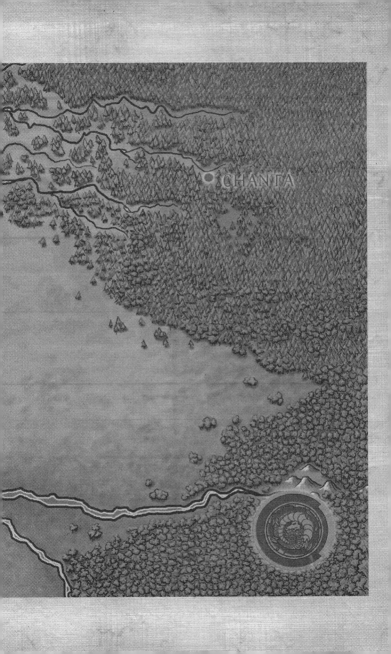

Author's Dedication
For Ellen Witte Rosenberg, who taught me to read.
Thank you, Mom. I wish you could have seen this.

PROLOGUE

Pain. Intense pain. Then darkness, and cold, so cold it stole the breath from his lungs, the heat from his blood, the thoughts from his mind. All that was left to him was the cold, the darkness, and the hatred. That it did not take. If anything, it fanned that flame, until his hatred carried him aloft.

You hate.

The voice shivered through him like a cold wind.

You hate, it said again, and he knew it was waiting for a response. He tried to speak, found that he could not. His lips and tongue would not obey.

You hate, it repeated, but it sounded fainter somehow, as if it were growing bored. And if it left, he suddenly knew, it would take his hatred with it, and he would be left with nothing. Just the cold and the darkness.

Yes, I hate, he thought, willing the words toward the voice. Since hate was the only emotion he had left, he channeled that, using his hatred to fuel his answer. And it heard.

I can help you, it told him. And suddenly there was light and color, as visions exploded in his head. Images of him exacting revenge over and over, in cruel and imaginative ways. Images of him taking what should have been his already, and destroying all those who stood in his way. Images of him, more powerful than he had ever been, so strong that no one could oppose him. And he knew that the voice was offering to make those visions a reality.

What do you want? He demanded. Nothing was free, he knew that well enough. That power would come with a price. And, right now, he was willing to pay it, no matter what it was.

Two things, the voice replied. *Allegiance, first. To me and mine. All that is yours becomes mine.*

Done, he replied immediately. He had nothing left now anyway, other than the hatred, and that was strong enough to share. *What is the second?*

It told him, and he almost laughed, it seemed so petty. *Why not?* he replied.

Give yourself over to me, the voice instructed. And, with only one brief burst of fear and doubt, he did. He let himself drift down into that cold darkness, let his hatred sweep across and through him, and allowed all that he was to bind itself to the voice and its owner. Now and forever.

And when his eyes could see again, and his mouth work, he saw what he had become. And a part of him laughed, while another part screamed.

He and his companion crept across the marshland from one patch of darkness to the next. Before them stood the manse, its tall, ornate doors shut tight. Most would see only a burial mound of unusual size, but his gaze cut through the piled earth to the stepped structure beneath. The high walls were shaped from massive stone blocks carved with suffering faces that almost seemed to shift and moan among the shadows, and the windows were narrow and tall and filled with writhing coils of smoke and fog. The citadel's height, particularly in this morass of low trees and oily plants, gave it a clear view of anyone approaching. He and his companion could only hope that their distraction had worked, and that no eyes were trained in their direction as they ran from the last patch to the carved awning above the door.

The doors were not locked, for no one would dare enter this place unbidden. Yet he and his partner did just that, pushing one of the enormous doors open and sliding past it into the long dark hall. A blast of heat evaporated their sweat in an instant, burning away the air in their lungs, and the breaths they took to replenish their supply were hot and dusty and filled with the smoke of an old fire. Sound echoed, and the faint cries of many children filled every nook and cranny. The floor here was polished black marble, smooth as water and slick as glass, but they had come prepared and their soft-soled boots made no noise as they padded down the corridor. Doors and halls branched off at random intervals, and several times they saw impressive staircases curving downward, but they continued in a straight line, focused entirely upon their objective. They met several of the mistress's creatures along the way, but she was not at home. Their own master had drawn her attention away, and she had left to deal with the matter—and without her there, the intruder's will was enough to control them. He allowed many of them to mill in place, but the more dangerous residents he sent away to other parts of the citadel.

At last he and his companion reached the end of the hall. There was no door, but the hallway opened onto a single square room. It had no windows and no other doors—getting to the rooms beyond it required taking one of the earlier paths around. The walls in this room were the same black marble as the hall's floor, but the floor here was rough black granite. At its center was a great gaping hole, more than eight feet across, ringed by a plain black metal railing. The ceiling was pierced with a matching hole. A simple wooden chair sat in the far corner, and next to it along the wall was a bookcase, which held a collection of large, thick books. Other than that the room had no furnishings.

He paused at the threshold, eyeing the hole. This was a place of great power, perhaps the foremost in this land, and that made it dangerous. The ceiling led to the mistress's throne room, on the highest level of the citadel, and any who visited her there would think that opening at the base of her throne led directly into the well below. Few knew of this chamber—even his master had only speculated that it existed. Now a small portion of the intruder's mind urged him to approach the railing and peer over the edge, but he refused.

He knew what was down there, as much as anyone could, and knew that to glance at it directly was to be lost beyond even his master's power to restore. Instead he skirted it, focusing upon the chair and the bookcase but being sure to keep the hole in view at all times. His companion did the same.

When he reached the bookcase he paused again. It held twelve books, each as large as his torso. The volumes were bound in black leather and clasped with glittering soulsteel. Their covers had no markings, and a thick strap kept each book tightly shut, but he could see that the paper was thick and rich, and still supple despite its age. These tomes seized the intruder's attention, and although his master had not spoken of them, he knew that his master would give much to study any one of them. The intruder's partner, whose skills had seen them safe and undetected this deep into unfriendly territory, voiced his misgivings about so much as touching the tomes, but the intruder paid him little heed. He conceded only that they could not bring *all* of them back, so he selected one volume, the first one in line. With that extemporaneous improvisation accomplished, the intruder clutched his prize then skirted the hole again to retrace their steps back out of the citadel. When she learned of the theft, the castle's mistress would be enraged, and it was best to get as far away as possible, while they still could. On that, both partners agreed.

They fled the building, and after that citadel and that pit, the shadow-shrouded marshes seemed pleasant and airy. Wasting no time, the intruder tied the book to his back and then broke into a steady run, heading toward the nearest border.

They were still running, hours later, when the air suddenly grew thick with insects. The sound of thousands of tiny wings blocked out any other noise, making it difficult to think. And then the insects were upon them, turning the sky black, coating skin and hair, clogging nostril and mouth. His partner raised both hands, gathering his will, then swept them down sharply, the loose fabric of his sleeves swirling and creating a clean space around himself and his partner.

Yet their respite was brief, for *she* came a short time later.

Only the intruder escaped, though not without loss. For reasons the intruder would never know, his partner sacrificed himself on the fool's pyre of honor. When they heard the sound of small feet splashing through the fens behind them, his partner shoved him under the exposed and clawlike roots of a massive tree and tied a cloak of shadows that not even sunlight would have been able to penetrate. The intruder could still see out from within his hiding place, though, and he was forced to watch as *she* caught up to his partner and tortured him beyond salvation or even dignity. When she was done playing, she ended him, taking his head back to her mistress as a trophy.

Nonetheless, the intruder waited two more hours before parting the obscuring veil his partner had laid over him. His partner's remains were still splayed across the ground, and he could do nothing but edge past it. Then he ran again. He kept running several hours after he had crossed the border, trying to outpace those memories.

But finally he stopped. Then he sank to the ground, untied his parcel, and laid it on his lap. For this, his partner had died—this tome and the impulse that had compelled him to steal it. Carefully he spoke the words and the lock sprang open. Darkness surrounded the book as if it were a torch and the darkness its flame, blackness licking around its edges. Resting the back on his right leg, he flipped the cover open and stared at the first page. Dark rolled off it like fog off a river, deepening the shadows around him, yet he could still see the words on the page as if they were glowing faintly. Or perhaps the darkness arose from the words themselves somehow, giving them more shape and clarity by darkening their outlines against the rich creamy paper. The book was written in a language he knew of but did not know beyond a few words. Yet what little he could read made his eyes pop open and his breath catch in his throat. Yes, despite the loss, his master would heap praise eternal on him for taking the initiative to steal this book. Even with just this one tome, his power would be immense.

And, thinking that, the Sower of Decay and Distrust smiled. His master had promised him power and revenge, yet he had stalled time and again. Now that he had obtained this book, his master would finally let him claim those prizes.

But not if he stayed here, so close to the border. He stood again, tied the tome to his back once more, and set off at a quick walk, but not back to his master's domain. He had a different destination, a place he had sworn he would return to and reclaim as his own.

CHAPTER ONE

"Ow."

Grendis Lam squinted, glanced around him, and quickly shut his eyes again. *What have I gotten myself into this time?* he thought. His arms and legs ached. Actually, his entire body ached, except for his head, which was throbbing, and the muscles in his shoulders and thighs, which were burning, and his wrists and ankles, which were rubbed raw. That was to be expected, though, considering that his arms and legs had been pulled taut when someone had tied him to long stakes planted amid the rice. The ground itself was hidden by the ever-present shallow water, and Gren was at least glad that the ropes held him above that surface. Better raw than water-logged, at least for the moment.

Now, what did I do to deserve this? Grendis—Gren even to his friends and associates—asked himself. He tried to ignore the aches and the disorientation that usually came after either hard drinking or a blow to the head and thought back to recent events. Ah yes. Now he remembered.

He and his band, the Scarlet Daggers—referred to by some as the Bloody Knives—had been hired by some would-be king in a backwater kingdom called Ortense. Gren hadn't met the man himself—that was Rangol's job—but had heard the man was an odd sort who'd insisted that he was merely "a sower of decay and distrust" and refused to give his name. More importantly, he had paid his silver dinars up front. This "sower" had wanted them to help him toss out the current king, which they'd done. Not that hard, really. The Daggers were good at fighting—it was the only thing most of them were good at, except perhaps for drinking, cursing, and generally breaking things—and Ortense's army was more used to policing its civilians than stopping an all-out invasion. Pretty soon the old king, Mariburn, was dead, and this Sower was in his place.

Then the Sower had given the Daggers a new job. He'd wanted them to ride out along the outskirts of his kingdom. Though not the largest of the Hundred Kingdoms, Ortense was large enough that its army was divided into local militias apart from the unit tasked with defending the capital. The Daggers had already crushed the capital forces, but many of the local militias remained, and their employer wanted those forces destroyed as well. "Teach them to fear me," he'd apparently told Rangol. "Reap the terror I have sown." Weird words but more cash, so they'd gone.

Most of the encounters were easy enough. What chance did local militia, who had rarely fought against more than small bandit groups, stand against hardened mercenaries? The Daggers would ride into a town, beat on anyone who presented armed resistance, announce that Mariburn was dead and the kingdom of Ortense now belonged to the Sower of Decay and Distrust, and move on. Sometimes they'd pause to loot a little, though these towns didn't have much worth taking—some rice wine, and sometimes a joint of meat or some fresh steamed buns. And then they'd ride back out again.

Gren had to admit, even in his current predicament, that it had been a good few weeks. Some of their jobs had left a nasty taste in his mouth, but one ruler was much the same as another, so he felt no remorse for removing this Mariburn guy. And nobody got hurt much in the towns. Only a few still had their own militia, who were easily defeated, and disarming them was as effective as killing them, since most of these men would never afford a second sword. As for the villages without defenders, it was more about scaring them than killing anybody. At least, that was how Gren saw it. A little mayhem, a few kicks and punches, a little shouting, and that was that. Not all of his cohorts agreed, though.

Letting his head sink back and the ropes take the weight off his shoulders and hips, Gren remembered the last town they'd hit. Hadovas, an old local word meaning "north" because it was the northernmost town in Ortense. Only a little bigger than the others—this one had an actual dirt road through the middle, instead of the usual string of wooden bridges, with not one but two rows of paper-and-wood buildings rising on stilts from the water on either side. Maybe four dozen people in all, most of them rice farmers and fishermen and simple craftsmen. But Hadovas also had a small shrine. It wasn't much to look at—a low pedestal, simply but handsomely carved from some local wood, and the symbol of the Scarlet Empress above it, with flowers and fresh fruits set on a wide earthenware plate at its base. But that was more than they'd seen in any other town so far. And it should have warned them that the people of Hadovas were better organized, and possibly more stubborn, than the peasants they'd terrorized before this…

The Daggers rode into town, shouting and waving their arms. Scamp was swinging his sword, and he demolished a porch column on the first house they passed, bringing the porch crashing down. One rice-papered wall actually separated from the rest of the frame and slid back into the water alongside, the plaited-husk joints unable to absorb the shock of Scamp's blow. Hud waved his bow, though he didn't have an arrow nocked—too valuable to waste on a ride like this. Enjy swung his eagle-headed mace above his head, not hitting anything but an impressive sight nonetheless. Lirat, Milch, and Rangol didn't have weapons out but were rearing their horses, who were lashing out with their front hooves. Gren kept his mount's feet on the ground, and contented himself with shouting and yelling at the top of his lungs.

Then they reached the center of the town. They'd passed a few people already, and Gren had enjoyed their startled looks as they were shoved back by a horse's shoulder or a well-placed kick. One strapping young man was carrying a bucket and swung it at them, but Enjy's mace shattered it without pause and the farmer fell back like he'd been killed. But apparently everyone else was over near the shrine, because that's where the Daggers found them.

Thirty or so people turned to face the Daggers as they rode up, and Gren felt a little prickle at the back of his mind. Fear? Not exactly—many of these peasants were burly, but none of them were armored and most had only walking sticks and clubs for weapons. There were a lot of them, though, and all in one place, and they looked less frightened than surprised, and maybe even annoyed, seeing the Daggers appear. That wasn't usual, and Gren didn't like surprises.

If his buddies felt similar qualms, they didn't show it. They reined in, and Rangol shouted down, "Mariburn is dead! Long live the Sower of Decay and Distrust, King of Ortense!"

And no one moved.

"Didn't you hear him?" Scamp demanded, pointing his sword at one of the men near the front of the group. "You have a new king!"

The man, a town elder, judging from the gray shot through his hair, shrugged. "So what?" he replied. "One king or another, what does it matter? And why should you care?"

Gren, stationed along one side of their group, had to agree. It didn't really make much difference to these folk. And the Daggers sure didn't care. They were just doing their job—which, since none of the villagers looked like soldiers and no one had contested the announcement of a new king, meant scaring them and moving on. He still wasn't sure why the scare was necessary at all. How did it help this Sower to make these simple people afraid of him? But it wasn't his job to think about such things.

"The Sower is paying us to care," Milch replied, walking his horse up so that its chest bumped the man back. "We're here to make sure you obey your new king."

"What's to obey?" another man called out of the crowd. His hair and beard were brown without gray, but the way the others parted for him, Gren could tell he had their respect. "The king sends his men to collect the tithe twice a year, and we pay it. That's all. He leaves us alone otherwise, and we live our lives. As long as this new king does the same, we'll stay loyal."

Scamp had been itching for a fight that day. Gren had known it from first light, when Scamp had tossed his food in Dyson's face and told him it wasn't fit for a cow to eat. Now Scamp's face turned red as his hair as he swiveled to face this second speaker. "You'll stay loyal because you're told to!" he shouted down, gesturing with his sword. "And because otherwise we'll cut you down!"

"There's no need for that," the first man started to say, but he never finished. Scamp swung, and his blade bit into the man's neck, spattering blood on the others nearby. As the man fell, Scamp raised his sword high.

"That's what happens to people who talk back! Shut up and obey, or you die!" Then, to drive his point home even more, he wheeled his horse around and charged the shrine. The people scattered.

In an instant, the horse's hooves had destroyed the pedestal, shattered the plate, sending the flowers and fruit flying. Scamp didn't stop, and the thin, carved walls of the three-sided lean-to behind the pedestal came crashing down. Then he was through it and on the other side, turning just before the low rope fence that marked where the ground fell away into marsh, and charging back through again.

Gren felt the change first. Oddly, the crowd had not reacted much to the death of their neighbor, perhaps because it had been so sudden. He'd heard a few moans as the blood struck, and some sobbing, but no one had moved. But when Scamp ruined the shrine, the crowd stiffened. People's faces hardened, and their fists clenched. And the sobbing changed to a low, sharp murmur. They weren't frightened, they were angry—angry enough to do something about it.

He noticed first, but his friends weren't far behind. They'd all been through enough fights to recognize the warning signs. Scamp's sword was still in his hand, and Enjy had his mace. Hud nocked an arrow to his bow, and Milch and

Dyson lifted axes from their saddlehorns. Lirat and Rangol drew their swords, and Gren did the same. He couldn't blame the villagers for their anger—neither the death nor the desecration had been necessary—but that didn't mean he would let them kill him, either.

"We are the Scarlet Daggers!" Rangol shouted, as if the name alone might stop them. "One of the deadliest fighting units in the world! We never lose, and we never retreat!" Both of which were lies, but of course these villagers didn't know that.

The crowd paused for an instant, and Gren thought the bluff might have worked. Then a man—the same one who had spoken about loyalty—stepped up with a heavy banded club in his hand.

"You ride in here, threaten us, destroy our shrine, and kill our own," he said quietly but clearly, "and then you expect us to let you leave untouched? I don't know what manner of man you've faced before, but you'll not find such people here." And, with no wind-up, he swung his club at Scamp. The thick wooden end struck the soldier square on the wrist with an audible snap, and Scamp dropped his sword with a low cry.

And then the fight truly began.

The Scarlet Daggers were more experienced, of course. They had been in plenty of fights for their lives, while most of these villagers had never faced anything worse than a drunken neighbor or a rabid dog or a starved robber. But there were a lot more villagers than mercenaries, and they were on foot, which meant they could swarm the horses. Each of the Daggers was pulled from his horse and forced to fight on foot, except for Hud, who had been near the back. He wheeled his horse around and started firing arrows into the crowd while keeping a safe distance from their staves and clubs. Rather than risk being overwhelmed, Gren dismounted deliberately, leaping down on one of the larger farmers and knocking him out with a blow from his sword pommel. He shoved his horse back, slapping its rump to send it running, and that gave him enough space to swing, but still he hesitated. Did these people really deserve to die? Uncertain of that, he used the pommel and the flat of the blade instead, administering knockouts and bruises instead of gaping wounds.

From what he could see through the chaos, none of his friends were as squeamish. Scamp had regained his sword and was swinging it with the other hand, making up for the lessened accuracy by using even more force than usual. People were trying to reach him, but they all fell back clutching bleeding stumps or pressing hands against gashed bellies and carved torsos. Dyson and Milch were swinging their axes, shearing through flesh and bone left and right, and Enjy was no less formidable with his mace, whose eagle head was already matted with gore. Dyson and Enjy were only targeting men who swung at them, or were about to, but Scamp wasn't as picky. Neither was Milch.

"That's enough!" Gren shouted, but his comrade-in-arms either didn't hear or pretended he didn't. At first Gren considered leaving it alone—anyone stupid enough not to get out of Milch's way probably deserved whatever came around—but he changed his mind when he glanced at the people near the big man. One of them was a youth, barely more than a boy. The kid had a small sickle but seemed more intent on standing protectively over his even younger sister than on wielding the thing. But that wouldn't stop Milch. Gren threw himself into the crowd, shoving people aside, and lashed out finally—

—and caught the brunt of Milch's axe, just behind the blade itself, on his own sword. The blow sent shivers down his arm, and he had to clench his fist to keep the handle from being jarred loose, but at least he stopped the stroke. The boy and his sister were right beneath it, staring.

"Enough!" Gren insisted, grasping Milch's axe handle with his free hand. "He's just a boy! Leave him alone!" Milch glared at him over the axe, then pulled it away and turned without a word. The boy, meanwhile, grabbed his sister and ran away from the chaos. He left the sickle behind. Gren turned to see how the rest of his friends fared.

Rangol had his back to his horse, stabbing anyone who got too close, and Lirat was carving a path to him, leading his own horse by the reins. Once the two of them were together, Lirat covered Rangol while he remounted, and then Rangol's horse menaced those nearby while Lirat climbed onto his own steed.

"To me!" Rangol shouted, wheeling his horse in a circle. The others made their way toward him and Lirat, Milch and Dyson leading their horses. Scamp's had bolted, Gren had sent his own out of the fray, and Enjy's had been captured by a bold farm boy with a nasty-looking knife clutched in one hand.

"You'll regret this!" Milch shouted as he swung onto his own horse and turned it toward where Hud was covering their retreat. The others formed up around him, Scamp and Enjy jogging in their midst. Gren was on the outer edge, just behind Rangol, and was just pushing a peasant out of the way—

—when, to his immediate right, he saw an older woman. She was just cowering there, hands over her head to avoid getting hit. Thin white hair flowed from under her cap, and her face was lined and tanned from years outdoors. She had her eyes shut tight, and tears were leaking out—

—and then she was on the ground, moaning, as one of Hud's arrows sank into her side.

Gren didn't even stop to think. He swerved away from his friends and dropped to the woman's side. The arrow wasn't in too deep, but it was solidly imbedded—if Hud knew anything, it was how to shoot a bow. A little blood was leaking out around the shaft, red but not too bright or too dark, which was good. The woman had fainted, and that was also good. She wouldn't fight him. Gren grasped the shaft with both hands, took a deep breath, and pulled hard and fast, twisting it as he did so. It came free, leaving a much wider wound and a steady flow of blood, but it didn't spurt. Another good sign. Gren grabbed the woman's cap from her head, wadded it up, and shoved it into the wound. That would staunch it for now, until someone could—

He hadn't noticed the shouts or the footsteps nearby. He did register the sudden pain in the back of his head, and then his vision went dark and he didn't notice anything else for a while.

And now here he was, staked out above the rice paddies. Because he'd stopped to help someone.

Well, he thought to himself, parched lips cracking into a faint smile, *Scamp always said my conscience would be the death of me. Figures he'd have to be right about something someday.*

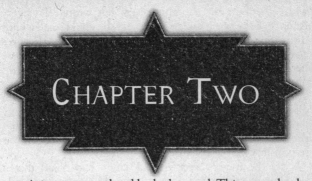

CHAPTER TWO

Arianna stopped and looked around. This seemed to be the place.

The gentle rolling hills she had recently traveled were smoothing out ahead, forming a shallow valley, and the tall, thin grass was giving way to taller, thicker stalks whose bases were hidden in a thin sheen of water. The ground felt softer, spongier, and the air was filled with moisture, glittering in the midday sun. The dirt road she had been following led to a long wooden bridge a few paces ahead of her, and she could see that the bridge ran to a small hillock, barely two paces wide. A second bridge led beyond that, and a third was barely visible among the plants in the distance. She could hear the sound of small wings, and saw several insects flitting among the grass and flowers. A flicker of movement below the first bridge was either a slow-moving fish or a lazy water snake.

It was not an ugly place, on the surface. She had never visited a marsh before, but she'd read about them. Marshes were fertile farmland, particularly for rice paddies, and teemed with life of all sorts. If this valley before her was any indication, she was entering a place full of life and activity and promise.

Then why did it feel so dark? She frowned as she glanced around, shifting the weight of her pack. The sun was high overhead, its light filtering through the trees behind in small patches but flowing openly upon the bridge before her. So why did it feel as if the way at her back was in light and this bridge in shadow? She closed her eyes and studied the land with other senses. Something here felt wrong. The very Essence of the place was sluggish, and she could smell a faint hint of mold beneath the moisture. When she opened her eyes again, Arianna also noticed that somehow the plants before her seemed grayed, as if they had been leached of color. A thin mist rose up from the water, curling about the plants and the bridge supports, its tendrils wafting across the worn wooden planks of the bridge. That was a natural product of such heavy moisture, she knew, but she could not shake the notion that the mist was as much shadow as water vapor, and that it was responsible for the color drain all around.

So the rumors were true. Arianna had heard that a kingdom near here had recently changed hands in a bloody coup. She had been curious what effect such violent political upheaval would have upon the tenor of the place, and particularly upon the Essence in its region. If she were as close to that kingdom as she suspected, this strange gloom might well be the result. And, now that she had marked it, she would have to examine it at its source, and study its progress or dissipation.

Arianna sighed. She had hoped to return to her other studies, now that she had parted ways with Swan—the first Solar Exalt she had ever met—but clearly that was not her fate. At least not yet. The sooner she investigated, the sooner she could find a nice quiet tavern and curl up with a bowl of good stew, a cup of hot tea, and one of her books.

She checked her daggers and her pack, took a deep breath, and stepped onto the first bridge. Instantly she felt a touch of cold, sending goose bumps dancing across her arms and neck, and the colors seemed to fade from her clothing and her pack, though her skin and hair were unaffected. The Unconquered Sun did look after his own.

Refusing to glance back, Arianna began walking, striding along the wooden planks without hesitation. Within a minute, the plants and the fog had swallowed her from view.

CHAPTER THREE

The sun beat down on Gren as he slid in and out of consciousness. At one point his head had sagged down so far that it had brushed the water, and he had a mild sting as the moisture dampened matted hair and blood. That was where they'd knocked him down. Had no one seen why he'd stopped, what he'd done? He'd saved a woman's life! Or had she died anyway?

The heat was intense, and Gren could feel the sweat springing up and then drying away across his heat-reddened skin. They had stripped him to his breeches, of course—no sense wasting a good suit of armor, and boiled man would be tough to clean out. He hoped whoever got his sword would take good care of it. Insects swarmed about him, sampling his exposed flesh, and already he was covered in bites that had begun to itch mercilessly. Not that it would matter soon.

He'd opened his eyes a few times, but the sun stabbed into them, blinding him, so he kept them shut most of the time. His breath was coming in short gasps as the heat burned the thick air from them, and his lips already felt like they'd been cured into hard leather. He'd tried struggling against the ropes, but they were thick and strong, and the knots were solid. His limbs had been pulled taut enough that he couldn't get any leverage anyway. For simple villagers, these people knew how to leave a man helpless.

As the sun rose and the heat grew more intense, Gren lost consciousness more often. When he did force his eyes open, his vision was blurry and random bursts of color swam before him. He was having more trouble breathing, and he could feel his heartbeat faltering. It wasn't unpleasant, though—like having a thick, warm blanket wrapped around you. His whole body tingled, and he didn't even notice the aching anymore.

And then he started to have dreams.

First it was his father, laughing and cursing as he kicked Gren out of the house. "Worthless sod, go sponge off someone else!" he shouted, his boot catching Gren on the side of the head and sending him sprawling in the dirt. "You'll never amount to nothing but trouble, and I don't need more of that! You're nothing to me! Come by here again and I'll cut you down like a beast and toss your entrails to the dogs!" That was less a dream than a memory, exactly as it had happened all those years ago, but it was so vivid, so real, that Gren could almost feel the blood along his face, and the tears in his eyes.

Then he saw Grendis Makan, the mercenary who had taken him in and taught him how to survive and how to fight. "Pathetic little thing, ain't ya?" The grizzled fighter leered, glaring him up and down with his one good eye. "I'll toughen ya up—or you'll die tryin'!" He owed Makan a lot, and had even taken the veteran's name to replace the one his father had stripped from him, but that hadn't stopped him from hating the man for his cruelty, his taunts, or his constant beatings. Yes, Gren had gotten tough, because it had been the only way to survive.

After that were images from fights he'd been in, jobs he'd taken, stints in different groups. Each one felt as real as it had then, and each time the image changed. Gren was surprised to realize he wasn't covered in blood after all, and that his sword wasn't in his hand.

Then he saw Rangol interviewing him for the Scarlet Daggers. "Quiet one, eh?" Rangol said, sitting across from him at the table in the back of that seedy little tavern. "That's fine. You don't have to talk much. I hear you're good with that blade of yours, and that you keep your head and do what you're told. That's what we want. We're not the nicest group, the Scarlet Daggers—some call us the Bloody Knives, and with good reason—but we get the job done, and we keep getting work. Stick with us and you won't go hungry or want for drink." And he tossed a dagger, its blade dipped in crimson, onto the table. After a second, he picked up the dagger and slipped it into his belt, then reached across the table to shake Rangol's hand.

And then, after reliving a few of the Daggers' jobs, seeing himself moving up through their ranks until he had been admitted to the top group, Rangol's own unit, the image had shifted again. Only this time it wasn't anyone Gren knew. Or anyone at all, really.

Instead, he felt the light beating down upon his face, and upon his closed eyelids, take shape somehow. Almost like mist turning to rain, solidifying and gaining a discrete form. But this was still hot enough to burn, and it was still streaming across him.

"Grendis Lam." The voice washed over him in waves, less a sound than the pounding of the heat against his skin.

"Open your eyes, Grendis Lam." Gren forced his eyes open, squinting against the light. The sun was directly overhead, and it felt as if one beam had narrowed to a spear and was jabbing through his eyes and into his skull.

"You have been chosen, Grendis Lam."

"W-what?" His lips were still cracked, and his tongue so swollen Gren wasn't sure he'd really spoken.

"Chosen to resume your rightful place in the world," the voice replied. And, at that proclamation, something deep inside Gren rejoiced—something he'd never known was there until now.

But I have no place, he screamed in his head. *I'm the son of a woodsman, and even he disowned me! I have nothing, no name, no family, just my arm and my sword and my scars.*

"No, Grendis Lam," the voice corrected, and Gren didn't even wonder how it had heard his thoughts. This was a dream, after all. "Your beginnings are lowly in this time and place, but that is not who you truly are. Your lineage stretches to an earlier Age. Your kind was great once and shall be again."

That deep, hidden something in his chest swelled, and Gren felt the urge to laugh, to shout with joy, to weep with gratitude. But why?

"You were rabble, Grendis Lam." The voice was disapproving, its waves striking his chest like blows. "You lived upon the pain of others, doing nothing in return. But that was your youth. You learned discipline and martial skill." And now the waves almost seemed to caress him. "And then you learned scruples."

Again Gren had images appear in his mind, scenes of various jobs with the Scarlet Daggers. Times when he had pulled back from killing someone who begged for mercy. Times when he'd suggested less final methods of getting the job done. Times when he'd stood up to Enjy and Lirat and even Scamp, stopping them from murdering someone out of spite or simple bloodlust.

"Yes." The voice approved of the visions, and his choices, and somehow that made him happy. "You have proven yourself worthy to be reawakened," it continued. "I restore you to your former potency, you who are now Grendis Lam." The voice swelled, its waves stronger but still gentle. "I cast my mark upon you for all to see, so that the world may know you for mine." And the spear of light shifted upward, to his forehead. And stabbed him, carving deep into flesh and bone.

The pain was intense, severe, blinding—if his body had still retained any moisture, Gren would have wept. As it was, he screamed. He might have swooned—he couldn't be sure— as he sagged back against his bonds.

"Now go forth, Grendis Lam. Serve my will, and your own. You are needed here, to right a great wrong and prevent a great evil. Go forth, and know that my blessing is upon you."

And then the voice was gone. And Gren remembered…

He was speaking—no, that wasn't quite right. "Speaking" wasn't forceful enough to match the passion that was pouring out in his words, or the way the phrases and sentences linked with such single-minded intensity. He was preaching.

Yes. He was preaching to the multitudes. His hands were upraised, calling down the blessing of the Unconquered Sun upon them all. And the crowd stood rapt, his words spilling across them like sunlight itself, brightening their hearts and uplifting their souls.

When his words were done, his speech at its end, he lowered his hands again, gripping both sides of the podium before him. Long, tapered fingers curled around the—

Wait, what? Gren tried to stare at his own hands, but couldn't move his head. It was like watching through someone else's eyes, powerless. And that's where he had to be, behind someone else's eyes, because his own fingers were anything but long and tapered. Short, thick, powerful fingers, good for grasping a blade or prying open a stubborn door or, folded into a large fist, pounding sense into a stubborn foe, but not these graceful digits he saw now. This was someone else.

But was it? If so, why had every word of that sermon felt familiar? Why, when he'd raised his hands and the sunlight had streamed between his splayed fingers, had Gren felt such immense satisfaction, such belonging? Why had it felt like that passion and devotion had come from within him?

Now he was turning to speak to the men and women gathered behind him on the dais, his assistants and acolytes. He towered over most of them—and that felt normal, since Gren himself was tall—but something about their posture and his, and the shadow that he cast against them, told him that he was slender, almost skinny. And that wasn't Gren, whose torso was solid and strong like his fingers. He also caught a glimpse, as he turned to talk to one of his senior disciples over his shoulder, of long, ash-blond hair, nothing like Gren's own battle-short crop of prematurely graying black.

Who was this man? And why, if he was so different, did it feel so normal to be within his skin?

He walked back from the outdoor amphitheater with his students, listening to each one's opinion of the sermon and thoughts about its meaning and purpose. Occasionally he answered a question or redirected a comment, and Gren was amazed at the wisdom of this man he had become. With a few well-placed words, he encouraged his disciples to focus on the true meaning of each sentence and thought, praised them for their insight, admonished them for their oversights, and urged them to look deeper and to follow his examples. This man was more than a mere preacher, he was a true priest, a link between the divine and the mundane. He was a man touched by the Unconquered Sun, greatest of the gods, and Gren felt both pride and fear at the notion that he was somehow linked to such a person, even if only in a fever-dream.

Then he was alone, the others having left him at the door to a small chamber. The walls within were simple paneled wood, plain but handsome. The floor was smooth granite. And the ceiling was an open square, and the light of the sun poured down, filling the room to capacity with its brilliance. The sun was almost directly overhead, and Gren felt himself sinking to his knees, face upturned, eyes open and staring straight at the sun itself, its light lancing through into his brain.

And the voice spoke to him, praising him, approving his sermon, and reassuring him that he was one of its favorite servants.

Then it gave him the knowledge he would need to finally weld his followers into a loyal congregation, the information searing into him through the mark burned into his forehead.

And Gren woke with a start, sitting bolt upright, his forehead feeling as if it were on fire.

Gren's mouth opened in a scream and his hands flew to his forehead, trying to massage away the pain. His fingers jerked back at first, hesitant to touch the raw, blistered edges of the wound—

Until he realized that there wasn't one. His forehead was fine, the skin unbroken. And the pain, that burning pain, was receding.

He lowered his hands slowly, taking a deep breath. And then realized that his breathing was back to normal—no more shallowness, no more searing pain, no more stifling heat.

Then Gren realized that he was sitting up. And had raised his hands to his head. And his legs and backside were wet.

And that made him open his eyes.

His vision had cleared. He saw now that it was just past midday, and the sun was no longer right overhead. It was still high in the cloudless sky, and the water that swirled around Gren was still warm to the touch, but it was no longer so hot it steamed. And he no longer felt overheated.

He glanced ahead and saw the tall stakes that had held his legs. Short pieces of rope still hung from the thick wooden stakes, tied through iron loops at the top—they probably used the same stakes to tie up their boats at night, he realized. But the other ends of the ropes, the ones that had been wrapped around his ankles, were—burned? Yes, they looked like they had been burned away, and the edges were still blackened. He glanced behind him, left and right, and saw two more stakes, both with equally damaged remnants of rope. Those had held his wrists. Gren rubbed first one wrist and then the other, gingerly at first, then a bit more forcefully. No pain. Studying each arm in turn, he saw that the skin had not been abraded away, as it had felt earlier. In fact, he didn't even have mild rope-burn. The skin on his wrists, and on his ankles as well, was as undamaged as elsewhere on his body. And none of that was harmed, or even dried out from exposure. A little reddened, perhaps, like he had gotten a lot of sun lately, but otherwise the same as it had been yesterday. Even the bug bites were gone.

Gren stood up slowly, in case the heat had left him dizzy. His feet sank into the sodden ground with a wet squelch, but his head remained clear. He stretched, swinging his arms from side to side, and realized that he felt good. No, not just good. He felt as if he had gotten a solid night's sleep after a hearty meal. He felt fit, strong, and ready.

Perhaps angry villagers should stake me out more often, he thought, then shook it away. No, he had survived the ordeal somehow—he didn't want to acknowledge that strange dream of the talking sun, not just yet—but that didn't change what the villagers had done. They had sentenced him to a slow, ugly, painful death. Without giving him a chance to defend himself. That wasn't right.

Gren grimaced and glanced around. Out here between the towns, one rice paddy looked much like another. But there weren't many trees in this marshy little kingdom, and he recognized the outline of one off in the distance, having seen it while approaching Hadovas. Which meant, judging from its position, that the town was ahead and to his right.

Time to get a few answers, and register my displeasure, Gren thought as he spotted the nearest of the ubiquitous wooden footbridges, and started in that direction. The people of Hadovas were in for an unpleasant surprise.

When he reached the village an hour later, however, it was Gren who got the surprise. He was the only one left who could feel such a thing.

Hadovas was still standing, which was a small surprise in and of itself. Gren had half-expected Rangol and the others to circle back and raze it to the ground. But then, if they had, they'd have found and freed him as well. Either they'd been too scared to return or something had prevented them.

The town looked much as it had before the fight, with minor damage to a few of the buildings along the road and the ruins of the shrine still scattered on the ground. Gren immediately noticed two differences, however.

The first was the tree, standing almost in the center of the road, not far from the shrine itself. Gren was sure it hadn't been there before. Most of the trees he had seen in Ortense were tiny little things, stunted and twisted because their roots could not find much purchase in the soft, soaked ground. But not this one. It was easily the ugliest tree he had ever seen. It was tall, well over three times his height, but so gnarled and twisted that some of its branches trailed the ground. Its bark was dark, black with splotches of gray, and looked somehow oily. Its leaves were long, black, and shriveled, and the ground was darkened as if by grease or soot where they touched the ground. If poison were a fruit, this would be the tree it grew upon, Gren thought, shivering slightly. At least it looked dead, though he wasn't sure what might have killed it. Then again, how such a massive tree could have appeared there so quickly was a mystery of its own.

The second difference Gren noticed was the bodies. Everywhere he looked people were stretched upon the ground or draped over a railing, a post, a chair. He recognized several faces. There was the man who had spoken of loyalty. There was another who had barely avoided losing an arm to Scamp's blade. There—Gren paused and choked back an unexpected sob, there, lying before a surprisingly well-carved wooden stool that she had probably been sitting on, was the old woman he had saved. He could see the bandage on her side, where a little blood had seeped through. She had survived the wound then. But, looking at her now, Gren couldn't help think that she might have been better off if he hadn't stopped to help her.

She was twisted about, her back so arched it was a wonder it hadn't snapped. Her hands were extended, the fingers hooked into claws, and one had dug deep furrows in the wooden railing beside her. Her face was a picture of agony. Mouth open as if to scream, lips pulled back, teeth bared like a wild beast, eyes rolled back, blood drying where it had dripped from her nose and ears. Whatever had killed her, it had been horrible.

Nor was she the only one. Every other body bore a similar grimace of pain and was contorted in a similar agony. Something had struck the entire town at once and killed every man, woman, and child there. Even the animals had not escaped, and though their faces were not normally as expressive, Gren could clearly see that they had suffered as much pain as their masters.

Standing there with the old woman's body at his feet, Gren clenched his hands into fists. No one deserved to die like this. Yes, they had left him staked out in the sun to die, but that was nothing compared to this. That had been cruel but understandable, given the circumstances. This was inhuman.

And many of these people had done nothing to anyone, not even to him and his friends. Who had killed them? Why had their lives ended in such a horrible way?

His insides burned with rage. Dropping to his knees, Gren stretched out his own hands, reaching toward the old woman. He hesitated, as his blood boiled, then reached out again, touching her face even as his own vision went red.

"Rest in peace, old woman. May the Unconquered Sun fill your soul with warmth and guide it to its next place in the Great Cycle." He didn't know where the words came from, but they felt right.

As his hands touched her flesh, Gren felt a small burst of warmth rush down his arm and out through his fingertips. And then he was stumbling backward, as a flare of white light enveloped her.

He could not see her within the glow, and raised his hands to shield his eyes from the heat he felt radiating from her corpse. And then the light faded, and only a small pile of ash remained on the porch before her house.

What just happened? Gren stared at his hands, which showed no signs of heat or flame. *I did that.*

Hesitantly, not sure he wanted to know how, Gren stood and walked toward another body. It was the young man who had shielded his sister from Milch's axe. Again he raised his hands and blessed the victim, and again he laid his hands upon the corpse—

—and again the body was enveloped in an instant of blinding light and burned to ashes.

Gren backed away more slowly this time, knowing somehow that the light would not hurt him. It was beautiful, clean and white, and it gave the pain-wracked corpse back a measure of dignity even as it consumed flesh, blood, and bone. It was a final cleansing.

Gren stopped, and one hand flew up to touch the spot on his forehead again. This time there was something there, less of the flesh than of the spirit, but his fingertips tingled as they traced an odd pattern that he knew was imprinted in his flesh, and his eyes widened as he finally understood.

I am Anathema.

But something inside him corrected that thought instantly, replacing the familiar, fear-laden term with the proper word—one that immediately felt right.

I am Exalted.

And the thoughts continued to flow, adding more detail. Again it felt right, as if he had known this all along.

I am a Solar Exalt of the Zenith Caste.

Even as that hidden part of him gloried in this rediscovery, the rest of Gren shuddered at the concept. An Anathema! The Immaculate Order told of them, and how they had been tyrants and despots who had bargained with demons for their unholy power. The Dragon-Blooded had displaced them, driving them from this world and tearing down their empire. The Realm had risen in its place, ruled by the Scarlet Empress.

But the Anathema—the Exalted—had never fully vanished. And their souls could not be silenced. They returned again and again, reborn, with traces of memories from their previous life and with their powers restored. The Wyld Hunt sought out each newly resurfaced Anathema and executed him or her before the monster could cause a problem. Gren had seen a few Hunts, though he'd never witnessed the battle between the cornered Anathema and the hunters. But he knew that Anathema were considered the worst kind of monster, and that any Realm soldier would attack on sight.

That had been before, though. Before the Scarlet Empress' disappearance. Before the return of the monsters. Now, although the Anathema were still considered an evil, they were not always the most pressing one. And many soldiers of the Hunt had been re-tasked, drawn back to the Blessed Isle to protect its people and serve its dynasts during the struggle for the vacated throne. Which, he supposed, was good for him, or else he'd have them chasing him even now.

He shuddered as he remembered his dreams. The Unconquered Sun, speaking to him. Choosing him. Telling him to awaken. And then those visions of another life, where he had been someone else. It hadn't been someone else now, it had been someone *earlier*. Himself in a previous life. During the First Age. When he had first been a Solar Exalt.

Gren wanted to retch. In a few short hours or days—he wasn't sure how much time had passed since the attack—he had gone from being a reviled but tolerated mercenary to a criminal and a blasphemous abomination. He had lost his friends, his job, even his identity. He looked down at his hands again, then walked over to another corpse, blessed it, and administered that burning touch. Yet the old Gren could not have done that. These bodies would still be here, their pain written on their faces, if not for his touch. The touch of an Exalt. And the visions—his old self had not seemed evil. Gren had been inside his head, and had felt the man's passion and sincerity. He was doing what was best for those people, just as Gren was now doing what these poor villagers needed. How was any of that wrong?

His head was spinning, but Gren forced himself to walk through the entire village, immolating each and every corpse. When it was done and the town was clean, he walked back to the center, righted the old woman's stool, and sank onto it, carefully avoiding the tree that seemed to cast a dark blot upon the village even now. He had planned to confront the villagers and demand to know why they had punished him for showing compassion. Instead he had helped their souls escape the wreck of their bodies, so that they could advance to their next incarnation.

And what would he do now? He had found his armor and his weapons in one of the huts—he could reclaim then and find the rest of the Daggers. They couldn't be too far. But could he really go back to being Grendis Lam, mercenary? He shook his head. Too much had happened, even in such a short time, for him to hurt people for money anymore. He had changed. Then he remembered what the Unconquered Sun had said to him.

"You are needed here, to right a great wrong and prevent a great evil."

Looking around at the little piles of ash on the walkways and porches, then risking a quick glance at that tree, Gren suppressed another shudder. Whatever had done this was definitely wrong, and certainly evil. Was this what he was supposed to correct and prevent? It felt like it. And, even if Exalted were evil themselves, this was something worse. Gren sighed. He had no idea where to start, no idea what he was looking for. He was sure the tree was connected somehow, though whether it was the culprit or another victim he wasn't sure. But at least he had something he needed to do. And he couldn't shake the feeling that he was the only one who could do it.

He sat there a little while longer, not really focusing on anything. Then he heaved himself out of the chair and, still avoiding the remains of the tree, walked toward the hut to retrieve his weapons and armor. He was probably going to need them.

CHAPTER FOUR

Arianna stared about her, clutching her pack's strap so tightly that the leather cut into her hands. She had known something was wrong as soon as she'd spotted the village, but nothing could have prepared her for this!

She tried not to look as she stepped between bodies, working her way over to a rough bench toppled in front of a house. Righting the bench, she sank down onto it. From that vantage, it was easy to see the corpses that littered the town's many wooden walkways, and she quickly squeezed her eyes shut.

What could have caused this? Every villager dead? And all the animals as well? And none of them bore a single mark, beyond the fixed horror of their expressions. This was not the work of bloodthirsty marauders. The damage here, the sheer scale of it, said that sorcery was involved. And sorcery far more potent than anything she possessed.

Leaving her pack upon the bench, Arianna stood and forced herself to look everywhere, study everything. Then she took a deep breath, forcing herself to relax as her mind and eyes focused past the physical. She gazed upon the Essence of the town, and it nauseated her.

Shadows were everywhere. Even though it was still daylight and the sun was strong overhead, she felt as if she had been wrapped in darkness. All around her the Essence oozed rather than flowed, and it had a dark, oily quality to it, like stagnant water mixed with stale blood. Every surface had a thin sheen of the dark Essence, but the bodies were literally coated with it. Death, horror, and fear could alter Essence, she knew, just as joy and life could reclaim it again. Perhaps these villagers' deaths had tainted the town's Essence themselves, but she could not help thinking that something else had begun the process. Their deaths had only made matters worse, here and in the surrounding area as well, because the tainted Essence was leaking past the town limits, corrupting more Essence beyond. The shadows were expanding.

The sight revealed something else as well. A massive, gnarled tree sat near the center of the town, erupting up through the lattice of wood and rope that formed a town square over the water. The tree was twisted and dark, its bark oily to the touch and its leaves a glistening black. An ugly thing, certainly, but nothing more to the mundane view. Yet in her sight, the tree demanded attention. It was limned in shadow, as if it radiated darkness, sucking light away from its surroundings and leaving the town ever dimmer. Somehow the tree was emitting tainted Essence, or else adding to the corruption in the Essence around it.

Arianna approached the tree. It did not resemble any tree she had seen before, and staring at it left her queasy. It could not be natural, with its bark and leaves and those thick knotted roots visible below. And why would anyone plant such a monstrosity, much less in the center of town? The planks and ropes had not been carved away to make room for its trunk, but were jagged and cracked. It was as if the walkway had been intact there, and the tree had burst through it. Surely that, combined with its central location and the tree's clear affinity for the tainted Essence, could not be a coincidence. Somehow, Arianna realized, this tree was more than just involved in whatever had happened here. The tree was its source.

She studied it carefully, memorizing the shape of the leaves and the pattern of its bark, but as she stared at one leaf it began to shrink and to curl in upon itself, the dark striations fading to gray. A quick glance confirmed that all the leaves were the same, and that the trunk was losing its luster as well.

Its light was fading. That strange dark glow surrounding it was dimming. The tree was dying.

"No, it's too soon," she protested, scooping up her pack and rushing to the tree's side. She had hoped to study it and perhaps discern its origins. But once it died, whatever energies it possessed would be lost, and with them any clues they held.

The tree curled in on itself even more. Its leaves began dropping in great fluttering crowds. Its bark turned grayer and began to flake off. Its roots disappeared from view, as if they were melting into the water below.

"Who did this?" she demanded of the dying tree, wishing she had some way to make it answer. "What happened here? What made you? I have to know!" Watching it, Arianna was sure that it had never been meant to survive. It had served its purpose, destroying the inhabitants, and then had faded back into the shadows that had spawned it. Which unfortunately also meant that it took any clues with it, leaving only dead wood and shriveled leaves behind.

She waited another two hours, to make sure the bodies were grouped together and arranged properly and in case the tree managed to recover somehow. Then she left the village's inhabitants burning on the pyre she had constructed from one of the larger houses. She had cut the ropes that held the walkways to it, so that it could burn without endangering the other buildings. Perhaps someone would want to live here, to breathe life into this place again. She could not imagine settling amid such shadows, but this was not her land, and she could see the taint more clearly than most.

Where should I go now? Arianna wondered. She had to know what had created that tree, and why. In gathering the bodies she had also studied the town itself. It was a strange place, with the shallow water flowing beneath it and the rice paddies on all sides and the buildings all on stilts, but perhaps that was the way of towns here amid the marshlands. Certainly the homes had been solidly constructed, but they were small and made from simple materials, vines, and bamboo and woven mats. It was hard to imagine this place had been a threat to anyone, or had held something that someone else had wanted that badly. Nor was it in a key location, unless the rice paddies hid something she had not noticed. Judging from their clothes, the people were simple as well, not starving but with few luxuries. Who had wanted them dead?

Arianna glanced around, shouldered her pack, and set off down the long footbridge, which would no doubt lead her to the next town. Perhaps someone there could tell her what had made this town a target. Or at least suggest someone else she could speak with. In the meantime, she focused upon the walk itself, the walking stick she clenched in one hand, the new book she had bought a few weeks ago and tucked into her pack. Anything but the twisted, anguished bodies she had laid on the pyre, or the deathly silence that had permeated the town, leaving her cold and tired and very much in need of live company.

CHAPTER FIVE

Gren reached the next town a week later. It had been a long, boring week. He'd seen no one on the interlocking footbridges that passed for a road, no one working the rice paddies that dominated this countryside, no one paddling down the shallow streams that flowed alongside. As the days passed, he worried that perhaps whatever had struck the people of Hadovas had hit everyone in Ortense. What if more of those odd black trees had appeared, marking each town as an open grave? What if he was the last man left alive in this little kingdom? But birds flew overhead from time to time, and he managed to trap frogs and fish (and once even a small crane) for supper, so at least *something* had survived.

Gren wasn't used to the solitude, which surprised him. He'd always thought of himself as a loner, but the week of walking taught him that that independence had faded away since he'd joined the Daggers. Now he found himself getting up in the morning and sighing when he realized there would be none of Milch's awful jokes, none of Lirat's repetitive stories, none of Rangol's overly involved schemes for making them all rich. None of the morning chatter he'd told himself he hated but now missed desperately. Somewhere along the line he had become a pack animal, and now that his pack was gone he felt like one of his arms had been hacked off.

The other problem with being alone was that it gave him time to think. As he walked, Gren found himself thinking about his life, about recent events, and about the one thing he really didn't want to think about—that moment when the Unconquered Sun had spoken to him and changed his life forever. Yes, if it hadn't reached out to him he would probably be dead by now. He realized that. The sun would have baked him instead of blessing him, and by this point even the insects would have finished picking at him, leaving nothing but the bones and a few scraps of cloth. And yes, what he'd done back in the village had been a good thing. Whatever had killed those people—Gren had an idea, but didn't even want to consider the possibility of it yet—leaving those bodies there was inviting disease to spread. The clean flame was fast, simple, and gave those poor villagers a little of their dignity back. And he couldn't have done that without the sun's blessing, either.

But all that did was prove to him that he wasn't the same man he'd been. And being alone after so much time with a tight group didn't help. Whenever Gren remembered anything from the past two years, he saw himself with the rest of the Daggers, smiling at something one of them had said, or shaking his head at what they'd done, or lending a hand to keep one of them from getting his fool head split open. But always it was with the group. That was who Grendis Lam had been, a quiet, solid man who looked after his friends. Who was this new man who walked the outskirts of a disease-ridden kingdom on his own, with only his armor and his weapons, and the deadly touch of his hand? Who was this Exalt?

At one point Gren studied himself in the water. He looked for signs of the change, but saw the same face looking back that he'd always seen. Square jaw, broken nose, deep-set eyes, a bit too much stubble on the cheeks, a little too much gray at the temples, a few too many lines around the mouth and on the forehead. He rubbed at the lines, frowning, wondering if that strange mark was somehow hidden beneath them. But if it was, it stayed hidden. Nothing about his features showed what he'd done in Hadovas. The changes were all tucked away where no one else could see them. But he knew they were there.

When he finally reached the next town, Gren was more than ready to stop thinking. And so, when he noticed that there were people walking about or herding oxen or cleaning fish, he didn't go straight up to the nearest one. Instead he glanced around, found what he was looking for, and practically sprinted toward it.

Thinking about it later, Gren admitted that it wasn't the first time entering a bar had gotten him in trouble. Strange that an establishment he liked so much should cause him so much grief. And yet he always went back, sometimes as eagerly as now, when he flung the bamboo-and-rice-paper door open with such force that it slammed against the wall, drawing the attention of everyone within.

"Well, look who it is." Everyone else had stopped talking when the door struck, so the voice floated easily across the room. "Is it a ghost, or is it real?"

"If it's a ghost, what's it doing here?" A second voice replied. "Ghosts don't drink, do they?"

"Maybe he wants the ghost of a drink," another voice offered. A loud slurping sound followed.

Laughter followed, and Gren joined in, more out of relief than real amusement. Seeing that everything was all right, the rest of the bar's occupants turned back to their drinks and conversations as he made his way toward the group clustered around a large table in the back corner.

"C'mere, you dog! What the hell?" Enjy was the first to kick his chair back, and met Gren while he was still a table or two away. The big man grabbed him in a rough hug, then shook him like a small animal. "Where the hell have you been? We thought you'd run off during the fight! Kept figuring we'd wake up and there you'd be, chewing us out for leaving so sloppy, but you never were."

"Almost was," Gren admitted, letting Enjy drag him the rest of the way to the table. For a minute it was quiet except for the hugs and the handclasps and the friendly slaps and punches. Even Milch muttered something like "about time," and Scamp almost smiled. Rangol had slipped away after a quick but sincere handshake, but now he handed Gren an earthenware cup of the region's excellent rice wine and slid a stool toward him, taking the one next to it for himself.

"Thanks." Gren downed it in one long swallow, to appreciative chuckles from the others. "I needed that!"

"Where did you go?" Rangol asked softly, sliding another drink his way. "What happened?"

"I got caught," Gren admitted, shaking his head. It all seemed like a bad dream now. Maybe it was. Maybe he'd been hit on the head and wandered for a day or two, and just imagined the rest. But that didn't explain how clearly he remembered it, and he could still feel that voice washing over him, and the energy that had coursed through him when he'd ignited those bodies.

"Hud shot an old woman," he explained, laughing with the others when Lirat cuffed the archer's head. "I stopped to pull the arrow out—"

"Fool," Scamp muttered with a scowl. "Why bother?" Gren noticed the heavy bandages wrapped around his sword hand and wrist, but didn't say so. It wasn't the first time Scamp's mouth had gotten him hurt, and probably wouldn't be the last. It was the first time in a long while, though, that it hadn't been Gren doing the bandaging, and he was a little annoyed to notice that whoever had done it did an excellent job.

"Cares more for nameless peasants than for us," Milch agreed quietly, but not so quietly that Gren couldn't hear him. And judging by the glare that accompanied the statement, Milch had wanted him to hear.

"Then someone smacked me with a club," Gren continued, ignoring their comments. "When I woke up—" he hesitated. What should he say? He couldn't tell them the truth—that he'd been staked out but freed by the Unconquered Sun itself. They'd never understand. Not that he did himself. "I was tied up in a hut, but not well," he said finally. "They must have thought I was half-dead, and nobody was watching me. I managed to get my hands loose and snuck out."

"You always did have a hard head," Hud commented, laughing. "Looks like it came in handy for once."

"Your horse is fine, by the way," Rangol told him. "She's with Dyson, but I'm sure he'll be back soon."

Gren nodded. He'd been a little worried about his horse, actually, but he'd hoped the band had caught her on their way out, rather than leaving her to the villagers. Apparently he'd been right. And now that Rangol mentioned it, he realized that Dyson wasn't with them in the bar. He started to ask where he was, but Enjy handed him another full cup, and it seemed rude not to drink it right away.

The next few hours blurred a bit around the edges as Gren's friends kept handing him drinks. At one point he realized that they weren't paying for the jugs of rice wine so much as scaring them out of the barkeep, but as Scamp always said, "If he'd wanted us to pay for them, he'd have hired bully-boys to keep us in line." The others asked him to repeat the story of his capture and escape several times, and each time Gren pulled himself together enough to stick to the same simple lie, but the details grew more exaggerated with each rendition. The others laughed and grinned and insulted him, each other, and anyone else within earshot, and they all had an excellent time—

—until the doors to the bar flew open again, and a minute later Dyson was standing over them.

"Dyson!" By this time Gren was feeling very good indeed, and he reached out to slap the other man on the back but missed and hit the table instead. "I'm back!"

"That you are," Dyson agreed. Enjy was up fetching a fresh jug, and Dyson sank onto the empty stool, his eyes never leaving Gren's face. "I thought you were meat for sure. "

"They thought he was dead!" Hud shouted across the table. "Left him in one of the huts, all on his lonesome! "

"Did they now?" Dyson smiled, but it didn't reach his eyes, and they were still fixed on Gren even as he took the cup Lirat slid toward him. "In a hut, hmm? Not out in the rice fields? "

Gren stared at him. How did Dyson know that? The others were glancing between them as well, and Gren forced himself to shrug, though his happy haze was quickly fading. "Yeah, they put me in the fields first. Then in a hut."

"Wait," Hud said. "You didn't say nothing 'bout a field."

Gren waved it off. "After they knocked me out, they hung me in the fields like a damn war banner. I was still dazed. I passed out, and when I came to... you know..."

"Why did they cut you down?" Dyson asked him, downing his drink between words. "Why not leave you there?"

"Dunno," Gren told him. "Probably thought I was dead by then. Or maybe they had something else planned next."

"You were passed out when they cut you loose?" Dyson leaned forward, studying his wrists. "I don't see any rope burns."

"It's been a week," Gren said, rubbing his wrists self-consciously.

"So you don't know how they removed the ropes?"

"No, I didn't see it. Must have cut through them."

"That would make sense," Dyson agreed. "Cutting them. Instead of doing something like this." His right hand jerked forward, and something fell to the table. Something short, thick, and scratchy.

Gren looked down and realized that the object was a piece of stout rope. One end had been cut through, probably with Dyson's dagger. The other end was burned away, and suddenly Gren knew exactly which rope it was.

"Whass this?" Enjy demanded, picking up the rope and waving it in Dyson's face. "Rope? So what? Gren's back!"

"I know, Enjy," Dyson replied calmly. "I can see him. I want to know how." His axe was still in his other hand, the flat of its blade resting across his lap, and now he hefted it and slammed it onto the table, hacking a deep gash into the sturdy wood. "And I want to know now."

"What's wrong, Dyson?" Rangol didn't sound drunk, but then he rarely did. And Gren realized with a start that their leader had also been watching him all evening.

"I went back to see if I could find you, Gren," Dyson began, standing up, lifting his axe again, and smacking it against his free hand while he talked. "Took your horse. I found this," Dyson gestured toward the rope with his axe. "This was attached to a stake a little ways outside the village. And three more like it. All of them burned away." He glared at Gren, and this time Rangol glared a little with him.

"Gren?" Rangol asked softly. "Want to tell us again how you got loose?"

"Yeah," Scamp added, leaning forward. He was definitely drunk, but unfortunately with Scamp that only meant he was more belligerent. "You ain't Dragon-Blooded now, are you?"

"I told you," Gren insisted. "I just got loose and got away."

"Got away how?" Dyson demanded. He scooped up the rope. "You didn't cut through this, and you wouldn't have had a hand free anyway. This has been burned away! What are you hiding?"

"Nothing," Gren fumbled. "One of the villagers must have—"

"That's another thing," Dyson snapped. "The villagers are dead."

"What?" Even Hud, who'd been lolling in his chair, sat forward. "Dead? How many?"

"All of them," Dyson replied grimly. "Everyone."

"Finally flying our true colors, eh? " Milch muttered. Gren ignored him, and so did the others. They all knew he was a mean drunk.

"Heh!" Scamp slammed his uninjured fist down on the table. "Good for you! Guess being staked got rid of that squeamishness, eh? Don't know that I would've killed *every-body*, myself, but most of those bastards sure deserved to be carved up."

"They weren't carved, Scamp," Dyson told him, and now Gren could feel a chill growing inside him. He wished he could stop Dyson's words from emerging, but there was no way, and he simply watched his friend's mouth as he continued, "They were all burned to ash."

Now all of the Daggers were paying attention. To Dyson's words, and to Gren.

"What's that about, Gren?" Rangol was as quiet as ever, but Gren could hear the disapproval in his voice—and the disappointment. And that, surprisingly, pissed him off. Who was Rangol to disapprove? They'd left him behind!

"You want to know what really happened?" Gren demanded, letting the warm rush of anger accentuate the fuzzy glow of the rice wine. "You really want to know?" He pulled himself to his feet, partially to get Dyson's axe away from his head, and stepped back so he could glower at all of them at once. "Fine, I'll tell you what really happened.

"I stopped to help that old woman," he announced, leaning forward to rest his hands flat on the table. "They clubbed me down like a dog. I woke up staked out and left to die. Left to die because you'd all run away! And I would have died, too, but the Unconquered Sun gave me strength." He straightened up again. "That's right! The Sun himself spoke to me! He gave me strength, burned through my bonds. I don't know what killed the villagers, but I burned them. I couldn't leave their twisted bodies lying around! And then I came here, wanting to find out what happened. Hoping to find all of my friends, who had run off and left me there!"

Those same friends were staring at him now, with looks that ranged from horror to disbelief to anger. *Oh boy*, Gren thought, watching them. *What the hell did I just do? I just admitted—no, bragged about—being Anathema! To hardened mercenaries! Even if they don't believe me and decide I'm a monster...* He half-expected Rangol to tell the others to disarm him, or kill him, or both. But once again it was Dyson who spoke.

"How did you get here, Gren? That's another thing. I had your horse."

"I walked," Gren replied, but Dyson shook his head.

"You couldn't have. It took me three days to get here. Even if you'd set out after the fight, it would have taken you three times that to get here on foot. No one can cover that much distance that fast."

"Well, I did," Gren insisted, letting his anger hold him up. "What other choice did I have? My horse was gone— and so were my friends." He glared at each of them in turn. "You all started this mess, and then you left me to deal with it. As usual."

"What's that supposed to mean?" Milch demanded. "We started it?"

"If you hadn't gone on a rampage, those villagers wouldn't have fought back," Gren snapped back. "I wouldn't have gotten knocked out. And none of this would have happened!"

"You weren't arguing when we rode in there!" Scamp shouted at him. "I didn't see you telling us to quiet down!"

"Because you wouldn't have listened!" Gren shouted back. The anger was burning hotter now, and he felt his blood boiling through him. He raised an unsteady hand to point accusingly at Scamp, and noticed vaguely that his skin almost seemed to glow with the heat of his rage. "You never listen! All you do is beat on things, and break things, and destroy things!" Now he was shaking almost entirely with rage, and he shoved back from the table. "You kill innocent people! " He glared at Milch again, who glared right back. "You kill helpless children—or you would have, if I hadn't stopped you! You're out of control!" Even his vision was hot, and this dark back corner of the barroom seemed to grow brighter. "The Unconquered Sun sent me back to right a wrong," he announced loudly. "I thought it was the village, but maybe I was wrong. Maybe it was you!"

The others were still staring, and Gren could tell that they thought he was crazed. That only made it worse. If they thought he was mad, they would discount what he had said, downplay their own guilt, ignore their own crimes. He couldn't stand to see that happen.

"You don't believe me?" he shouted at them, taking a step forward. "The Unconquered Sun chose me and marked me as his own. I'll prove it!" And with a control he hadn't realized he possessed, he concentrated on the mark he had felt burned into his forehead. Suddenly the bar brightened, and his friends' shadows filled the walls behind them as his forehead burst into light again. This time it did not burn, or feel unpleasant—instead he felt a warm rush across his forehead, and his energy flared with the light. Even through the wine's effects, he could see about him with extraordinary clarity. Every nuance of his friends' expressions, every hint of the horror they felt, was plain to see.

Surprisingly, it was Hud who reacted first. Though still drunk, he stood up, not grabbing for the unstrung bow and quiver behind him but for the scarlet dagger at his belt. Drawing the blade, Hud leapt over the table, the dagger poised to imbed itself in the top of Gren's head. "Demon!" Hud cried as he leapt.

But Gren saw the attack as if it were slowed. With one hand he snatched the latest jug from the table and tossed it up and forward, spinning beneath it even as it left his hand. Hud's dagger sliced downward—right into the open mouth of the wine jug, which trapped his blade. And then Gren's other hand found the airborne archer's stomach, adding new momentum and turning his leap into a toss that sent him smashing into the bar six feet away.

"How dare you!" Gren was furious at this betrayal, and the light from his forehead flared with his anger. The room grew bright as the day outside, and people at other tables fell from their seat, stunned by the waves of light rolling off him. He could see his friends perfectly now, their faces and features lit in the glow. Dyson was standing a few paces away, axe half-raised to strike. Rangol was behind him, one hand on his sword hilt and one on his chair. Milch was on the other side of the table, axe in hand but still at his side. Same with Enjy and his mace. And Scamp—Scamp was trying to stomp through the table, his sword in hand.

"Draw your blade!" Scamp was shouting at him. "Draw it, or I'll cut you down like you are!"

"No." His anger had cooled, turned cold and hard, and Gren didn't need to shout anymore. "I won't draw it." Then he smiled, and he knew it wasn't a pleasant smile. "I don't need my sword to deal with the likes of you."

That enraged Scamp, as he'd known it would, and his former ally swung at him, putting all his considerable strength in the swing. His sword curved around in a deadly arc, its blade gleaming in the light—

—and Gren spun into the blow, stepping inside Scamp's reach so that his shoulder brushed against Scamp's upper arm, shoving it and the blade back and stealing some of his momentum. Gren shoved Scamp with both hands, his open palms connecting with stomach and chest, then spun back the other way. As Gren moved, his own cupped hand lashed up and out, catching Scamp's sword just below the guard. Gren continued to move away, his hand exerting heavy pressure on the sword guard, and stripped the sword right out of Scamp's grip. He stopped spinning then, just beyond Scamp's reach, tossed the sword forward over his shoulder, caught it properly in his other hand, and then tossed it back over his other shoulder. He barely noticed the thud as it smacked point-down into another table.

Scamp was beyond words now, and he jumped at Gren, hands outstretched to throttle him. Gren slapped the hands down, and then struck Scamp across the face with his own open palm. Scamp reeled back and collapsed across the table, an angry welt already forming where Gren had touched him.

Dyson swung then, but Gren side-stepped the axe. It imbedded itself in the table behind them, and Gren tugged it free with one hand while his other grabbed Dyson's shirt collar. Then he tossed the axe aside, and its owner after it. Dyson collided with Enjy, and the two of them dropped to the floor, groaning but already unconscious.

Hud had recovered from his collision with the bar and made his way back to the far corner. He had his bow in his hands, and was almost finished stringing it, an arrow already clutched between his teeth. Gren leaned across the table and snatched the arrow free, slashing it downward before flinging it aside. The sharp arrowhead cut cleanly through the bow-string, which gave with a loud twang. Hud hadn't expected that, and when the taut bow sprang upright he lost his grip on it. Gren slapped the bow to one side, and it struck Lirat's jaw, knocking him out. Lirat's sword had been raised to strike, and now it fell from his limp hand—Gren lashed out with one foot, kicking the sword as it dropped, and sending it full force into Hud, slamming him back against the wall. His head collided with the corner, striking solid bamboo instead of thin rice paper, and he slid to the ground, unconscious.

Gren turned, and there was Rangol.

"Come on," Gren snarled. "Don't you want a piece of me, too? Look, I'm a demon, like Hud said!" He gestured toward his forehead, and the light from the mark there blazed even brighter.

But Rangol left his sword in its scabbard. "I won't draw my blade against a friend," he said quietly, and that hurt more than any of the others' attacks. "And Grendis Lam is still a friend, no matter what has happened to him. Still the same man I could always count on to back me up, and to watch my back, and to keep Scamp from getting too crazy." Rangol took a step closer, both hands at his sides still. "I don't know how this happened to you, Gren. But I know you're still in there. I know you're angry at us. And you're right, we should have stayed. But I don't think you'll kill us. You're not like that— at least, my friend Gren isn't. Not even when he's drunk."

Rangol stepped closer still, and looked Gren straight in the eye. And Gren felt the anger begin to wash away, as if he had been splashed with cold water.

"You'd better go," Rangol told him softly. He raised one hand toward Gren's forehead, and seemed to trace something there, though without touching him. "Watch your back, Gren. And be careful. What just happened, the Wyld Hunt will be here soon. You'd best be gone when they arrive."

The Wyld Hunt! The name shot through Gren like a bolt of frost, freezing his guts. He stared at Rangol a second longer, then turned and fled.

Gren ran out of the bar. His horse was tethered just outside, and he grabbed up its reins and flung himself into the saddle. Then he wheeled the steed around and galloped out of the town. He rode for hours before it became too dark to continue safely. Then he directed his horse off the footbridge and through the shallow water to a small mound of dirt that held one of Ortense's rare trees. He managed to tie the reins to the narrow trunk before collapsing against it. Gren's last thought, before he passed out, was that he really was alone now. And despite the blood-tinted blade still at his side, he was a Scarlet Dagger no more.

CHAPTER SIX

The Sower of Decay and Distrust leaned back into his throne and smiled. Those close enough to notice backed away, and his smile widened. They were frightened of him. Excellent. Many of them had laughed at him before, he remembered. Others had whispered insults behind his back. And then there were those who had simply ignored him altogether. Well, no one was ignoring him now. They were focused upon his every move. As they should be.

His right hand rested upon the arm of the throne, and he idly stroked its newest ornament. All was proceeding according to his own design and with his master's approval. True, those trumped-up mercenary thugs had failed at Hadovas, but that was acceptable. In many ways, it was ideal. Word of the town's rebellion had reached him, though not by normal channels. It would be many days still before the courtiers knew of it, and by then they would also be hearing about the town's spectacular fate. Soon everyone would know what happened to those who dared oppose him. Let the rebels think on that fate for a while!

He knew about the rebels, of course. What kingdom did not have them, after all? He had been one himself once upon a time, not even that long ago. If he had not assumed that such rebels existed, they would sweep in and dispatch him, and it would be only right. A good ruler was always cautious. Even Mariburn had known that.

Mariburn! The Sower's jaw suddenly clenched so hard his teeth ground together, and his fingers tightened upon the item decorating the end of the chair arm, threatening to shatter it completely. That swine had dared to laugh in his face! What was worse, the man had opposed him, and even defeated him. For a time.

But all that had changed now. Mariburn would trouble him no more. Best to focus his thoughts upon the future instead.

Glancing out over his throne room, the Sower watched the courtiers mill about, unsure what to do with themselves. Good. They were useless except as a sop to his ego, but that was the way of courtiers. Right now they could not decide the best way to win his approval, flattery or imitation or blithe ignorance, and that troubled them. And he preferred them that way. He already knew which of them could be most useful. Later he would weed through them, selecting those who had some spark of intelligence and some self-control, and he would begin to mold them. Eventually they would be worthy to serve him. But that was later.

For now, he needed to move forward with his other plans. The mercenaries, for example. They had been useful in taking the throne, certainly, but their strongest team had failed to take Hadovas, a simple farming town. And that meant that, once the word spread, other towns would stand against them as well. Because nothing spread as quickly in the country as gossip, soon everyone would know that the deadly mercenaries had been cowed by a bunch of peasants with big sticks. No, the Bloody Knives had only one use left in them.

But that was acceptable. He had known from the start that he would be rid of them eventually, and now was the time. To take the throne from Mariburn, the Sower had required standard muscle. It wouldn't have done to have revealed his other allies so early in the game, and it would have turned the people against him. (Taking the throne was hard enough without every peasant and merchant plotting to block his path as well.) But now that he had the throne, he did not need to hide his potency. He could unleash his new servants, and they were far deadlier than mere fighters. Many of the mercenaries he could even use, converting them into his own style of army. The people would be frightened, as they should be, and would obey him all the more quickly, but it was too late for them to stop him. And the rebels—well, they would sit in their hideouts and plot, but what good would that do them? Their blades might have served against normal guards, but not against the army he would soon have surrounding him. As the Bloody Knives would soon demonstrate. And, as an added bonus, the courtiers and their ilk would have clear proof of what happened to any who betrayed him, or outlived their usefulness.

Yes. The Sower smiled again. Everything was moving smoothly, and his master was well pleased. True, losing his partner in enemy territory had been unfortunate, but the tome he had retrieved was proving most useful. Ortense was firmly under his control, and soon it would belong fully to his master as well. Already the Essence of this place had grown thick and dank, darkening as the unnatural deaths poisoned it. The land was ripening with death and decay. Soon it would slide into the Underworld, forming a shadowy border between that place and this. And then his hold over Ortense would be complete. He had promised his master this, and his master had allowed him his mortal revenge over Ortense at last. In fact, when he had told his master what illicit treasure he'd retrieved from the Mound of Forsaken Seeds, his master had practically *insisted* he stay and take his revenge before returning home. Relaying his instructions by Infallible Messenger, his master had even taught him the basest rudiments of the language in which the tome was written so that the Sower could touch the surface of its power. The mercenaries' might had won him the throne, but it was by the dark necrotic power of the stolen tome that he would keep it and punish those who had sought to deny him it.

And as for any who stood in his way…

The Sower stroked the ornament again, and his smile widened, revealing sharp white teeth more like those of an animal than a man. Anyone who opposed him would merely become another decoration. His fingers caressed the skull that hung from the arm of his chair, dancing around the empty eye sockets. Mariburn had never left the throne, and never would. But at least now he added something to the room, as did his wife on the other arm. The Sower laughed, a low sound that grated like rusty metal, and continued to admire his own handiwork. This palace had been so dull before, but he had such plans for it now! It would never be dull again.

Even the courtiers would have to agree with that.

When he finally woke the next morning, Gren didn't bother to get up. He simply rolled onto his back and lay there, eyes clenched tight against the sunlight, thinking.

CHAPTER SEVEN

Where could he go now? What could he do? Who would he be? He felt like all of his identity had been stripped away, and nothing left in its place. A few days ago he'd known who he was—mercenary, fighter, officer of the Scarlet Daggers. Now who was he? An Exalt. An Anathema. A monster. A criminal.

That brought back Rangol's last words to him, and suddenly Gren was sitting up, gulping for air to fight the panic. The Wyld Hunt! They could be after him already! He leapt to his feet as if to run, but why bother? Everyone knew the Wyld Hunt always got its quarry. Its soldiers were among the greatest of the Dragon-Blooded, focusing entirely upon finding and destroying new Anathema before they could wreak havoc on all Creation. If they really were after him now, he was a dead man. So why run?

Besides, perhaps it was better this way. He had lost his friends, his career. All he had now was this curse the Unconquered Sun had laid upon him.

Why did you do this to me? he demanded silently, glaring at the sun high above.

It didn't answer him. Why should it? It just stared pitilessly back at him like Makan had often done after knocking the wind out of him in sword practice. *You gonna cry?* The sun seemed to sneer in Makan's growl. *Go on. I'll give you something to cry about.*

"Fine," Gren finally grumbled, running a hand across his face. "What am I supposed to do then?"

After finding the people of Hadovas dead, he'd been afraid he was dealing with some sort of epidemic. But then the people at the second town—Gren realized he'd never even bothered to learn its name—had been fine. And so had his former comrades, who had been in Hadovas with him. If it had been a disease, wouldn't they have been infected? And wouldn't it have shown itself after a whole week? So maybe it had been an isolated incident. Perhaps their food had been contaminated. That would explain why none of the Daggers were affected at least.

Gren felt a little better now that he had something else to think about. He'd been worried about what could have killed an entire village like that, and so quickly. And the one answer that had leapt to mind was something he hadn't really wanted to consider. But since the nearest neighboring town was okay, it must have been something at Hadovas itself.

Of course, if he really wanted to be sure, he could go to the nearest town on the other side of Hadovas and make sure everyone there was okay as well. But that meant riding all the way back to Hadovas first, and then passing it. Gren paused as he realized something. He had no idea where he was! He hadn't really been paying much attention last night when he'd fled the bar—he'd simply started riding. Now he looked up at the sky, to gauge the position of the sun, and then checked for any landmarks. What he saw surprised him.

Over there, to the right, that odd little sandbar—he'd seen that before. When they'd first approached Hadovas, back before his life had fallen apart. He pulled himself up into the tree, balancing on the highest branches thick enough to support him, and peered around. Sure enough, he was near Hadovas again! He must have ridden that way without realizing it.

Well, if that was really the case, he might as well check out the other town. It wouldn't be far, perhaps a day or two away. And if everyone there was still alive, he could get some food, some clean clothes, even something to drink. His hand rubbed the heavy pouch at his belt, which contained not only his own money but whatever he'd found in Hadovas, since they clearly hadn't needed it anymore. Perhaps he could trade his horse for one of the small shallow-hulled boats the locals favored. And if those people had been stricken... Well, he'd deal with that if it happened.

So Gren stood up, stretched, checked his horse, tightened the saddle, and swung back into it. Then, with a gentle nudge of his heels, he turned the horse back toward the footbridge and the towns that waited beyond.

"Not again," Arianna whispered, shaking her head to control the shiver that crept down her back. She looked down from the hill, toward the town below, but already she knew that she was too late. Too late to save them, at any rate. Perhaps not too late to gain the information she needed.

If only she didn't have to enter the town to gain it, she thought with a sigh. The last one had been almost more than she could bear, particularly when she had come across that family. They had been clutching one another, as if to ward off the threat by their proximity, the parents gathered protectively around their children. They had died together, and she had built a small pyre around them without even trying to separate them or drag them over to the other bodies. Let them be as close in the next life as they had in this one. But her hands had shaken so badly, and her eyes had been so filled with tears, it had taken several attempts before she managed to light the pyre. And several more before it was burning properly. Her stomach lurched and her breath caught at the thought of facing that again. This was not the first time she had seen horrors, but it was the first time she had been forced to face them alone.

I have no choice, she reminded herself. No one else knows what has happened here. No one has survived these towns, and that meant that even their closest neighbors were unaware of the danger. If she did not find out what was causing it, and put a stop to it, all the Hundred Kingdoms could be affected.

So, with a deep breath, she shouldered her pack again and started across the next bridge at a brisk walk. Time was of the essence, after all. Not that it would help those below, but the sooner she reached the town, the more chance she had of reaching the tree before it had faded completely like the others. She was sure the trees were the key to each town's demise. If only she could study them in time, she might find a way to stop this from happening elsewhere. The ritual she was contemplating was long and intricate, and even one mistake could spell her own painful death. But it might help her solve this riddle, and that was worth the risk. No more families like the last one. No more pyres. Keeping that thought firmly before her, she increased her pace, almost running toward the town and the grisly sight she knew was waiting.

CHAPTER EIGHT

When his horse finally staggered to a stop hours later, Gren found himself facing a shallow valley—a decent-sized stream, almost large enough to be a river, with a thick, wide bridge arching over it. On the far side, the ground rose slightly, and instead of the usual bridges, he saw a series of short wooden landings, arranged like an enormous staircase. The town, he remembered, was just beyond, in a second valley. He was there.

Might as well leave the horse here, Gren decided. He dismounted and tethered the horse to the thick wooden post at the start of the bridge. Then he dropped to the wood of the walkway and stretched his legs out in front of him, leaning back and letting the sun dry the sweat that clung to his face and arms and had drenched his shirt. It was a pleasantly warm day, the sun was high overhead, the sky was clear, the river was quiet, and the valley was peaceful. Not a bad way to spend an afternoon.

After relaxing for several minutes, Gren rose again and set out across the bridge. It took less than an hour to reach the top landing on the other side, and he paused there to study the village below. It was smaller than Hadovas but had more dry land, which was precious in Ortense. A single row of buildings stood on either side of a narrow dirt path, perhaps twenty in all. From this distance they looked to be mostly wood and bamboo, with some stone near the bases and simple rice-paper roofs. Only a handful had the stilts he had come to expect. At the center of the town, the path widened, making a real village square. Patches of green behind several buildings indicated gardens. It looked like a quiet, pleasant place.

So why did it feel so wrong? Something about the town made his skin itch. The air smelled strange, stale, and the river and the surrounding buildings looked pale, as if the color had been scrubbed away. Nothing looked or smelled quite right. Or sounded right.

Gren frowned as he realized that he hadn't heard a single sound or seen a single movement since he'd crested the hill. No one was stirring. No animals were barking or chirping or bleating. The town was utterly silent. So was the river, which would normally be teeming with fishermen. He began walking down the hill. He already suspected what he might find, but he had to know for sure. The closer he came to the town, the thicker the air felt around him, and it was almost oily—he tasted grit, and his skin felt coated with a thin layer of filth.

He was still a stone's throw from the outermost building when he saw the first bodies.

Gren stopped beside two of them. Men, a little older than him but still fit. Judging by the bamboo rods, reed baskets, and small nets near them, they were fishermen. Both had the same look of horror he'd seen on the people of Hadovas. Which meant the disease or whatever it was had spread this way as well. Damn!

Gren touched each of the bodies in turn, reducing them to ash, and then moved on. He found several more before he was in the town proper, including several animals. As with Hadovas, it didn't look like anyone had escaped.

Then he caught sight of the town square, and two things stopped him in his tracks.

The first was an enormous tree right in the center of the square. It was gnarled and twisted, its bark black and greasy-looking, its leaves long and oily and gray-green. It was a match for the one he'd seen in Hadovas, and this tree was also dead. Two dead towns, two dead twisted trees. What did the trees have to do with this?

But the second thing stole Gren's attention away from the tree and everything else. Because there was someone else in the square with him, a tall figure leaning against that odd tree. And judging from the faint movements, and from the fact that he was barely touching the gnarled trunk, that person was still alive.

"Hey!" Gren started off toward him, thrilled to meet another survivor. How had he survived? What had he done to save himself? Had he seen what had caused all this?

Arianna glanced up at the sound of someone shouting. She was surprised. Had someone survived after all? She saw a bear of a man stomping toward her, however, and quickly tossed aside any hopes that he was a local. Not in that armor. No villager could have afforded it, or the hefty sword at his side. The armor wasn't clean enough, or pretty enough, to be part of any Legion. He clearly wasn't from here, which meant he was simply a distraction. Maybe a local soldier who'd stopped by to check on the town. She'd speak to him in a moment.

As he drew closer, Gren slowed down again, noticing new details that tempered his excitement with innate caution.

He realized as he approached that the figure was not a "he" at all. Though slender, the body was clearly female. A woman? How had a woman survived?

Then, when he was closer still, Gren saw that she was wearing clothes that, while not new, were very well made and cut from expensive, sturdy fabrics. No one who lived in this crude village could have afforded such clothes. She was not a local.

But then why was she here? Gren stopped a few yards away and studied her more closely. She was lovely, but it was a cold beauty that did not fit with this place. Her long, silvery white hair was pulled back into a thick braid. The pack at her feet suggested that she was well traveled. And her hands were long and slender—

—and one of them was being tugged by a small child at her feet.

No, not a child. It was the right size, but the shape was all wrong. This thing was twisted, hunched, almost as gnarled as the tree beside them. He had thought it was simply in shadow, but now he realized that its skin really was that dark red, like drying blood. And he caught a glint of yellow as it glanced over at him. A demon!

What manner of woman would consort with such a creature? The answer came to him immediately: the kind of woman who had unleashed the tree on these villagers in the first place. The kind of woman who could command it to slaughter an entire village.

"Hey!" He put a hand on the hilt of his sword. "Lady, step away from the tree!"

Arianna glanced up again. She had been listening to the demon explain its findings, and the soldier had come much closer. His gear looked oft-used but well treated, and he looked like he was ready to draw his sword.

Not that that mattered to her right now. This tree was rapidly dying, and she needed to learn from it while she still had the chance. Plus, though she had compelled the demon to her service, only her will held it in check. If she loosed her attention too much, it might escape or find some way to hinder her investigation. Whoever this soldier was, he would simply have to wait a little longer. She waved a hand at him, urging him to give her a little space. And a little time.

The woman glanced at him for an instant, then turned her gaze back to the demon, raised her free hand, and shooed Gren away. The negligence in that gesture, the arrogance, made Gren grind his teeth.

"Lady!" Now his right hand tightened around his sword hilt. "I'm not kidding! Now!"

She glanced at him fully this time, actually looking at his face, and he was startled by the blue of her eyes. They didn't look evil but they were cold and barely focused upon him. "Hush," she said, shooing him again. Then she returned her attention to the demon at her side. "Not you, slave," she said.

Though her voice was soft and sweet, indicating that she was still as much girl as woman, her tone was enough to break his temper. And the motion had revealed the long daggers sheathed at her belt. "That's it!" he shouted. Gren lifted his sword.

What is with this man? Arianna wondered. Shouldn't the *demon* now kowtowing to her have sent him dashing away screaming into the marshes in abject terror by now? Barring that, shouldn't the soldier at least be *curious* about the bodies strewn everywhere? But perhaps, the thought occurred to her, perhaps he didn't pay attention to them because he already knew about them.

Perhaps he had something to do with all of this.

Certainly he was out of place here. His armor and sword said as much. Perhaps he was here as a guard after all—for the tree. Perhaps if keeping her conjured demon in check wasn't dominating her attention that might have occurred to her already...

She did not have time to pursue that thought farther, however, because the warrior was charging toward her, sword raised above his head. The sight of that massive blade shattered her concentration, and in that instant, the demon broke free.

"Yes!" it hissed as it snapped the bonds of the spell. Then, inexplicably, it lunged directly toward the charging warrior.

Gren saw the demon to protect its mistress. Its wide, lipless mouth opened to reveal row upon row of tiny, triangular teeth, and its hands opened, showing its long black claws. At the sight of such an obscenity, Gren exploded with rage. This creature did not belong upon this earth! Heat flowed through him, and burst around him in a flare of colored light.

Arianna, watching the impending collision, gasped as the man's anima flared, and a golden disk appeared upon his forehead. An Exalt!

The demon, seeing the sudden glow, came to a sudden stop, and cowered back. It was afraid of him! No, Gren realized as he closed the distance. It was afraid of his light. Something about the glow—the same one he had experienced when freeing the dead, and again in the bar, only stronger now—terrified it. He lowered his sword, though he kept his hands firmly about the handle, and concentrated upon the demon, and upon the light. And a memory from the First Age rose within him. A snippet from a sermon he'd given in another life.

Those who do not belong upon this world cannot withstand the light of the Unconquered Sun.

He focused, channeling his rage and bringing it to bear on the demon. His body glowed brighter, and the demon shrieked, covering its eyes. Then Gren felt a spark leap from his anima to the creature before him. It convulsed, fire pouring from its mouth, ears, and eyes, and then it blackened and burned away, leaving only a dark smudge upon the ground. Gren felt almost like singing as he relaxed and let his anima fade again. He had done that! He had destroyed that creature! He had felt the same each time he had sent one of the dead on to the next turn of the Cycle, but this was fiercer, more intoxicating. He had banished something unnatural from this world. He had cleansed the land of a particular blot.

But the creature had not come alone; its mistress was still here, watching him quietly. He turned back toward her, raising his sword again.

Arianna nodded as the man swiveled to face her. "I'd rather you hadn't destroyed him," she admitted, "but no great loss. I found what I needed."

"Why did you do this?" he demanded, stepping closer, and looking at his face, seeing the anger written there, she suddenly realized what he meant. What he thought he had seen.

"I did not do this," she told him, raising her hands to show that she was unarmed. "I am trying to find out who did."

"You lie!" the man shouted, taking another step. She forced herself not to back away. "You summoned a demon!"

"I was testing for demonic *influence*," she explained, biting back fear. The soldier was so *big* up close. "What better judge could I have petitioned?"

Gren thought about that. He hadn't seen her tell the creature to attack him, and it had looked more sullen before that. Was she telling the truth? More to the point, would a demon-worshipping cultist confronted by an obviously superior power be able to spew out such a terrible bald-faced lie without a hint of fear?

"I am an Exalt as well," she informed him, and suddenly a golden circle appeared upon her brow. The upper half of the circle was solid but the lower half was empty. The glow was strong enough to make him wince, but it was a clean light, tinted with rose.

Then another memory resurfaced, awakened by the divine, guiding providence of the Unconquered Sun...

He was sitting in a small study—his study, he knew—speaking with two other men. Two of his acolytes, he remembered their faces from the sermon memory, and his earlier self knew them well. They were discussing something, someone.

"He has been tainted," Gren was saying. "His soul has been touched by the Abyss, and fouled by it."

"How can we be certain?" The first acolyte, a woman named Mira, asked. "He does not look changed, nor does he speak strangely."

"We must ask the Unconquered Sun to grant us its wisdom, so that we may hear only truth," Gren replied. "Summon the accused, and you judge for yourself." The second acolyte, Tetran, went to the door, which he opened just wide enough to whisper to someone on the other side. A moment later, someone knocked on the door and a man entered.

He was middle-aged and average height, thick around the waist but still fit. His clothes were traveling silks, worn but cared for. The topknot that crowned his half-bald pate was shot through with thick gray streaks. His face was solid and pleasant, and his cheeks and chin shaved clean.

"How may I be of service, Exalted Lord?" the man asked, bowing low. Gren waved his hand in benediction.

"Come, sit with us, brother, and let us speak of the things you have seen on your travels," he said, and the man sat beside him. Mira and Tetran took chairs to either side.

"Unconquered Sun," Gren's former self intoned then, and all four bowed their heads. "Shed your light upon us, and grant us the gift to hear truths as they are spoken!"

A burst of light filled the room, as if the sun had descended through the low ceiling, and it was bright as midday in the small chamber. With the light came a clear tone, as if a bell had been struck. Then the light faded, and the tone died away, but in its wake, sounds were clearer and crisper and carried more meaning.

"You say that you resisted the lure of the shadows?" Gren's former self asked the visitor, and his acolytes leaned forward to hear the man's reply.

"Yes, holy one," the man said. "They offered me much, but I refused them. I trusted in the power of the Unconquered Sun, and it protected me."

But beneath his words, they heard something else. The sounds echoed strangely, harshly, and those echoes revealed the lie.

"You have been corrupted, my friend," Gren's other self told him sadly, and the man jumped from his chair, producing a thin dagger from his sleeve and driving it down toward Gren's chest. But a golden glow turned the steel aside, and…

Gren found himself back in his own body again suddenly, and knew from the woman's postures that only an instant had passed. She had not noticed anything. But he knew what to do now.

"Unconquered Sun," he called out, feeling a little foolish, "shed your light upon us, and grant us the gift to hear truths as they are spoken!"

His head rang as if it had been struck, but that faded quickly, and his hearing felt unusually sharp, as it did after an illness when the stuffiness vanished and sounds and smells returned full-force.

"Did you create the tree or kill these people?" he asked her.

Arianna felt the power in the words he'd spoken, and she relaxed. "I did neither," she answered clearly. "I was studying the tree for clues as to its origin and its purpose."

Gren listened, but her words rang cleanly, and the echoes were soft music. She told the truth.

"But you were consorting with a demon," he said. "And you kept shooing me away."

"I was busy, and you were interrupting," Arianna replied without expression. "But at least the demon had a chance to tell me the tree did not come from Malfeas—the demon world. For what it's worth, I believed the little miscreant."

Again her words were true, and Gren finally sheathed his sword. "There. Sorry," he told her. "My name is Grendis Lam."

"Arianna," she replied. "I suppose I would have doubted had our situations been reversed." She frowned. "I wish, however, I had a chance to learn more about who did this, and why."

"Not who," Gren corrected. "How. How did they die? What killed them?"

"That did," Arianna said, gesturing back toward the tree. "I'm not quite sure how yet," she went on as if reading his thoughts, "but the tree was definitely the cause. And I highly doubt the villagers planted it."

"They didn't," Gren confirmed. "At least, in Hadovas they didn't. It grew overnight somehow."

"So you've seen another town like this?"

He nodded. "So have I," she said. "Several, in fact."

Now that he had relaxed, Gren took the opportunity to study her. She was tall for a woman, though still a head shorter than him. Her hair had suggested that she was older, but her voice showed otherwise, and her face and hands matched that. She was barely more than a girl, though the lines around the eyes suggested she'd already seen more than most. Her clothing fit her well, but it was dusty from travel, and she had no jewelry or ornaments except a strange acorn pendant hung around her neck. The mark on her forehead had faded now, but she was still an arresting sight, with her piercing blue eyes frankly meeting his green ones, and with some amusement. The thin scar that began above her right eye trickled across the bridge of her nose and ended just below her left eye and highlighted the delicacy of her features.

For her part, Arianna examined him as well. He was tall and powerfully built, a man who had been gifted with size and strength and was active enough to maintain it. His features were not handsome, especially with that nose—she wondered how many times it had been broken—but they were solid and open. The gray-green eyes still watched her warily, and the mouth almost hidden within the thick black beard, shot through with a few strands of silver, was still tight. He had put away his blade, though, which was something.

"Let us compare information," she suggested, seating herself on the ground a few paces from the tree's roots. "Shall I start?" He nodded as he sat down himself.

"I noticed that this land's Essence felt strange," Arianna told him, "and decided to investigate."

Gren frowned. "Essence?"

"Essence is the energy of the world. It's all around us, and in us, and in everything. Without Essence we die. But we, you and I, can use Essence in other ways. As when you destroyed my demon."

"Ah." Gren nodded as something suddenly made sense. "Is that why the air feels oily, gritty... dirty, somehow?"

"Yes, exactly. The Essence here has been tainted... By that." She gestured at the dead tree behind them. "Someone, or something, is corrupting the Essence of this land. The question is why." She looked over at him again. "And you? What are you doing here?"

"I am—I was—a professional soldier. A mercenary." That had never embarrassed him before but now, with this strange girl watching him so intently, he was glad that was in the past. "We were hired to help a man take the throne here in Ortense."

"Ortense?"

"This kingdom." He saw her look of surprise, and laughed himself. "You didn't realize you were in another kingdom?"

"They all look alike," she replied, frowning a little. "It isn't as if they have signs and gates. Perhaps they should."

"No, I guess that's true. Though Ortense is damper than its neighbors. Which way did you come from?" She pointed, and Gren squinted in that direction, trying to remember the map Rangol had shown him. "I'd guess it's a week's walk to the border from here, going that way. Where the footbridges start, that's the border."

Arianna frowned again, more deeply this time. "That would be right about where I felt the taint."

"Huh. Well, I was left to die outside Hadovas, that's the village northwest of here. And then I was Chosen. When I walked back into the town, everyone was dead. Just like they are here."

She nodded. "I've seen two other towns as well, also like this. Whatever it was must have swept this entire region. Perhaps it started at the border and is working its way in." But Gren shook his head.

"There's another town," he explained, "a week west of Hadovas. Everyone there is fine. But it's about on level with this one. If something was coming down, they would have been hit as well."

"What if it was coming from the east, though?" Arianna pointed out. "It might not have reached that town yet."

He hadn't thought of that. "You're right," he replied, standing up quickly. "We have to warn them!" He couldn't help thinking of Rangol and the rest. They had cast him out, and they might try to kill him if they saw him again, but he still thought of them as friends. He couldn't let them die, not without trying to save them.

"We're probably too late," she warned him, standing up herself and brushing the dirt from her clothes. "But you're right, we should go. If there's another tree, I might get to it soon enough to ask it questions." She glanced sidelong at Gren. "Assuming no one distracts me this time."

Taken aback by the girl's casual callousness, Gren only said, "We can't just leave them like this, though."

"It will take too much time to build pyres," Arianna said. Gren smiled, though it wasn't a happy expression. He walked over to the nearest body, whispered his prayer to the Unconquered Sun, laid his hands upon the corpse's forehead, and then stepped back as a flare of light consumed the body.

"I'll take care of it," he assured her.

"Yes, I suppose so," she agreed. She had to admit she was impressed, as much with the way he handled the matter as with his ability to immolate the bodies so quickly. Each prayer was the same, and very short, but from where she stood, she could tell that he really meant each one. He was definitely not the mindless thug she'd first thought him to be.

After Gren had dealt with the bodies, he walked back over to her. "My horse is tethered just beyond the river," he told her. "We could take turns riding her, maybe even ride double for short periods."

Arianna lifted her chin. "Thank you, but I can arrange for my own transportation." She whistled, an eerie sound that seemed to hover before them. The sound intensified, as if a small wind was blowing there, and the sunlight caught on specks of something in the air, producing a warm glow flecked with pinpoints of brighter light. The lights were swirling about, and the glow thickened, until it almost had substance. The lights continued to dance, weaving about this strange misty shape, and it became even more substantial. Legs were formed, white with hints of gold, and then a back, a strong neck, a long, graceful head. Finally the last of the light settled forward and back, turning gold and red, and the shimmering became a glowing, golden, flame-maned stallion. This time it was Gren's turn to be surprised and impressed as Arianna grabbed its mane with her hands and swung gracefully onto its back.

As they left the town, Arianna found herself liking the fact that they would be traveling together. She had thought that she could be comfortable alone, and she *had* been more or less fine since she had last seen Swan, but that parting had not been entirely her choice, so the resulting solitude was just something she'd had to get used to. Gren was no Swan, not by any stretch of the imagination, but he seemed friendly now that he'd overcome his initial distrust, and she was sure she could count on him in a fight. And for now it was just nice not to have to travel down the road alone.

CHAPTER NINE

The palace was silent, its darkness broken into shards of shadow by the guttering torches placed here and there around the edges. All of the courtiers had fled at nightfall, and even the servants were now asleep in their quarters, huddling against one another for scant protection from the chill that had nothing to do with the weather.

Perfect. The Sower uncoiled from his throne, where he had remained the entire day, watching the throne room from behind steepled fingers. He stepped off the dais and moved quickly down a narrow hallway, his soft-soled boots making no noise upon the hard paving stones. Only the rustle of his robes against his flesh offered any sign that someone was passing by.

Reaching a small, heavy wooden door deeply inset in the wall, the Sower paused. He glanced about, assuring himself that the palace's other occupants were all asleep, then muttered several words under his breath. The door gave an audible click as the latch rose, and he pushed it open and stepped within, sliding the door shut again behind him.

It was a vast chamber, its walls made of rough-hewn stone blocks and the floor similar but smoother. Two steps ran all the way around the walls, so that the room was much taller than the low doorway suggested, and the walls tapered in as they rose, finally angling in toward a wide open square. During the day he avoided this place, as the sun caught flecks of crystal within the stone and transformed the chamber into a bath of light. But now, with the cool night air filtering down and nothing but darkness overhead, the Sower felt more comfortable. Nor was the darkness entirely mundane.

In the center of the room he had torn up many of the paving stones, revealing the old dirt beneath. It was toward that gap that he headed now, and toward the tree that grew from it.

The tree towered overhead, its branches brushing the walls and its highest leaves well above where the ceiling would have been. Its bark was a glistening black, as if coated in thick oil, and its thick limbs twisted about like strands of smoke or twirled rope. The leaves that covered it were wide and pointed and dark gray streaked with red. Their edges were sharp enough to draw blood. The tree's roots filled the gap in the floor, and had grown enough to force up several more stones around the edge, as they burrowed deeper into the earth for sustenance and purchase.

But it was the seeds that the Sower wanted now. Hanging from several branches were pear-shaped objects the size of a child's hand, gray and black and red swirled together in patterns that shifted if you stared at them. The Sower reached up and clutched one of these seeds firmly, then twisted it free from the tree, whispering an incantation as he did so. Released as much by the spell as by the physical tug, the seed dropped into his hand. It felt grimy, as if dipped in soot, and it sucked away what little moisture his skin still possessed. The darkness around the seed writhed and unfurled slightly, answering his own dark aura.

"Come, my beauty, we have work this night," the Sower whispered to it, turning away from the tree toward the simple pedestal. It had stood in the center of the room, its base carved from the centermost paving stone and the rest constructed of the same material, but he had moved it to one side when he had prepared space for the tree. Resting atop the pedestal was his tome.

Even now he felt a thrill and a small chill as he slipped the binding strap free, spoke the proper words, and opened the cover. Darkness poured up from the book, bathing both the

Sower and the seed in its reverse-glow, and both of them absorbed the Essence and grew stronger for its presence. More tendrils of smoky night billowed out around the edges of the pages and curled around the pedestal, creeping across the room and curling into its corners until nothing below the Sower's knees could be seen. Those shadows that reached the tree grew stronger still, wrapping around its trunk and roots and sliding up among its branches like man-thick snakes at home among the oil-black limbs.

Gently the Sower turned the pages, more from reverence than from any fear of harming them. He had first thought they might be human flesh, but they were too thick and too smooth to come from any man or woman or child. Some other creature had given up its skin to make this tome, perhaps several creatures, since the book was thick with many pages. Whatever its materials, the tome had been carefully crafted, and even after centuries its paper was sturdy and flexible, bending easily at the touch and not crinkling or cracking in the least. The words and images looked almost as if they had been graven into the flesh rather than merely drawn. Their edges were still so crisp, so distinct. The tome was truly a thing of unholy beauty, and the Sower rejoiced in its details, and in his possession of it.

He turned the page again, revealing the incantation he wanted, and settled it gently, smoothing the page with the hand not cradling the seed. With what little his surprised master had taught him of the language, he had still deciphered only a few passages in the book, but this was the one had used most often. And now, tonight, under the cover of darkness, he would use it again.

Holding the seed aloft in both hands, the Sower recited the spells. The darkness poured forth from the book in response, wrapping itself around his hands and the seed within them. The seed wriggled as if alive, the colors under its skin swirling openly now. And then it unfurled itself, spreading its skin the way a bat releases its wings, thin panes of crimson-laced flesh stretched to each side. Beneath them the seed was angular and jet-black, small protrusions sprouting from it like tiny legs, and it looked very much like a spider with extra legs and bat wings grafted to its back.

The Sower drew his hands back toward him, so that the seed was level with his nose, and he stroked the wings gently with one forefinger. Then he leaned closer.

"Holoko Chia," he whispered to it. "He lives in Anaka, my pet. Destroy him. Destroy Anaka." And he blew upon it, a gentle breath as one would blow upon a dandelion.

His breath caught in the seed's wings, billowing them and lifting the seed high into the air. In an instant it was sailing up through the opening, past its parent tree, and flying off into the night. The Sower watched it go until he could no longer see it in the darkness, a small smile upon his face. Soon that town, too, would know death.

He closed the tome again, and strapped it tightly. Then, running one hand idly along the tree's trunk as he passed, the Sower crossed the room again, opened the door, and slipped back out into the hall. Tomorrow would be a busy day, and although he no longer needed sleep, now was an excellent time to plan while his subjects slept. He returned to his throne room and resettled himself in his throne.

His only regret, he mused, was that he had not been able to single out King Mariburn with one of the seeds and come to power that way. Doing so would have forced him to plant his tree somewhere else in Ortense, though, and nowhere else in the kingdom would have been safer or easier to defend against the inevitable pedestrian rebellion. Plus, he simply hadn't been able to resist the dramatic symbolism or planting the instrument of Ortense's doom right in the center of this castle that should have long since been his. Ah well. Perhaps some day he would have the leisure to carry one of the seeds to its destination by hand and then stay to watch the resulting doom settle upon that location. At that time, he could let his chosen victim stand in effigy of the deposed king.

But for now he needed to handle matters here, and Anaka was near the very edge of his domain. A domain that fell more firmly under his control with every seed he sent forth. The Sower smiled again and leaned back, letting his eyes slip closed. Soon the shadows would cover this land completely, and then his minions could move about openly, devouring the land in the name of his vengeance and his master. The seeds were merely the first step. One day the tree would stretch its branches from border to border, and all beneath it would succumb to the darkness.

CHAPTER TEN

Gren's horse and the steed Arianna had created moved quickly, and they made excellent time. As dawn broke on the second day of their travels, they could see buildings peeking up from behind a hill just ahead.

"It's not a big place," Gren mentioned as they approached. "Maybe half a dozen buildings in the center, houses scattered beyond that, the same walkways you find throughout Ortense. It's got a bar, though." He said it with such a mixture of longing and regret that Arianna found herself fighting a smile.

"You can get a drink later, if everything is still all right there," she assured him, surprised that the suggestion didn't win more approval. "But our first priority must be the inhabitants."

"I know. It's just… I like bars," he told her. He added something else, which sounded like "despite everything," but she wasn't sure and didn't press it.

The last two days had been interesting ones for both of them as they'd adjusted to each other. Both were used to traveling with other people, but ones completely different from their current companion. For Gren's part, Arianna had proven to be very quiet when not discussing the current situation, and she'd spent most of the evenings buried in one of the seemingly endless supply of books she had pulled from her pack. She was pleasant enough when she did speak, if a little cool, and she was an efficient traveler, setting up a fire or cooking a meal quickly and easily. Gren was happy to admit that her cooking beat Dyson's hands down. But he missed the joking and laughter of his friends. Arianna reminded him most of Rangol, but Enjy and Lirat and Milch and Scamp had always been there to offset their leader's quiet with their boisterous humor.

Arianna had grown accustomed to traveling with Swan before this, and she kept having to remind herself that he was a trained diplomat and an expert in dealing with other people. Gren was only a fighter. True, he had shown himself to be smarter than she had expected, given her previous run-ins with warriors, and he was far less hot-tempered than she might have thought. They hadn't had much problem since leaving that last town, but he'd handled the travel and its usual concerns easily and practically. He was very gruff, though, and he lacked Swan's poise and wit. The few times Gren had tried telling a joke, it had been crude and rough and he had trailed off into silence after a few sentences.

On the other hand, she did appreciate his calm, imposing presence. Once they had heard a rustling in the reeds that could have been bandits, and Gren had simply stood and stretched, then announced, "I'd better sharpen my blade before it goes dull." He'd unsheathed the massive sword and begun honing its already-sharp edge, and the rustling had quickly faded away. Arianna was sure she could have handled whatever had been watching them, but she was relieved that she didn't have to. And she appreciated the fact that Gren had dealt with the matter without actually crashing into the foliage.

She still didn't know much about him, of course. She had made a few attempts at social niceties, as much to parry his questions about her as because she was curious about him. After his first few rebuffs she had stopped. She had the sense that he didn't want to think about his childhood much, and she could certainly understand that. (Thoughts of the tower where she'd grown up, and the spoiled young men squandering its knowledge while she toiled in secret, still haunted her occasionally.) But all she had to judge him by was what she had seen thus far, and the few tidbits he'd provided since then. She still wasn't sure she could predict him, or trust him to understand a situation, particularly if it involved magic. But at least now she knew she could trust him when they were in danger.

Drawing closer to the town, both of them breathed sighs of relief when they saw a farmer leading a row of ducks toward a feeding trough by the river. Whatever might happen, the town and its people were still alive this morning. Arianna and Gren reined in just shy of the trough, and dismounted without discussing it.

"Guess that horse'd be pretty obvious in town," Gren mentioned with a grin, tethering his own horse there.

"I'm afraid so," Arianna agreed. "Best not to draw so much attention if we can avoid it." She stroked her horse's nose, then pushed it away gently. "Off with you now, my friend. I thank you for bearing us this far, and I may call upon you again, but for now you must return to the Unconquered Sun." She added a few words in that familiar but strange other language, and with a puff of golden dust and a twist of light, the horse unraveled like a loosely woven shawl, threads of flame and white flesh spinning outward and fading into nothing, until no trace remained.

"Good thing you weren't still riding him," Gren muttered.

"Shall we?" Arianna asked, ignoring the joke. Together they turned and started walking up the hill toward the town proper. They passed several people along the way—the sun was just rising, and people in the country rose with it—and nodded to each in turn. A few of the men looked startled to see Gren in his armor and sword, and several of the women looked almost as frightened to see Arianna walking beside him in her long white robe, blue-edged jacket, and silken veils, but most nodded back. Gren just hoped that the men who had been in the bar had passed the fight off as the product of too much beer too early in the day. He wondered if his friends were still here, or if they'd moved on already, and unconsciously set his left hand on the dagger still stuck in his belt. He wished there was some way to take back what had happened the last time he'd seen them, but he knew there wasn't.

As they entered town, the walkways became more crowded, and not just with foot traffic. People had laid brightly woven blankets out upon the planks, and atop those colorful spreads they displayed wood carvings, reed flutes, paper kites, and other items. Here and there men had set up rough plank tables, piled high with fish or hard little plums or glistening sugar cane or some other food. A few people were cooking rice or stew, or grilling fish or duck, or steaming buns. Children were darting between the tables and blankets, waving streamers and playing flutes and shouting and laughing.

"What is all this?" Gren asked one man who had bumped against him, and the older man grinned, revealing a mouth with only three remaining teeth.

"It's the Spring Festival," he said, pressing a small sweetcake into Gren's hand and another into Arianna's. "Time to celebrate life and the harvest." And with a smile and a wink at Arianna, he disappeared into the crowd again.

Gren began glancing around, looking for any sign of the Daggers. He started to mention his concern to Arianna but broke off as she grabbed his arm.

"Look," she hissed, and pointed.

Ahead of them the walkways and footbridges intersected, and in their center was a rough circle, the only dry land in the town. The major buildings were arrayed around it, and it had been left clear of booths and stalls. Apparently it was too sacred a spot to use for selling food and trinkets. In the center of that circle stood a heavyset man of middle years, dressed in silk robes that, while not grand or ostentatious, radiated a certain dignity and sense of rank. The man was just in the midst of raising his arms to call the crowd of onlookers to attention, when Gren finally noticed what it was that Arianna was pointing at. A small, basket-sized shape was dropping down out of the sky right toward the man. Before either of them could do anything, even shout a warning, the black object crashed into the man's neck and shoulders, driving him down flat on his face.

The onlookers fell back in shock, and someone shouted, "Mayor Holoko!" Before anyone could rise or move to help, an inky black vapor exploded into the air, obscuring the central area in unnatural smoke. Gren and Arianna could only gape along with the other gawkers until the black vapor swirled and suddenly seemed to be sucked into the ground right down through the fallen mayor's back. The horror was not over, though, as those closest to the scene realized first. The mayor lay unmoving now, black blood seeping from his nose, ears, and mouth, and something small was writhing in the ghastly wound that had dashed his back open between the shoulder blades.

People farther away began to notice it as well, and they all froze in horror. A man and his wife stood staring, holding forgotten bits of salted fish to their lips. A little boy had dropped his toy flute, and was clinging to his mother's leg through her skirt. An older man had paused from tying string to a kite, and a stray breeze pulled the kite from his hands, sending it spiraling out over the water unnoticed. Everyone had stopped what they were doing to look at the strange thing writhing in the body of their dead mayor.

"What just happened?"

It was a voice Gren knew well, so he didn't have to turn and look. He did anyway. Milch had come around the side of a house, where he'd been relieving himself in the river, if the way he was buckling his pants back up was any indication. He noticed the mayor's dead body first, because it was closer to him. But then he saw where some of the other people were looking, and his gaze swiveled around to Gren. And Gren watched as the mouth hardened and the eyes turned cold. This was a man who had, until recently, been a good friend. A trusted companion. An ally who had saved his life several times, and whose life he had saved many times in return. But to see the look on Milch's face now, he was looking at a poisonous snake or a rabid bear or a cutthroat willing to sell his entire family for the cost of a single drink. And when

Milch turned and dashed back through the bar's front door, Gren knew that he was running for the rest of the group. He'd be facing all the Daggers shortly, and he suspected most of them would have the same expression.

Except, that didn't matter anymore. The object that had fallen from the sky was now finished unfurling from the dead man's back and had revealed itself to be a tiny sapling with two spindly branches, one on either side and each sprouting a single oversized leaf. But even as Gren watched, the sapling began to grow. It widened as it shot up, and in a single blink it was several feet tall and as thick as a man's arm. Several smaller branches sprouted off the sides, and the original two grew thicker, roughly as thick as his thumb. Then it was as tall as a man, and as wide around as his chest, and its two large branches were as thick as his arms. They had lengthened as well, but were no longer growing straight out, nor was the trunk straight anymore. Instead the entire tree seemed to curl in upon itself as it grew, and its branches curved in like arms wrapped protectively around its body. In moments, dozens of root fingers swarmed over the dead mayor's back and enveloped him, pushing his corpse into the ground and hiding it from view. It took only seconds.

"Come on!" Arianna tugged at his arm, dragging Gren closer to the tree. When Gren didn't move quickly enough, still transfixed by the sight, she released her grip on him and ran forward herself, dodging between stunned locals. Her mind was racing, trying unsuccessfully to flood out the horror of the death she'd just witnessed with icy analytical detachment. She could feel taint spreading through the Essence around her, the mystic current growing gritty and bitter, and that corruption was much stronger than she'd felt at the towns she'd come upon after the fact. It undermined her resolve and planted a seed of panic in her.

Could she stop it? She drew one of her daggers and slashed one of the smaller branches as hard as she could. The blade definitely connected, she could feel the shock run up her arm as the metal struck wood, but it left no mark and her hand ached from the impact. Normal weapons would not be enough. Even Gren's sword, if she could convince him in time to swing it, probably wouldn't have any effect. Which left magic.

"Unconquered Sun, hear your child," she called out, throwing her head back and her arms wide. She heard gasps and cries of alarm around her as the locals were only just reacting to what had happened, but she blocked it out. "Grant me your light to guide my way, and to expunge the darkness that threatens us!" She began to glow, the holy mark blazing upon her forehead as light licked around her hands and torso, slowly covering her body. But the square still grew dimmer. Right where she stood, inches from the tree, was an oasis of light, but the shadows quickly spread across the rest of the clearing, and reached out to envelop the buildings on either side.

"Gren! Help me!" She called. But he did not respond, and a glance over her shoulder told her why.

Milch had returned, and as Gren had predicted, he was not alone. Scamp was right behind him, sword in one hand and broken bottle in the other. Behind him Dyson hefted his axe and Lirat his sword. Enjy looked less enthused, but still dutifully carried his massive eagle-headed mace, and after him was Hud, an arrow already nocked and a snarl on his usually sunny face. Rangol was last, and though his sword was still sheathed, his hand was on its hilt. Those locals nearby wisely shook off their daze to clear a wide berth around the mercenaries.

"Came back for more, huh, demon?" Scamp demanded, waving his blade as he spoke. "Got the drop on us last time, but not this time. Let's see if you at least bleed like a man!"

"Why did you come back, Gren?" Rangol put his hand on Scamp's arm, and Scamp lowered his sword a little to let their leader through. "Did you come to finish the job?"

"I came to warn you," Gren told him, keeping his hand well clear of his own sword. "I came to warn all of you," he told them, wishing they'd believe him.

"Warn us of what? That we're damned for even knowing you?" That was Hud, and it didn't surprise him. Hud had always been the closest to religious of any of them—or at least the most superstitious. "Get away from us!"

"You have to leave," Gren told Rangol. "All of you. Right now. It's not safe here."

"Leave?" Dyson laughed at him. "Why? The Wyld Hunt won't be coming for us—just for you."

"It's not that!" Gren wished he knew some way to convince them. "It's—" and then he saw the looks on their faces as they stared past him, and noticed that they were suddenly standing in shadow even though it was early morning on a cloudless day. "It's too late," he whispered to himself, turning back to see what his former friends had already seen.

The tree was twice his height now, and its trunk was as wide around as a cart, wider than the dirt it sprouted from. The mayor's body was nowhere to be seen, and the people who had been standing closest to the tree were running now, finally screaming in the fear that shock had temporarily squeezed out of them. The tree's longer branches were as thick as he was, and their tips brushed the buildings to either side. More branches curved down the ground, creating a massive tangle of dark wood. Leaves had sprouted all along them, long triangular leaves ending in wicked points, black with faint streaks of crimson, as if they were blood long since dried and hardened. The tree's bark had thickened and grown black with splotches of gray and more crimson, and it gleamed wet in the faint remaining light. Its roots pushed the bridges and walkways aside and ringed the tree in an irregular circle of knots and bumps, like dark creatures swimming below ground, their backs breaking the surface. The entire tree glistened as if it were wet, and those tiny glimmers were almost the only light left. All around it, everywhere beneath its still-spreading branches, was darkness. This was no normal darkness, either. It was the pitch black of the dead of night, the strange eerie gray of the oncoming storm, the dank cold quiet of the musty cellar, the chill void of the ancient tomb, all mixed into a single smothering presence. Everything beneath that tree felt cold and dry and drained, as if the air itself had grown thick enough to choke.

Everything save one. Still only feet from the tree was Arianna, her skin glowing as if on fire, a golden light blazing from her forehead, the only splash of color in the dismal scene. Her hands were in front of her, and Gren saw with a start that they had changed somehow. Gone were the pale, slender, delicate fingers of a scribe or scholar. Instead her hands now seemed oversized, the fingers far too long, and jagged like claws or broken branches. They had darkened as well, and from here they resembled wood more than flesh. She slashed at the tree with them, and he heard the scrape of wood upon wood, and the sob of frustration that escaped her. Leaving his friends standing, Gren rushed to her side.

"What can I do?" He asked her, taking her hand and trying not to pull away from the grotesque wooden appendage as the glow spread from her flesh to his. His own body began to glow, and the pure light grew stronger, creating a small space around them. But still the tree grew. Now its branches had reached the outer buildings, and its shadows had deepened further. People were beginning to drop without a mark upon them, even those who were running and screaming. Tables were overturned, and food and crafts went everywhere, adding to the chaos.

"I don't know!" Arianna said, and he could hear the despair in her voice. "It's happening too fast!"

Gren closed his eyes and searched within himself. The memories of the man he had been were there, most still buried, a few like that sermon rising to the surface. Many of them still felt foreign to him, as if he were listening to someone tell tales of another's life, but as each one rose it became clearer, more colorful, and became a part of him again. Over the past few days, several memories had returned to him, but he didn't have time for the slow method now. Yet now that he wanted some direct guidance, nothing arose to enlighten him.

"Okay, Sun, what do I do now?" he demanded, opening his eyes again. And wishing immediately that he hadn't.

The tree had stopped growing. Its trunk was now as wide as a small building, and its branches covered the entire town.

And from those branches, Gren realized, hung fruit. Strange round fruits, so dark they stood out even in the gloom. So dark they seemed to generate darkness, turning the shadows around them still deeper. And, as he watched, one of those fruits fell.

He saw it bounce down through the branches as if it was in slow-motion, and he reflexively took a step toward it as if to catch it. But something deep within pulled him back—perhaps the man he had been, or perhaps just his own instincts.

Instead, the fruit struck the ground by the kite-maker's blanket. It made no sound when it hit, but flattened like a giant water drop. Then it burst open. Or perhaps it simply lost its form, released by the impact. The globe dissolved, and in its place were tendrils that writhed and spread. They were darker than dark, so dark the eyes hurt to look at them, and as they moved they carried the dark with them, obliterating even the memory of life. And then one of the tendrils touched the kite-maker, who had simply dropped off his stool, unable to get away. Its edge tapped his foot once, reared back, then struck like a snake, driving itself into his flesh.

The kite-maker jerked upright, his whole body going rigid. His skin darkened, mottling with black and red and gray, and his limbs spasmed. Fingers clawed at his chest, tearing cloth and flesh alike, trying to dig the darkness loose. But it had hold of him now. Gren and Arianna stood petrified as the man's eyes bulged and rolled back in his head. His mouth opened in a silent scream, teeth bared, spittle flying. Blood began seeping from his ears, nose, and eyes. The spasms were growing more rapid, more severe, and he thrashed on the ground. And then, with a last gurgle, he arched his back and stopped moving altogether.

Nor was he the only one. Other fruits were falling as well, and tendrils were everywhere. People fled, the festival forgotten, trying to escape the deadly plant, but they died quickly, unable to avoid the tendrils or resist their lethal touch. One tendril reached toward Gren and Arianna, and he instinctively raised his hand to ward it off.

"Get away!" Gren shouted, letting his anger and horror well up and out through his palm. There was a flash of light, and a small burst of flame—red and orange rather than the white flare he had used to release corpses—leapt from him toward the tendril. It caught fire, there at the tip, and shrieked as it fell. It was a sound that cut through the silence, through the darkness, and shivered people where they stood. The rest of the tendril broke free, leaving its charred tip behind to dissolve away, and retreated rapidly. The rest followed suit, and soon Gren and Arianna found themselves standing in the only clear spot in the town, their light providing a faint respite from the darkness all around.

"Help me!" A woman, one of the last villagers left alive, staggered toward them, grasping at Arianna's arm. "Please! Save me! Save my baby!" She had a little boy clutched in her arms, and thrust the baby toward them, even as the tendrils homed in on them both. Arianna reached out for them, but the glow did not pass from her to the woman or her child. She had one hand on the baby when a tendril struck the woman, causing her to jerk back, and the little boy fell between them. In an instant, three tendrils had converged on him, and he was lost amid the darkness, only his faint cries giving any indication of his presence. Those stopped soon after.

"Gren!" He turned to see Enjy only a few feet away. Hud and Milch had fallen already—he saw their bodies not far from the tavern door—and Dyson was nowhere in sight, but he could see Scamp and Lirat battling against the tree's feelers some distance away. But Enjy was much closer, and so far he had not been harmed. A few tendrils wavered around the big man, and he swung his mace at them. Even though the weapon passed harmlessly through them, the tendrils seemed to pull back from his force. "Gren, help me!"

Gren reached out, as Arianna had done. He grasped his friend's hand, wishing that some of his light could pass to his friend. But nothing happened. Gren could feel the energy flowing around him, but it refused to transfer to his friend. The tendrils seemed almost to realize this, and massed just beyond the two men, gathering around Enjy so thickly that the very air beyond him seemed to turn black with malice.

"I'm trying," Gren whispered, unable to speak any louder.

Enjy looked him in the eye, and said only, "Damn, Gren." The mace dropped from the big man's hand unnoticed, and a second later the tendrils had claimed him as well, so many of them converging that even his massive form was buried beneath them. He only screamed once, near the end.

"There has to be something we can do!" Gren vented his anger toward Arianna. "Anything!" The tendrils seemed uninterested in them as yet—or maybe they were powerless to affect the Exalted—though that didn't help anyone else.

"What, then?" Arianna demanded in return. "It's happening too fast for me to *think*!" Gren hissed and glared in impotent rage. What else could he do?

"Gren." The voice was as soft as always, but Gren heard him nonetheless. He turned.

"Rangol." He faced his friend and former leader and didn't bother hiding the tears that came to his eyes. "Rangol, there's nothing I can do."

"There is," his friend insisted. "Dyson told us the villagers in Hadovas were burned to ash. This," he nodded toward the tree, "didn't do that. Did you?"

Gren nodded. Somehow Rangol had evaded the tendrils thus far, and as one quested toward him he flicked it aside with the tip of his blade. But Gren knew that could not last. From the look in his eyes, Rangol knew it too.

"Do that for me, Gren," his friend insisted. "Burn me to ash. Right now."

"You're—it's—they were dead already," Gren protested, shocked at the thought. But his friend shook his head.

"Doesn't matter. You can do it. Dead or alive makes no difference. I need it, Gren. Don't make me die like that." He glanced toward where a man and his horse were twitching mere feet apart, shuddered, and looked away again. "Please."

"I—" Gren started to say something, then realized that what his friend had asked was impossible. "It doesn't work that way," he admitted miserably.

"Then use your blade, Gren," Rangol begged, desperation showing on his face for the first time Gren had ever seen. "That I *know* you can do. Please. Give me a warrior's death, at least."

Gren nodded and drew his sword, but found that he could not raise it. Deep in his heart he knew that what Rangol was asking was what he would want for himself, and that he owed him that and more. But something in him would not let him raise his blade against a friend, even out of mercy. He struggled against his own resistance, but finally his head dropped, and the tip of his sword scraped the ground.

"I can't," he whispered. "I'm sorry."

"It's all right, Lam," Rangol said softly, using Gren's given name for the first time. He blinked away a tear from the corner of each eye, and then he was himself once more. "I understand." He saluted Gren with his blade, and smiled a sad smile. "Take care of yourself. You're a good man. The best of the Scarlet Daggers." And then he turned and leapt toward the waiting tendrils.

"No!" Gren couldn't help shouting as his friend and leader charged to certain death. It was an amazing display, as Rangol spun and dodged and wove between the deadly plant limbs, and for a moment it looked as if he might somehow make it. But then one of the tendrils struck his left arm, paralyzing it, and another wrested his sword away, and then a third stabbed into his open mouth, the blackness rising through his head and pouring in dark tears from his eyes and nose and ears. And then Rangol jerked, twitched, and collapsed.

"Damn it, no!" At Rangol's death Gren felt the paralysis leave him. His sword lifted again of its own accord, his body searching for something to kill, but there was nothing but the tree, and he knew that his blade would be useless against it. But his rage had built as the villagers had died, and overflowed as he watched his friends perish—rage at the tree for killing them, at the Unconquered Sun for putting him in this situation, at Arianna for leading him here, at Enjy and Rangol for demanding his aid, at himself for being unable to spare them their pain. Rage at everything. But this was not like some of the anger he had felt in the past, when he had been younger and cruder. This was a clean rage that swept through him and left him feeling more whole, like a valley after a much-needed rain. This rage was pure and good, and it focused his mind and his power. And Gren finally knew what could do.

"Close your eyes!" he shouted to Arianna, and she hastily obeyed, for she could feel his energy increasing, the Essence pooling about him in a golden glow that burned through the shadows. Then Gren turned toward the tree, tilted back his head, and bellowed. It was not a word, merely a sound, all of the rage built up inside him pouring out in that one utterance. And with it came the fire.

Sparks flew from Gren's anima, and shot straight for the tree itself. They ringed it, a glittering dance of light about its base, and where they touched the bark flames leapt up. The fire quickly spread, racing up the trunk and out along the tendrils, and though the main tree was too strong to be destroyed by such flames, its tendrils shriveled and vanished in puffs of greasy smoke, taking their darkness with them. The flames took hold elsewhere as well, jumping from tendrils to overturned tables, small stands, wooden stools, even the bodies that lay heaped about. Soon everything within sight was on fire. Only Gren and Arianna were untouched, as they had been all this time.

Exhausted and spent, Gren lowered his head and looked around through tear-stuck eyelashes. The tree was shriveling, curling in upon itself as the others had, its time done. And the darkness had been swept away by the flames. The flames themselves were across the buildings now, consuming the footbridges and walkways, blackening the heavier support beams, and reducing the rice-paper walls to charred cinders. As the light from the fire grew, the tree's shadow dispersed, and the warm sunlight touched them again. It chased away the last of the darkness, and between that and the flames, the devastated village was filled with color and warmth, and fragrant wood smoke mixed with the faint smell of the countryside.

"Too late," Gren muttered to Arianna, right before he collapsed at her feet.

CHAPTER ELEVEN

"Can you hear me?"

Gren blinked and opened his eyes. Arianna was leaning over him. "What happened?"

"You passed out," she told him, kneeling down beside him. "I'm glad you woke up finally, though. I don't think I can move you again. It took everything I had to drag you out of there."

"Huh." He sat up and looked around. He was lying at the foot of the long bridge that crossed the river, near where they had tethered his horse. The fire was still licking along the bridge's length, but the moisture here was holding it at bay, and though blackened in places the bridge was still intact. Everything on the far side, however, had been consumed by the flames. The smell of burnt wood, flesh, and leather still hung in the air. "How long?"

"An hour or so. I thought it would be best to let you rest." She studied him carefully. "That was a lot of energy you expended. Are you all right?"

"Think so." He rose to one knee, then stood up slowly. "Yeah, I'm alright. A little weak."

"I would imagine so." She handed him a water skin and a hunk of bread with some dried meat. "This should help."

"Thanks." Gren busied himself with the food and drink as he glanced around. "Guess we didn't do so well, huh?"

She considered that. "You stopped it from spreading, which is good. We know more about how it works now, which is good." She glanced up at him. "But in the final accounting... no."

"Okay, so now what?" He finished off the bread and meat, and took another swig of water. "Even if we find another tree, I doubt we can stop it from killing people. We couldn't stop this one."

"If you had unleashed that flame before it had grown, it might have died," Arianna suggested, but shook her head when she saw the look on his face. "No, don't blame yourself. I should... I should have thought of it. Or anything." She sighed and accepted the water skin back from him, taking a healthy swallow herself.

Now it was Gren's turn to think. "Well, what do we know so far? These twisted trees are killing whole villages. It's happened five times so far, that we know of. Each time, no one's survived—except this time. It takes someone's death to make one grow—"

"That could be coincidence. That man just happened to be standing on the largest plot of dry ground in the center of the village."

"Fine, sure, but I don't buy it. Anyway, the trees grow incredibly fast, then they die when everyone around them is dead. Or when they've used up all the blood in their victim. What else?"

"It has only happened here in Ortense," she pointed out. "And this entire land is being tainted."

"Okay." Gren scratched the dirt with the tip of one boot. "Hey, wait a second." He scratched again, this time deliberately, drawing a rough circle. "This is Ortense, here. Here's Hadovas, up north." That was a scuff mark. "Here's this town." Another mark. "Here's where we met." Another mark. "Where are the two you found first?"

Arianna glanced at the crude map and shook her head. "I have no idea," she admitted, and Gren could tell that she hated to say such things. "I have no sense of this land yet."

"What did it look like?" She described it to him, and Gren frowned. "And it took you a week to get to the last town from there?" When she nodded, he drew another mark. "You were probably in Tillien, then. Here." She told him about the other town she'd seen, and he made an additional mark. "Lanting, there." Together they studied the results.

"Okay, all in Ortense, like you said," Gren agreed, staring at the marks. "That first one you found, though—that's a ways from these others. So it's not just spreading evenly."

"Those trees are the cause of each town's destruction," Arianna pointed out, "but something—or someone—is sending the seeds on their way."

"Right." Gren was still looking at the map, and now he nodded. "If we figure that someone's staying in one place doing… whatever he's doing, his reach has got to be long enough to hit each of these places."

"Or *her* reach," Arianna added.

"Or hers," he admitted. "So if he can hit Hadovas and this town over here," he indicated the first place she'd found, "he could just be right in between the two. Though that would put him," he scuffed a final mark in the center of the circle, "right about here. In Ortense."

"I thought you said we were already in Ortense," Arianna said, frowning.

"We are. Ortense is also the name of the capital." Gren shrugged. "I know, people with no imagination. But that's right in the center of all these others—and the whole kingdom. I don't like where this is leading…"

Arianna considered it. "It makes sense. Whoever is doing this has some goal in mind, something he or she hopes to gain. And if that is the capital, it would be the center of the kingdom's wealth and power. Anyone after either would do well to go there." She nodded. "All right then. Let us make our way toward Ortense. With luck, we will find something to lead us to the one causing this."

"I hope so," Gren told her, fingering the dagger stuck in his belt and looking at the ground. "Because even if those trees won't succumb to my flames, I'm betting the one who made them *will*."

Gren insisted on going back into the town, to make sure the bodies had all been fully consumed by the flames. Arianna did not try to dissuade him, and walked beside him without saying anything. But once they topped the hill again, they saw that the flames had done their work. Fed by the wood and paper, the fire had burned hot enough to reduce the corpses to ash, though perhaps not as cleanly as Gren would have done. He walked among them anyway, blessing each one in turn, and his voice caught when he reached the spot where Enjy and Rangol's bodies had fallen. The other Daggers were not far away, and Gren blessed them as well. There was nothing to gather from the town, so they left immediately after that. Gren did consider bringing Rangol's sword, but decided against it.

Back by the river bridge, his horse snorted in annoyance at being left alone so long. Gren quieted it, bribing it with a dried plum from his saddlebag, and then wordlessly mounted and offered Arianna a hand up. Agreeing silently that it would be better to leave that place as soon as possible, and not willing to risk creating another steed from the town's tainted Essence, she accepted the hand and swung up behind him. Then they took off at a gallop, heading toward the center of the kingdom.

It took them ten days to reach the capital, since they had decided that summoning another of Arianna's phantom steeds would take too much energy and draw too much attention. Gren had tried to insist that Arianna ride his horse the rest of the way, but she had refused to ride more than half the time, pointing out that she was used to walking. The trip was surprisingly pleasant and useful for both of them.

Arianna had initially thought of Gren as almost a tool to be used. He was a trained warrior, and knew how to handle himself in a fight, which was useful. His ability to immolate the dead was invaluable, and he'd demonstrated at that last village that the flames could serve other purposes as well. But she had assumed that he was crude, rough, and not particularly bright, based largely upon his size and his former profession. Later she admitted to herself that she should have known better—the Unconquered Sun would have chosen more wisely.

Over the days that followed, she learned that Gren was far smarter than she had first realized. She discovered that the second night. They had stopped to set up camp, and she had immediately pulled a book from her pack and started reading. That was how she had spent the previous night as well, only looking up when Gren had asked her a direct question. This time he sat down across from her and asked a question right away.

"What is that you're reading?"

"A book," she'd replied, still reading. But he laughed.

"I know that." He reached out and took it from her, and though that annoyed her, she didn't stop him. Then he glanced at the cover and frowned. "*Annals of a Corsair?*" He grinned at her. "Interested in pirates, eh?"

That surprised her, both that he could read and that he knew what a corsair was. "That's right. This is a history of Iona Sailstream, one of the greatest corsairs to raid the Realm in his day."

Gren nodded and leaned back. They were camped on a tiny spit of land jutting out between two bridges, and he had sat with his back against one of the bridge posts. "I've heard of him. Raided to the south mainly, didn't he?"

"Yes, he was feared all along the southern coast," she admitted. "It took an entire fleet of Imperial ships to finally bring him to justice."

"Why read that?" Gren scratched idly along his jaw. "He's long since dead, the desert tribes are probably completely different from the ones he faced."

"I like histories," Arianna replied, but knew that wasn't the whole truth. "This author thinks Sailstream might have been Anathema—Exalted," she finally added. "The evidence is intriguing. By reading about it, I can learn more about those Solars who emerged after the end of the First Age. What they were like, what they knew."

"Ah, I understand." Gren nodded again. "It's frustrating, knowing we can do things and not knowing what they are. I guess any hints would be helpful."

It was a simple statement, but it impressed her. Clearly he had considered the matter since his Exaltation only a few weeks ago. And just as clearly, he had understood her interests and intentions from what little she had revealed. Not stupid by any stretch, then. And now she found herself intrigued by him even more than the book, enough so that she actually set the slim volume down on her pack again.

"Where did you learn to read?" she asked him, and he laughed.

"Weren't expecting that from a dumb grunt, eh?" But he didn't sound bitter. "Long time ago, I signed on with a group that was fighting a siege. One of the men in my camp had been trained as a minstrel in his youth, before some... indiscretions forced him to take up the sword instead. He taught me to read and write a little, in exchange for my watching his back. Not that it did him much good." He turned somber again for a moment. "Rangol taught me more. He said it was nice to have someone else in the Daggers who could actually write out a list, or read a message."

That conversation forced Arianna to re-evaluate her companion, and she was impressed by what she saw over the next few days. After they had recovered from the events of the last town she saw that her new companion was methodical and patient, but not in a plodding way. He studied each situation, examined the options, tossed out the ones that were not possible for him, chose the one he felt would be most effective, decided how to implement it, and then began. There was very little wasted thought, and little wasted motion, either. And many things that she thought were difficult, like selecting and setting up a campsite, he seemed to do almost out of habit, without much conscious thought. He didn't talk much, particularly without prompting, and often he seemed almost asleep on his horse, but she noticed that his eyes were rarely completely closed, and he snapped awake at the slightest sound or movement. He did not miss much around him. That was certain. And yet he remained calm and collected. In that way he reminded her of Swan, who had rarely been ruffled. But Swan had been full of energy and grace and words, whereas Gren was quiet and thoughtful and solid. She found herself wondering if the two would have gotten along. Perhaps some day she would have the chance to introduce them and find out for certain.

Gren, for his part, had seen Arianna as an arrogant young woman, cold and quiet and uninterested in being more than civil but filled with knowledge he could use. The latter part was correct, he found, but there was a lot more going on with her than just distance and egotism. Arianna had an amazing capacity to focus all of her thoughts and senses upon a single point, he discovered, and her intensity was just shy of frightening. She had immense knowledge stored away beneath that long white hair, but little of it was practical, and she fumbled at collecting wood and lighting fires so much that Gren had to laugh the first few times he watched her. But she knew a great deal more about being Exalted than he did, more than he suspected many of their kind did, and he knew he could use that information.

What surprised him, however, was how much he began to enjoy her company. She would be silent for long stretches, then suddenly burst out with a flurry of conversation, or more often a lecture, and he soon realized that she was busy thinking the entire time and collected her thoughts into these random spates of words. But as the days went on, he began to realize that her coolness was merely a front. She was still very young, and he guessed that she had been forced to fend for herself for a long time. With her looks, she must have attracted a lot of unwanted attention even before becoming Exalted. So she had acted cold and haughty to keep would-be admirers at bay.

Gren found himself doing most of the talking, which was all right with him. In the Daggers he had been one of the quieter ones, and the change helped him distance himself from the pain of thinking about that unit. He told her about his misspent youth, his rough training, and some (though certainly not all) of the things he'd done as a mercenary. At first he had merely been talking to fill the silence, but one day he glanced over and realized that she was actually listening to him. He was so surprised he stopped in mid-sentence.

"What happened next?" she asked him quietly after a moment.

"What?"

"The raid on the pigs," she said, glancing away. "The farmer had woken up and come after you with a pitchfork. What happened next?"

After that, Gren found that she was actively enjoying his stories, and she even began asking him to tell her about certain aspects of his life. And slowly, very slowly, she began telling him about her in return. She told him about her life in the tower, taking care of the kitchen and the books and sneaking into the library each night to read tomes those empty-headed scholars could never understand. The more she said, the more Gren understood why she had acted so distant at first, and the more he both admired her and pitied her. And the more they talked, the more Arianna seemed to relax around him, and the more comfortable they became together.

They made a surprisingly good pair. Arianna was pleased to discover that Gren did have a sense of humor, and though rough and direct it was less crude than she'd feared. She was the better cook by far, and had no qualms with handling that chore, but while neither of them enjoyed cleaning up afterward, Gren handled it quickly and efficiently and without fuss. Arianna had spent too many years sweeping and washing for thankless boys to handle the same tasks without grumbling. He was also far her superior at setting up camp and building a fire, and she stayed out of his way for such things, watching as he handled them with quiet competence.

"I don't see why you do that," she told him one morning, as she watched him removing traces of their camp.

He shrugged but continued what he was doing. "No harm in it, and it may be useful," he replied. He dug a small hole beside the remains of the campfire, tossed aside the rocks he had ringed it with, and then scooped the ashes into the hole and tamped the earth flat again.

"On the road, one horse hoof is much like another," Gren said, straightening and brushing the dirt from his legs. "But campsites are different. Anyone who knows such things could read one and tell when it was last used and even by how many." He winced at those last words, as it occurred to him that each night he had been building a fire much larger than the two of them needed. He had been setting a fire the way he always had, when it was him and the rest of the Daggers. "Better to be safe," he finished, wiping his hands on his pants and heading toward the horse.

Arianna could see that something had upset him, but she didn't know what, so she decided to keep silent. She simply followed his lead, and mounted the horse, wheeling it around as they started down the trail again.

Two days into their journey, they met the first person they'd seen since the village. And heard their first rumors.

"A great black boar, it was," the old rice farmer told them, leaning on his hoe. "Tore them to pieces, everyone. Y'can hear it roarin' through the forest at night, y'listen closely."

"Have you seen this boar?" Gren asked politely, but the man shook his head.

"Nah. If I'm lucky I won't, either. Worth a man's life to avoid such a beast, that." He eyed Gren carefully. "Best keep that blade ready, man, and keep her close, and sleep wit' one eye open, hey?"

Gren simply nodded and patted the sword's hilt, as if to reassure the man. There was little else to say, and they were 10 minutes away before Arianna could no longer contain herself.

"A boar!" she burst out, glancing back in the farmer's direction though he was long out of view. "How could a boar have done all that, even a giant one? It's ridiculous!"

Gren laughed. "Not used to people much, are you?" he asked her, then shook his head. "He said he hadn't seen it, and I'm sure he hasn't seen any of the destruction, either. He's just saying what he's heard, or what he thinks may have caused whatever he did hear. Who knows what people are saying happened at those towns? Though," he added with a frown, "I reckon we'll find out soon enough."

And they did. As they encountered more people—and none of the homes or small villages here had been attacked— they heard yet more stories of what had happened near the border. "A hailstorm, out of nowhere," one old woman told them solemnly, "with hailstones larger than a man's head. Tore right through the buildings like they were straw."

"Drought," a middle-aged ox herder recounted, his older companion nodding sagely, "drained them dry in a fortnight, withered their bodies almost to dust."

"Wyld barbarians," another said, eyeing Gren uneasily. "Big ape men with goat-demons leadin' 'em. They been raidin' all over Verdangate, Nishion, Freeden, and Tulpa. We got to be next."

"Balls of fire from the sky," was the one that stopped them. It was a younger but clearly travel-worn man who said it, and he was sitting by the river's edge at a small town one day as they stopped to water their horse and take some lunch.

"What did you say?" Arianna asked him, leading the horse closer. It was the first time she had taken the lead in a conversation.

"Balls of fire from the sky," the man repeated, nodding politely to her and to Gren. "I seen it myself. Well, not the fire, but the aftermath."

"What do you mean?" Gren asked, walking up behind Arianna. The man clearly noticed his sword and armor, but didn't seem too frightened by them.

"I took some wares to Anaka a few days back," the stranger told them. "Pots and bowls, spoons and chopsticks— I make them and sell them hereabouts. But when I got there, nothing was left. Just blackened ruins. Like a giant fire had burned the place out."

"Perhaps someone left a cooking fire unattended," Arianna suggested, but he shook his head.

"Nah, too much open space for a fire to cross. And no cook fire would have burned that hot. This was more like the fire I seen used to melt metal. It burned them to ash, everyone, and the walkways, too. Most of the buildings as well. Even the supports were charred black."

"But why balls of fire from the sky?" she pressed, watching him carefully, all else forgotten. "What makes you say that?"

He shrugged. "What else could it be? The area past the town was untouched. Even just beyond the buildings, the bridges weren't harmed. No regular fire would have stopped like that. And the ground was clear beneath. I scraped at the soot with my toe, and under it was regular dirt. So it must have come from the sky." He glanced up, almost as if expecting a fireball to strike him for revealing such information, then chuckled. "Least, it's the only thing I can think."

"No one really knows what happened," Arianna said as they rode away an hour or so later.

"Why would they?" Gren replied. "If we hadn't seen those trees in action I don't know that I'd believe it, either. All people know is that something's been killing whole towns before anyone can get away. And, thanks to our fires, they don't even know what killed the people. Which is for the best," he admitted, shuddering as he thought again of the expressions on those people as they had died.

"Yes, but we'll never learn anything this way," she said, sighing. "I'd hoped someone might have some idea of who had done this, or why."

"They're just villagers," Gren said, glancing back at the one they had just left behind. "They don't know much beyond their own town and their animals. I know—I grew up in a place just like it."

The people of Ortense did know one thing, however, as Gren and Arianna realized when they reached the next town. They knew fear.

"Morning," Gren said, nodding to an old man leading an ox down the same dirt path they were riding. The man took one look at them and fled, leading the startled animal along with him.

"You are a bit imposing," Arianna pointed out when she saw the look on his face. "Particularly in your armor."

"Yeah, well, you should see me when I've got it *all* on," Gren replied, patting the helmet, facemask, and gloves tied to his saddle. "Still, I've gotten weird looks and people backing away before. Not usually outright flight."

The next person they saw was an old woman who was hanging up some washing along the riverbank. "Good morning," Arianna called out, but the woman glanced up, saw the two of them, and backed away, knocking over her laundry basket in her haste. Her hands flew up as she clambered back to her feet, and made some sort of gesture that was clearly meant to ward them off.

"Not just me, then," Gren commented as they watched the woman dart back into a nearby house and slam the door. "And you're a lot less scary-looking than I am."

"A lot *less*?" she responded, but her mind was elsewhere. "Could someone have mentioned us? Maybe someone did survive Anaka?" But she shook her head, answering her own question.

Gren had a few ideas, but figured he'd wait and see, so he held his tongue as he led Arianna and the horse across the final footbridge and on into the town. Not everyone fled when they saw the pair of them, but those who didn't did back away quickly and avert their eyes. Gren was used to people disliking him, and even people being afraid of him, but this was more than that.

"You," he finally called out, pointing at a young man who had been grilling a pair of fish until they'd arrived. "Come here. Now!" he added when the youth did not respond immediately. Something about his tone, or perhaps the sword at his side, made the stranger comply, though he wouldn't look at them or their horse.

"What's your name?" Gren demanded, leaning down so that he was closer to eye level.

"Harper," the youth said finally with a loud gulp.

"All right, Harper. Suppose you tell me why everyone's running away from me and my friend here." Gren frowned. "That wasn't a question, Harper."

The boy looked panicked, and his skin paled visibly. He wrung his hands, looking everywhere but them. Finally he burst out with, "Don't kill us! Please! We didn't do nothing!"

"Kill you?" Gren's frown deepened. "What? I don't even know you."

For the first time Harper glanced up at them, and both Gren and Arianna could see the tears in his eyes. "You mean, you're not—?" but he couldn't finish his question.

"Not what?" Arianna prompted.

"Not the—" Harper looked around, and his voice dropped so quiet that Gren wasn't sure he heard it right. "—not the Sower?"

"The Sower?" Now Gren straightened up. "No, we're not. He's in Ortense playing with his new crown, isn't he?"

The youth gasped at that, and backed away a step, staring about to make sure no one else had heard. Unfortunately, everyone was watching the exchange, which meant that everyone else nearby had heard Gren's words. When Harper realized that, he turned even paler. "Don't talk like that!" he gasped. "We're loyal! We do what we're told! We don't want to die!"

"Die? What—?" Gren stopped as he understood. "You think this Sower character is causing towns to die?" he shook his head. "Trust me, boy, he uses steel like any other man. I should know." *I worked for him*, he started to add, but thought better of it.

"What's that?" This was an older man who straightened up from where he'd been hiding behind a nearby screen. "That's not what we heard!"

"And what did you hear, exactly?" Arianna asked him. Gren noticed that she didn't bother to hide her interest, or to act all womanish and non-threatening. It was one of the things he liked about her. She couldn't be bothered to pretend that she was weak or slow.

"This Sower is the new king," the man told her anyway, though he didn't leave the shelter of the thin rattan screen. "Anyone who gives him trouble dies horribly. And he doesn't stop at a single person. No, if one person gives him grief, he kills their whole family, then their whole town. Overnight. Leaves nothing but ashes."

Gren started to argue but couldn't, because it did make sense. He knew that the Sower had used the Daggers to win the kingdom, so clearly the man had needed normal muscle to take the throne, but the timing was convenient. And they had been spreading terror so that people would be frightened enough to obey their new king. And Hadovas had been one of the first towns to be destroyed. He glanced over at Arianna, and saw that she was thinking much the same thing. Perhaps they had found information after all.

Harper had backed away when the older man had joined the conversation, and now Arianna dismounted and watered their horse. They didn't bother to question anyone else, or even to look around, which is why they were both surprised when a hand suddenly thrust a basket at them.

"Here, take it." It was the old woman they'd seen before, and from the covered basket came the unmistakable smells of fresh steamed buns, fish, and roasted bird. "Sorry about before. I thought you was the Sower."

"Thank you," Gren told her, accepting the basket. "We didn't mean to frighten you."

"Not your fault." The woman shrugged. "We all been scared lately. Jónas," she nodded at a man sitting on a stool carving something, "seen what happened at Tuaric. And we heard from folks in Linnea 'bout the new king and all. 'Obey or die,' they said. Figure them others didn't obey." She glanced over at Arianna, back at Gren, then looked away again. "You two came riding in on that horse, you ain't from here and neither are they. Figured you was with him. Or you was him."

"I understand," Gren assured her. "It's all right. Really."

"Best to get out," the woman told her, though not meanly. "Outta Ortense. Safer. Way you two look, might get the Sower after you, too." She backed away then, and they let her go. Arianna remounted shortly after and rode out quickly, the basket in her hands and Gren walking right beside her. The villagers watched them go, and no one tried to stop them.

"I don't like this," Gren admitted later, when they'd stopped to enjoy the lunch the woman had given them. "If the Sower could do all this, why bother hiring us at all?"

"Perhaps he needed you at the time," Arianna suggested, neatly piling a piece of meat and several slices of plum onto part of a bun. "Perhaps he's come into more than just temporal power."

"Maybe," Gren said, taking a bite of quail himself and washing it down with the water skin he'd refilled in town. "But Rangol didn't say anything about this guy being Exalted." He was pleased that he only paused for an instant on his friend's name.

"What makes you think he is Exalted?"

"Well, these trees are magic, right?"

"Definitely. And powerful magic, at that."

"So that means Exalted. They're—we're," he corrected himself, "the only ones with magic like that. Aren't we?"

She was already shaking her head. "Not at all. Creation is filled with spirits and creatures that can work magic, some far better than we can. The Fair Folk, for example." Gren nodded at that—he'd heard stories of the Fair Folk, though most of it he'd dismissed as beer-induced. But she was still talking. "The only thing we know it *isn't* is demonic magic, as I ruled out when we met. But there are other Exalted. We, you and I, belong to the Unconquered Sun. But the Moon has its own champions. And the Dragon-Blooded can work spells, though I doubt this belongs to them." She frowned, trying to tug free a scrap of knowledge that was tickling the back of her brain. "Something about his name reminds me of something. It's such a strange title for such a backwater kingdom."

Gren snorted. "He is a pretentious one. 'Sower of decay and distrust,' Rangol said he called himself. Wanted to put fear into people, I'd say, and figured his name was the place to start."

"There's something more to it than that," she insisted, accepting the water skin from him and taking a quick swallow. "I think Swan... an acquaintance of mine once told me something about someone with a similar name. It will come back to me." She sighed and turned away to hide an expression of self-reproach. "I just hope I remember in time for it to do us some good this time."

CHAPTER TWELVE

"Yes, Cytel?" The Sower glanced up from the scroll he'd been studying, his gaze flickering across the courtier who stood shivering before the throne. Even that brief glance was enough to make the man's knees weaken, and he was all but in tears.

"Sire—Sower—sir, your troops…"

"What about my loyal troops?" He set the scroll aside for now, rolling it and tucking it into Mariburn's convenient left eye socket, and gave the terrified courtier his full attention. He was actually surprised that the man did not run away, as so many of his friends had in similar situations. This one might almost be worth keeping.

"They are—sir, they are terrorizing the people!" *Impressive*, the Sower admitted to himself. *Not only brave enough to withstand my gaze, but he actually dares to question my warriors.*

"And what are they doing to them, exactly?" he asked lazily, leaning back and running his fingers idly across Mariburn's skull. The motion was not lost on Cytel, and he turned even paler, his skin now even whiter than that same ornament. "Are they attacking any of my citizens?" the Sower continued. "Beating hapless old men? Raping defenseless women? Devouring small children?" The courtier had to shake his head at each accusation, as the Sower had known he would. "Are they taunting people, casting insults at them? Laughing at them? Making lewd gestures?" More head shakes. "Perhaps they are creating too much noise, keeping the citizenry awake all night with their drinking and singing and shouting? No? Then what, exactly, is the problem?"

"Sire—sir, they are—that is, they were—well, but you must know that they—"

"Yes?" He leaned forward, his face mere inches from the courtier's. Cytel's courage finally broke, and he backed away, tripping when his foot missed the first step and sprawling onto the floor. He hastily pulled himself to his feet and backed away farther, stammering apologies, then finally gave up all pretense and ran for the door.

Yes, the Sower thought, watching him go. Definitely some potential there. He would have to convert this Cytel, and soon. Or else break him.

The throne room was empty now. None of the other courtiers would approach it, or the palace in general, as long as his guards stood watch. And they always stood watch. He glanced around, noting the ones who stood ready in each corner, and the two on either side of the door. More stood on the palace's front steps, and still more were clustered by the city gates. The remaining handful waited in the guardhouse near the city walls, in case he should need them. Not that he did, really. But it was always good to have spares.

It was astonishing, really. Just before setting his plan into motion, he had lacked faith that he could take Ortense with only two-hundred mercenaries, but his master had given his blessing to the endeavor and it had worked. The Scarlet Daggers had defeated Ortense's entire army, and basically handed him the throne. Two hundred against more than four times that number. Not that the two forces fought directly. No, he had been impressed by the tactics of the Daggers and their leader, the one called Rangol. The mercenaries were broken into small fighting units, and these had each targeted specific locations, striking quickly and then disappearing. They had whittled away at the local militia, using their own size and established patrol routes against them. Many of the Daggers had been placed around the kingdom, harrying the militias based there so that the soldiers could not come to the aid of the king. Rangol's own unit, plus five others, had struck at the capital itself, carving away at Mariburn's guards. The Sower had walked in unopposed while all of the guards had been occupied elsewhere, and had killed the king and his family personally. Then he had laid claim to the throne. The guards were too disorganized to stop him, particularly without a king, and any other claimants had either died or gone into hiding. It had worked beautifully.

That done, he had doubted that he could maintain the city and keep all the people in check with only fifty guards. That was half the number Mariburn had kept.

But his guards were… different than Mariburn's guards.

Those who manned the city gates and patrolled the marketplace and the other major locations were mere shambling hulks, suitable for little more than crude tasks. But they sufficed. And their appearance, the way the flesh rotted from their bones and the light of the Underworld shone in their empty eye sockets, was enough to send most people screaming. Yes, his guards were effective.

And here in the palace he had others, even more useful. No mere zombies to guard him!

He glanced at the nearest Servitor, who stood stock-still in the corner just past the hall that led to his chambers. Tall and broad, the warrior waited without motion, and had for hours on end. And would for hours more, if necessary. They did not need to eat or drink, his Servitors. And they did not sleep. Nor did they complain, or drink, or swear—or, for that matter, speak. All they did was follow orders. They were the perfect soldiers.

And yes, the people were frightened. They were supposed to be. These guards fed on fear as most men fed on beef and bread. Fear was their nourishment, and their only form of pleasure. And the more people feared them, the stronger they became, and the more fear they generated in return. And the more easily the handful of them could keep the town under such tight control.

The Sower smiled, nodding at the guard. The guard did not nod back. He gave no indication that he had even noticed the Sower's movement. That was fine. They did not react to anything except perceived threats, these guards. Those they dealt with quickly, however.

And there had already been several. Several courtiers, who had meekly accepted the death of Mariburn and his replacement by the Sower, had decided that these guards were simply too much to bear. Four of them, along with their own guards, had walked into the throne room together shortly after the Sower had summoned his new warriors. Their foolish bravery had stirred uncomfortable memories in the Sower at the time, but he was able to look back on it now with more of a sense of humor.

"This is an abomination!" The oldest of them, a middle-aged man named Ristan, had shouted. He was wearing a mail shirt and had a sword buckled at his side, and even though those items had probably sat idle for twenty years, Ristan still looked like he knew how to use them. "We will not stand for this desecration!" His followers nodded and shouted their agreement.

"Oh, really?" The Sower had said, leaning back and watching them behind almost-lowered lids. He knew that it made him appear bored, which only angered Ristan further. "And in what way have I offended you, my noble courtier?"

"These—things," Ristan had replied, gesturing with one mailed hand toward the nearest guard. "They should not be here. They should not be walking! Get rid of them at once!"

"Or what?" he had replied, looking up fully now. Ristan had backed away a step, but then rallied.

"Or we will return to them to their rightful places, and you with them," the courtier had replied quietly, hand going to his sword.

"I take it we cannot discuss this?" he had asked then, just to annoy them and to show how little he really cared. Ristan had not bothered to reply. "Oh, very well." He glanced at the guards nearest the throne. "Kill them all."

It had been amusing to watch. His guards had converged on the courtiers and their men, swords raised and ready. Ristan had known exactly what he was doing, the Sower had to admit. He had quickly organized his men so that they all stood in a tight circle, their backs to one another, weapons drawn. This way no one could attack them from behind, and they didn't have to worry about clashing with each other or getting in each other's way. Dealing with a handful of normal guards, that tactic would have worked. But these were not normal guards, or even normal men.

The first guard had gone straight for Ristan. The courtier had struck first, a nasty slash across the belly. The sharp blade had torn cloth, mail, and flesh, leaving a gaping wound. A normal man would have collapsed then, clutching desperately at his intestines as they spilled free. But the guard did not even slow down. His sword stabbed forward, piercing Ristan's chest, and everyone in the room could hear the splinter of bone as the steel shattered his breastbone. It split his heart and then continued out through his back, leaving the fiery courtier a limp weight that flopped mindlessly on the sword like a fresh-caught fish on a stick.

The other men, seeing this, had broken their formation and tried to run, but the guards were on all sides. They had no choice but to fight. A few managed to strike first, but it did them no good. Others tossed down their weapons and begged for mercy, but the guards did not hear. Each strike of a guard's sword connected, and each one felled an opponent, often shearing off limbs in the process. In less than a minute, the entire battle was over, and none but the guards were left standing.

Since then, none of the other courtiers had dared oppose him. Most did not even approach anymore. They had taken to hiding in the nearby taverns, he knew, grousing about his commands and what he had done to the throne room, the palace, the city, the kingdom. Let them complain. They were useless anyway, and this way they were all in one place, and mostly drunk. It kept them out of his way.

Reigning in his wandering thoughts, the Sower eyed the guard again. He often found himself admiring his warriors, their single-mindedness and efficiency. Before, he might have been as frightened as the rest, seeing the tattered, crumbling clothes, the rusted mail, the moldy flesh, the yellowing bones that thrust through in places. Certainly he would have found their faces unnerving, with their fixed expressions, bared teeth, shriveled flesh, and ragged hair. The fact that many of them lacked eyes, but all of them had a red glow deep where the eyes should be, could have given him pause as well. Now, however, he found them comforting. The living were far too much trouble. The dead were easier to control.

The guard to his right was a perfect example. Alive, Ristan had been an annoyance, a pest, possibly even a danger. Now he was silent, obedient, and useful. His chest, where it had been split open, was now a dark mass of rotted flesh, and from the right angle the Sower could see the ribs and the shriveled organs beneath. His hand, where it clutched his sword, was little more than bones within the mailed gauntlet, and what remained of his skin was mottled with mold and blackened from decay. But his eyes bore the red gleam of awareness, and he moved quickly enough to defend the Sower when required.

Yes, these warriors were the perfect army for him. And the best part was, even if someone killed several of them, he could always add new members to the ranks. Most likely, the fallen from those same attackers. So every time anyone attacked, they were actually increasing his army.

It was the perfect use for old fighters. And unlike the hired swords he'd had before, these warriors did not complain when there was no action. And they never demanded more money. Or any money. Or anything. They did exactly what they were told.

The Sower smiled absently, fingers still caressing the skull, eyes looking at and through his attacker-turned-guard. Skulls on the throne, blood in the seams between floor tiles, the raised dead for guards, the heavy black drapes that covered the windows and the columns… it was beginning to take shape. Slowly but surely, he was bending Ortense to his will—altering it to suit his desires and honor his master who had allowed him this personal indulgence. When the city and then the kingdom matched the place he had imagined, then the kingdom would be utterly in his control, and its place among the shadows would be complete.

For the meantime, he contented himself with remembering the look on Ristan's face when he had died, and the look on everyone else's face when he had brought the man back and made him a mindless fighter under his total control. His guards weren't the only ones who lived on fear, and lately he was filled to the brim.

And it would only intensify, as his control over this land tightened.

CHAPTER
THIRTEEN

Several days later they were on a long, broad wooden bridge traversing a wide but shallow river when Gren spotted a dark shape heading toward them. He squinted at it.

"Boat," he told Arianna, his hand straying to his sword hilt. "Maybe more than one. Be ready."

As the boat grew closer, Gren saw that he had been right not to assume. Behind the first small punt he could see a second, larger boat, carrying at least four people. There was no break in the bridge, which meant the boats would have to be emptied and carried across—and the two of them were too close to the middle to reach either side before the first boat arrived. Gren slowed his pace and Arianna slowed the horse, until they were moving at a slow walk. He had his sword loose in its scabbard, and a glance showed that Arianna's right hand had strayed closer to her dagger, but they did not draw yet. Gren hoped they wouldn't have to. His encounter in Hadovas had demonstrated that, no matter how good you were with a blade, you'd lose if you were outnumbered enough.

"Might as well be up-front about it," he muttered, more to himself than to his companion, pausing halfway across. "Ho there!" he shouted, holding up his free hand.

"Hello," the man in the first boat replied, paddling up to the bridge. Now Gren could see that it was an older man, worn thin by the years but still handling the boat well. The man's clothes were fine but dirty, and the sword at his side looked more ornamental than useful. Nor did the man reach for it as he swung the boat up against the bridge, and Gren reached out a hand to steady it for him.

"How are things the way you came?" the man asked, stepping up onto the bridge. The second boat was almost upon them now, and Gren could see that the man was traveling with five others, two of them women, and that the second boat was heavily laden.

"Not bad," Gren replied, trying to relax his face into a smile. "Clean, wet, and nobody on it but us. What about your way?"

"Much the same," the stranger replied. "We passed a few fishermen, but nothing more." He studied Gren's armor and sword openly. "Are you a mercenary?" He didn't sound contemptuous or just politely curious. Actually, Gren recognized that tone, and it relaxed him still further. Anyone looking to hire him wasn't likely to be a threat without him.

"I was," he admitted. "But I gave that up." He saw the other man smile past him to where Arianna sat on the horse. Let him misunderstand why Gren had quit. That was fine.

"Shame," the man said, looking at Gren again. "My master would have hired you to guard us on our journey."

Master? Gren glanced where the man gestured, to one of the men sitting in the second boat. Yes, he had the bearing of someone important, and his clothes were even finer, though just as dirty. In fact—

Gren looked more closely, then stared openly, forgetting all about the man next to him. "I know you!" he bellowed, startling everyone else. The second man, who had not been paying much attention, glanced at him when he shouted, then turned pale. He glanced around anxiously, but there was nowhere for him to go, and one of the other men in his boat was already stepping onto the bridge, holding a stout rope to anchor the boat there. Gren stepped over to him and helped tie the rope to one of the bridge supports.

"I'm not here to hurt you," he told the noble, who was still shrinking back from him. "I quit that sort of work."

"Oh, did you?" It was the first time he'd heard the man speak, but his voice was definitely that of a noble—cultured, educated, and arrogant. "Not before you'd butchered our army or helped put that madman on the throne!"

Arianna and the first man had approached by this point. "You know each other?" she asked Gren, nodding politely to the noble.

"We've met," Gren replied, offering one of the women a hand out of the boat. She hesitated, glancing back at the noble, who finally nodded. Then she accepted the aid and quickly moved behind the first man. "Though I don't know your name."

"Lord Trellan," the noble replied, then added, "or at least it was. There's little of my estate left now, thanks to you and your friends." He ignored Gren's hand and stepped across, then turned to assist the second woman and the boy behind her. The other two men had already lifted the punt and carried it to the other side of the bridge, and now they began unloading the bundles from the second boat so that it could be portaged as well.

"A pleasure, my lord," Arianna said, managing to almost curtsey while still on horseback. Her manners had an immediate effect on the nobleman.

"Charmed, my dear." He bowed back. "Clearly you are a young lady of good breeding, despite your attire. How, if I may ask, did you find yourself with this rogue? Are you in need of assistance?"

Arianna laughed, amused by the notion that this flimsy-looking man, even with his two old servants and the youth and the two women, could possibly hope to stand in Gren's way. "No, but thank you. This man and I are traveling together toward Ortense."

"Ortense!" One of the ladies gasped, and the other actually fluttered her hands as if she were about to faint. Arianna tried not to let her derision show. How could women stand to be so foolish? Look at those dresses! She remembered wearing such swathes of cloth, how confining it had been, and reveled again at being free of such fripperies.

"I would not go there, young lady," Trellan warned her. "Not unless you absolutely must. Even with this... man at your side, it is not safe."

"Why not?" It was Gren who replied with a frown.

"Horrible things," the first servant told him, shuddering. "Terrible things!"

"He is correct," Trellan told them. He eyed Gren again. "Much as I detest what you and your rabble did to us, at least you were men. You fought for coin and drink. I can understand that. But these things that guard the city now..." he shuddered as well. "They are not human."

"Is this the Sower's doing?" Arianna asked, and Trellan laughed a short, humorless sound.

"The Sower? What a ridiculous name! But then, he was always a fool, that one. I can't imagine why he thought changing his name would alter that. Though I must admit," here he shuddered again, "he is certainly changed, and not for the better. Would that Mariburn had done the job properly!"

"Wait, you knew the Sower before this?" Arianna drew closer. "And he had a different name?"

"Oh yes," Trellan assured her. "Belamis. He was a minor courtier, more an annoyance than anything, and quite laughable. I sometimes think he was the court fool, or as close as we had to one. But he thought much better of himself than that. Such men always do. He thought he was good enough to be a lord—even a king."

Gren was trying to remember what Rangol had told them when they'd taken the job. "He said he was reclaiming the throne, that it belonged to him. Not that we believed him, necessarily, but he seemed pretty set on this particular throne."

"He tried to take it once before," Trellan explained. "A year ago. Belamis drew a few other fools to his side, and they hired as many men as they could afford and attacked the palace. But Mariburn knew they were coming, and he bought off the soldiers beforehand, and the other would-be rebels as well. When Belamis burst into the throne room, he was all alone."

"And Mariburn didn't kill him?" Gren shook his head in disgust. "He was a fool then."

"I agree," Trellan said, which surprised them. "Letting Belamis live was taking a risk. Even as useless as he was, if he found someone to back him he could be a threat. As he turned out to be." Again he glared at Gren, but most of the rancor seemed to have fled his gaze.

"You're sure it's the same man?" Arianna asked him quietly.

"Yes, quite sure. I knew Belamis well enough. He was always trying to curry favor with myself and the other nobles. He still looks much the same, though those thick curls of his are gone now. Actually," Trellan paused, and frowned a little, "he does look different. More angular. Perhaps Mariburn had him confined and starved this past year. He looks very… hungry. But it is definitely him."

"Does he go by both names now, or just the one?" Arianna seemed very intent upon the answer, and Trellan blinked, surprised by the question. He eyed her again, clearly realizing now that she was more than a pretty face and a soft voice.

"No, he refuses to acknowledge his old name," he admitted. "A few of the others called him 'King Belamis' when he took the throne. He snarled at them that he was the Sower of Decay and Distrust, and should only be referred to as such. They died shortly after." The look on his face told plainly that he did not want to think about how his friends had perished. "After that, no one dared use the name 'Belamis' again."

"I take it he wasn't happy to see you either," Gren commented, glancing pointedly at their little group. Trellan snorted and raised his chin defiantly.

"I would not know. After your bloodthirsty little band put him on the throne, I gathered my family and my most trusted servants. We took everything we could carry, set our affairs in order, and fled the city." He shuddered again, and once more the one woman almost swooned. "We were almost too late, at that. I lost three good men and one boat to the horrors that bar the gates, and the rest of us have had unquiet sleep ever since. But if we had stayed—well, Belamis was always a vicious little brute beneath his curls and smile. I saw at once that he would be even worse now. I know I was right."

"Where are you going now?" Arianna asked them.

"I have a country estate, not far from the border," Trellan told her. "We will shelter there and hope that, what Belamis did to Mariburn, someone does to him in turn."

"Don't stop at your estate," Gren warned him. "Get out of Ortense for now. It's safer."

Trellan opened his mouth to protest, but Arianna cut him off. "Gren is right," she told the noble. "The Sower's arm is long, and he has already struck down Hadovas and several others. You are best served leaving the kingdom for a time."

"Hadovas?" Trellan blanched. "I had heard stories on the river—whole towns destroyed, but surely—?" He cringed when both Gren and Arianna nodded grimly. Then he pulled himself together and nodded as well. "Perhaps you are right. My cousin has a home a week's ride past the border. We can stay with her for a time, I think."

"Good luck," Gren told him, grabbing one end of the larger boat and hoisting it out of the water. The two servants and the youth barely managed their end, but together the four of them carried it across the bridge and dropped it back into the water on the other side.

"Thank you." Trellan led the ladies back to the boat, but paused and looked at Gren before stepping down himself. "I remember now. You and your friends cut our soldiers to ribbons." Gren didn't deny it, and the noble favored him with a small smile. "Yes, and I do not fault you for that. It was your job. But you—you stopped them from killing those who surrendered, didn't you?"

Gren nodded. Lirat and Scamp had wanted to finish them, of course, as had Milch and Hud. But he had protested, and Rangol and Enjy had backed him.

Trellan gave him a nod, that of a man to an equal. "I can respect that." His look turned sad. "They are all dead now, though. Belamis saw to that. I am sorry." And he stepped into the boat and pushed it away from the bridge. The first man had already steered the punt clear, and now the other servant took up his paddle and propelled the second boat after it down the river. None of them looked back.

Gren and Arianna watched them go. "You said you and your friends put him on the throne," Arianna remarked, "but I had not realized that the eight of you had defeated an entire army."

That brought a laugh from him. "Not quite. The Scarlet Daggers are a full mercenary group. I think we have—had—close to two-hundred men when we took this job. Within that, the Daggers are broken into patrols of twenty to thirty, and then units, usually five to ten men. Rangol is—was—in charge, and each patrol leader answered to him. I was in his personal combat unit—we were the top of the heap—but it took all the Daggers together to take the kingdom." He remembered the fighting. "The militia's biggest problem was organization. They had one large force at the capital, and then smaller forces scattered around the border, but no way to bring them together effectively. And even within each force, they didn't work well together—too used to facing small threats. Thieves and raiders rather than soldiers. Plus they had regular patrol routes, which were easy to learn and then either avoid or ambush. We'd send a unit to make some noise, get a band of them after us, turn around and cut them down, then do the same thing to another band. Pretty soon there wasn't anyone left." He had been proud of their tactics, but even then the actual fighting had left a sour taste in his mouth. He didn't mind going up against someone, blade to blade, but those ambushes had been more like slaughter than combat. He'd told himself then that it was necessary, part of the job, but he wasn't sure he'd believed it. And he knew he'd never agree to such a thing now.

"Well, I am glad we met Lord Trellan," Arianna commented, turning to look at Gren again. "Now we know a good deal more about this Sower, and about the man he was before."

"We still don't know why he changed his name," Gren pointed out, and she nodded.

"That's true, but we know what his name was, and what he was in this kingdom before. The more we know about his past, the more we can decipher his plans for the future." She sighed. "And everything we have learned has also shown that we were right in our choice. The answers will lie in Ortense."

"Right." Gren looked toward the end of the bridge, where a small stretch of land offered a break from walking across weather-beaten boards. "Let's get there, then." And he started walking. Arianna nudged the horse after him, and for a time neither of them said anything, just enjoying the weather and the ride and the quiet company. They both knew the peace would vanish soon enough.

CHAPTER FOURTEEN

Gren and Arianna stopped at the base of the hill. "That's it," Gren said, gesturing ahead of them. "That's Ortense."

They both looked at the city perched atop the hill. This was the only large stretch of dry land in the kingdom, making it the ideal location for a capital. A thick wooden palisade, some forty feet high, surrounded the entire city, and from here they could see two gates, one on either side. Both gates had wide, flaring arches above them, which Gren recognized as a dedication to the local gods. The river ran around the base of the hill, and they could make out the end of a long pier allowing access to it. Several boats were tied up there, from small punts to large sailing ships. The upper stories and roofs of many buildings were visible above the wall, and smoke from the many chimneys mingled to form a small cloud about the city. Arianna frowned. At least, she thought it was smoke. What was she really looking at? Not smoke, but shadow. A dark shadow covered the city from wall to wall, and it was slowly seeping outward.

Along the outer edges of Ortense the darkness was not that severe, no worse than a cold, cloudy day, the kind that brings out fatigue and anger and regret and introspection. The center of the town, however, was so dark she could not be sure what lay within, and the Essence of this place was dark and dank and tasted of mold. One building stood taller than the rest, and she guessed that it was the palace, but she could barely make out its outline, much less hope to navigate it. Nonetheless, she pointed the peaks out to Gren.

"That's the palace, all right," he agreed. "It's not that big though, really. Throne room, king's chambers, dining hall, council room, and a handful of spare rooms. That's about it."

"Well, it is where we can find this Sower," Arianna pointed out. "And find out how much of what we've heard is true. Then we can decide what to do about it."

But Gren wasn't listening anymore. He was staring at the city, more specifically at the nearest gate. "What the hell is that?"

She followed his gaze, and stiffened as she saw something swaying from the arch at top. The way it moved in the breeze, it was something tied to the arch itself. She shuddered as she realized that it was the right size and shape for a body. A similar ornament hung from the arch's other end.

Gren stalked forward, eyes locked on the sight. Finally he was close enough to see for certain that, yes, they were bodies. Men's bodies. Missing the heads and tied under the armpits. Judging from their state of decay, they had been there for at least a week.

"Cruel," he muttered as he watched the corpses sway. And particularly to hang them there, from that arch—it was a deliberate desecration.

Then he dropped his eyes and noticed for the first time the figure standing before the gate. It was a warrior, armed with sword and shield, but Gren could see immediately that something was amiss. "He doesn't move right," Gren grumbled, but Arianna could tell that it was far worse than that. The thing that stood there had the form of a man, and the tools of a man, but it was no man. At least not anymore. Tainted Essence curled about it in a dark cloud, seeping from every gap in its armor and clothes, billowing up from its chest to create a protective ring around its head, and from that darkness twin spots of red glowed. This was a corpse brought back to some semblance of life.

Gren could not see the Essence as she did, but as he moved closer he realized what he was seeing. This man was dead, yet he still stood and still bore arms. It was an abomination. Gren's mind was whirling, and his emotions with it. He had known that the Sower was most likely the cause of the destruction they'd seen. It made sense, though he'd avoided thinking about it. Now, looking at this creature before them, though, he could ignore it no longer. The Sower was to blame. He raised the dead to do his bidding. The trees were objects of death and evil, much like this corpse-warrior. The Sower must have created the trees. He had killed the towns. He had killed Gren's friends. He had hired Gren's friends, and then discarded them and killed them. He was to blame for their deaths.

Gren's rage was building with each thought, the blood rushing through him and creating a pounding in his head and behind his eyes. He let the rage come, welcomed it, stoked it, built it to a blaze.

"He created the trees," he said out loud. And his sword was in his hand.

"He killed the towns." He was only a dozen feet from the gate, and the guard had turned toward him, perhaps recognizing the threat.

"He killed my friends." Gren's anger spilled over as blinding light, and his anima erupted around him, casting a brilliant glow across the gate. The guard raised its shield, sword forgotten, to guard its eyes from that illumination.

"This is all his fault." Gren was almost within reach of the guard, which was cowering back against the gate support, mouth open in a silent scream.

"He must pay!" With that last bellow, Gren found himself upon the unliving guard before the gate. His anima flared brighter, as it had when he had faced Arianna's demon, and then a spark of light leapt from it and enveloped the walking corpse. The creature wailed, a horrible sound torn from its ravaged throat, and then collapsed in upon itself, crumbling to dust. But Gren had already moved past it and through the gate.

"Must pay!" He was barely coherent now, his vision red with rage, his anima dancing around him, and all of his attention was focused on reaching the Sower and destroying him in turn. Several more guards stood just beyond the gate, and as Gren stomped through, they rushed to meet him. These were of a kind with the first, and Gren let his anger and his light wash over them as well.

The first guard to reach him swung his sword at neck-height, but Gren blocked it, knocked the blade aside, stabbed his own sword through the creature's stomach, and then sliced upward, pulling his blade free as it exited alongside the neck. The creature collapsed, its torso sliced in twain, and Gren let his anima consume it as he stepped over the body. The next guard tried a downward stroke, sword held in both hands, but Gren simply moved inside the blow. He used his shoulder to shove the creature back, and then spun and removed its head with a backhanded blow. The third creature advanced, sword at the ready, but Gren knocked the blade aside and cut him diagonally across the chest, putting so much force into the blow that the creature literally fell apart as it dropped. He didn't give the next guard a chance to swing, but simply stabbed it and then ripped it open before getting close enough for the guard's shorter sword to reach him. Each body disappeared in a white flash as it dropped, leaving only ashes around him.

That left the front gate clear, and before the last guard had been incinerated Gren had already forgotten about them. He continued on toward the palace, sword at the ready, still letting his rage control him. All thought of strategy was gone, as was any sense. All he knew was that he was going to have his revenge, for his friends and for the people of those towns.

Arianna sat mounted by the gate, staring at the city laid out before her and the disappearing back of her companion marching through it. She had seen Gren angry before, when he had attacked her, but that had been nothing. The speed with which he had dispatched those four guards was awe-inspiring. It was not the way she would have chosen to enter the city, of course, and she was not completely sure he would succeed. But she was impressed by his strength, and his determination. And there was nothing she could do to stop him at this point. Instead she tethered the horse outside a nearby inn, then she followed the direction Gren had taken. If they were lucky, he might actually finish off the Sower before she even reached the castle. If not, she would be inside the city, and perhaps in a position to help. As Arianna moved away from the gate, she glanced back at the small piles of ash there, and couldn't help a small smile. It was hard to tell, but the Essence there seemed less sluggish now, and less stale. Even in his rage, Gren was a champion of the light.

Iuro sat with his companions, nursing a glass of wine. Of late they had found little to say, and had simply gathered to drink and commiserate in silence. There wasn't much more they could do. None of them dared enter the throne room anymore, or even approach the palace, not while those things still patrolled it. And that meant they could not get to the Sower, either.

He cursed softly, scratching at the table with a well-manicured nail. Damn him, anyway! His cousin Mariburn had been a decent man, and a decent king. And Ortense had been a quiet little kingdom. It was out of the way, being among the easternmost of the Hundred Kingdoms, and not worth anyone's trouble to conquer. Their people had been happy and fed well, their city had been clean and prosperous, and they had spent their days speaking with the king and looking for new ways to win more money and prosperity for themselves and for all of Ortense.

And then Belamis, stupid, arrogant, egotistical Belamis, had returned. But this time he'd brought mercenaries with him, and they'd made hash of the army. Not that Ortense had needed much of a military before this, just guards to keep the peace and kill anything that crawled out of the hills. But Belamis had killed them all, he and his men, and he had claimed the throne for himself. And now there he sat, the so-called "Sower of Decay and Distrust," in an empty room with dead soldiers to defend him. And towns were dying, and people were fleeing, and no one could do anything about it.

Iuro slammed his fist down on the table, toppling his glass. If only they had some way to banish those walking corpses, maybe they could reach the Sower himself, and put an end to him as well! But how?

They had thought of sending a messenger to the Realm or to Greyfalls, asking for its help. Not an army—no one wanted Ortense to become an Imperial satrapy—but perhaps a few Dragon-Blooded. Even one of those powerful, magical heroes might be enough to rid them of the Sower and his foul stench.

Just then Iuro heard a commotion outside and rose to investigate. Racing down the street was a giant of a man, clad in heavy armor that did not even slow him down. He held a massive sword in one hand, and a corona of light danced about him. As Iuro watched, the charging warrior reached the edge of the marketplace, and the four guards waiting there. The first guard advanced quickly, sword already stabbing, but the man's own sword dropped down, shattering it with a single blow. Without pausing the giant spun in a tight circle, sword rising and moving parallel to the ground, and the guard's head flew off, bouncing against one of the market's border posts before careening off down the street. The body collapsed, and a spark of light leapt from the giant to the corpse. A burst of pure white light enveloped it, and then the body was gone and only ash remained.

Iuro stared, redefining his long-held beliefs in fate, providence, and serendipity. He had seen one of those guards kill four men without difficulty, yet this stranger had just dispatched one with a single blow. Now two, as he flicked another guard's sword aside and drove his own blade through its eyes and out the back of its skull. He had to kick the head off his sword then, and one of the two remaining guards took the opportunity to lunge, but the giant stepped back and to the side. The thrust missed him by a few fingers, and then he spun into the blow, removed the creature's arm with one blow, and then its head with the return swing. And then there was one guard left, and he dispatched that one just by staring at it. And as each one fell, it was consumed by a flare of light and turned to ash.

Iuro could scarcely believe it. Who was this man? Already this stranger had moved on, heading toward the palace itself. Iuro turned around and quickly rallied his friends. This could be the chance they'd been waiting for!

Four more guards stood among the columns that decorated the front of the palace. Gren stoked his anima brighter as he approached, and they cowered from the sight. Sparks burst forth, and each of the four was destroyed before he had even reached them. The effort left him panting, however, and his anima dimmed slightly. It was as if each burst, each spark, was a heavy sword swing, and he was reaching the limits of his endurance. He had enough left to deal with the Sower, however.

Gren kicked the heavy bronze doors open and ducked the expected blow as he entered. Sure enough, another of the unliving guards stood just inside and attacked him as he passed through the doorway. A second was on the other side and swung a second later, but by then Gren was already past them. He flung his arm out to the side, the sword arcing back with it, and one of the guards fell, its head rolling away. The other struck at him again, a powerful overhand blow, but Gren curled his arm back in time to block it. He was in no mood to fence, so he kicked the creature in the thigh and impaled it as it staggered for balance.

The throne room was darker, and he quickly saw that the windows along the upper walls had all been covered by dark drapes. A handful of black candles provided faint light, but most of the wide space was cloaked in shadows that fled before his holy light.

Four guards approached him, and Gren knew that his anger was fading. If he let them all reach him together, they might actually hurt him. So he stepped quickly to one side, closing the distance with one of the four. The guard stabbed at his belly, but Gren was already past the sword's tip and he simply twisted and grabbed the creature's wrist, trapping its sword arm. A quick tug and the creature bent forward, where Gren's sword promptly removed its head.

The next two reached him at the same time, and both thrust together. Gren backpedaled quickly, the tips of their blades just grazing his armor. His own sword was much longer, and he swung it from the side, too high for their necks but low enough to catch the first one in the temple. This creature's helmet stopped the sword from carving clean through, but the force of the blow knocked it into its companion, and Gren quickly chopped one and then the other across the chest, downing them both.

That left a single guard, and its first blow was easy enough to parry. Gren did not allow it a second chance, but batted the sword aside and decapitated it. Then he lowered his blade slightly, and glanced around again, looking for the man he knew had to be there.

"Impressive." The voice floated free of a deeper, persistent darkness in the center of the room, and Gren raised his sword again. The shadows pushed back against his blazing anima, and the voice did not seem to come from any one direction. "I had thought my guards more than a match for any rabble this kingdom might raise against me," the voice continued. "Clearly I was mistaken." It had a raw, rough coldness to it, that voice, that set Gren's teeth on edge. It reminded him of the sound metal made when it grated on bone.

"And have you come for me, now?" the voice inquired, no hint of fear in it, and Gren all but growled.

"That's right," he said, turning in a slow circle. "Come out! Meet my blade, if you can."

"I don't think so," the voice replied, and something about it seeped into Gren, cooling his fire and chilling him to the bone. "I am sure I am no match for you... with a blade."

A form slowly resolved itself out of the shadow, drifting toward him, seeming to glide through the darkness. It was tall, as tall as him, but skeletally thin, draped in long dark robes whose edges merged with the dark around them so that the figure seemed to be wearing the shadows themselves. Gren could make out a long, thin face, and a head that had been shaven bare but was covered in strange markings. The flesh was so pale it might have been ivory, or bleached bone, and looked as warm. A golden crown perched atop, its warm gold and handsome stones completely out of place in this land of dark and shadow. The man's hands were empty, and he wore no weapons at his belt.

"Defend yourself," Gren demanded, kicking one of the fallen guards' swords toward the man, who had now stopped a few feet away.

"I will not contest you with the sword," the Sower replied, and again his voice stole away what little warmth Gren had left. He began to shiver.

Standing just beyond the palace door, Arianna saw all of this. She had followed as quickly as she dared, approaching only after she was sure no other dangers were left outside and that no one was watching the palace entrance. Now she watched Gren confront the man who could only be the Sower. Had he really tattooed his entire head? It certainly looked that way in this light. But more worrisome was the way the Essence focused around him. The Sower was a dark hole in an already preternaturally dark room, but the darkness around him was not still. It was constantly shifting, swirling protectively about him and extending feelers that darted about like fish through the shadows. And right now two long tendrils of it were coiling themselves around Gren and slowly dimming his light. The cold probably had something to do with it as well, for the throne room was so cold she could see Gren's breath. As each plume of steam emerged, however, it was pulled across and disappeared between the Sower's lips.

Gren was clearly in trouble. The only problem was, what could she do about it? Obviously the Sower would recognize Gren if both parties survived, which meant he would never be able to get close again. That also meant that she couldn't afford to be seen. Unfortunately, most of her spells worked only on herself, or for someone holding her hand. There was no way she could extend the spells to reach Gren, or even attack the Sower effectively. Not without exposing herself.

She did know a few spells that worked from a distance, however. None of them was what she would have considered tactically appropriate, but they might at least serve as a distraction. And one, in particular, might even help Gren fight back the darkness around him. She had to act soon, or he was liable to get himself killed or, worse, turned into the captain of the Sower's guard. Stepping back away from the door, Arianna took a quick look around. No one else was nearby, and the corpses had already turned to ash. If anyone else was watching, they were staying safely hidden. Keeping one eye out toward the street, Arianna began to summon her Phantom Steed once more. She just hoped it would appear before Gren grew too weak to take advantage of it.

"There is no need for such hostilities, I am sure," the Sower said softly, gliding a few steps closer. The temperature had noticeably dropped, and Gren could feel the goose bumps all along his arms and face. "Release the blade and we can discuss matters as gentlemen."

The words sounded reasonable, and Gren was so cold and so tired. His breath was steaming before him, creating a faint trail that glittered even in this darkness, and somehow it seemed to be drawn to the Sower. And with each breath he could feel himself failing. His fingers started to relax, the sword dipping toward the ground. But then he remembered his friends. And the faces of those townsfolk. And the dead who had stood against him only a few seconds ago. And he realized that the Sower's words had been laced with more than reason.

"No," Gren said, stepping back a pace and raising the sword between them. "You'll not bewitch me. Your evil ends here!" Focusing, he poured his remaining strength back into his anima, which flared up again, though not half as bright as it had been at the gates. And he lashed out with it, willing it to consume the man before him the way it had destroyed those guards. A glittering spark the size of his fist spewed forward and enveloped the Sower's head—

—and winked out as the darkness smothered it.

"Is that what you used on my guards?" The Sower laughed. "I am made of stronger stuff." He raised his hand and a bolt of crackling energy shot from it, so dark it left an after-image as it burned through the shadows.

And then a searing pain cut into Gren's side, and his back arched as his insides froze. He staggered back, and his sword would have fallen if the cross-guard hadn't caught under the lip of his metal bracer. The wound was like nothing he had felt before, as if a rabid beast had clawed its way through his armor and into his belly.

Arianna, standing by the door, almost cried out as she saw the arcane bolt strike her friend, the darkness lancing into him. She could see Gren's light dimming. *Just another second,* she prayed, her fingers finishing the last gesture. There! She whispered the last word of the incantation, and added a silent call to the Unconquered Sun to help protect Gren.

The Sower was stepping closer, one hand raised to blast the rebel a second time. He did not know who this man was, but clearly he was a Solar Exalt, and too dangerous to leave alive. Once he was dead, perhaps he could be raised to replace the guards he'd slaughtered. What a fine Servitor such a giant would make! But first things first.

Suddenly the room was filled with light as a gleaming white horse galloped into the chamber from nowhere. Its body glowed with a warm golden light, and its mane and tail were golden fire.

The Sower reeled back, both hands flying up to shield his eyes from the sudden illumination. He could feel the protective darkness peeling back, and he cowered away from the beast's flying hooves. What was this?

Gren had been fighting to stay on his feet, fighting through the pain in his side and the growing numbness in his arms and torso. He could dimly see that the Sower was moving closer, but he couldn't lift his feet or even turn his head away. It was as if his body had turned to ice.

Then, suddenly, the room grew bright as midday, and a glowing horse barreled toward him. Its light drove away the shadows, and Gren discovered that he could move again.

In the light he could see the Sower clearly. The usurper was rail-thin, and his arms where they were raised before him were little more than skin and bone. Almost Gren would have thought him a walking skeleton, but flesh still clung to his limbs and he still had ears and nose and lips. His eyes were clenched tight now, trying to block out the unexpected light, and Gren knew that the Sower was utterly defenseless now. He stepped forward, raising his sword to strike, but could not hold the blade steady. His arms were too weak, and the movement sent fresh pain stabbing through his side. He was in no shape to finish this. Best to leave before this unexpected relief faded.

Turning, Gren saw the open palace door behind him—and a figure darting away from it, down the steps. A tall, slender figure with long white hair. Of course. If he had not been so gripped in rage before, he would have realized that Arianna would have been right behind him. The horse was hers.

And now it was his turn to follow her, as he pulled himself onto the horse and gripped it as tightly as he could with his legs. He lacked the steadiness to sheathe his blade, and so he kept it in one hand and wrapped the other in the horse's fiery mane. Fortunately the steed needed no instructions from him, as it wheeled and raced back out into the courtyard. As they cleared the doorway Gren turned and glanced back at the Sower, who had retreated to his throne and was cowering there, robes pulled up to shield his face.

"This isn't over," Gren muttered. "Next time I'll finish you."

Then they were outside, and racing down one of the streets, toward the corner where he saw Arianna waiting.

The Sower sensed the warrior's departure, but there was nothing he could do to prevent it. The light of that accursed animal had blinded him, and he had been unable to think, let alone strike, in the face of its glow.

Who was that man? He had seemed vaguely familiar, but the Sower could not pin a name to him. Surely he was not from here, though—such a warrior would have stepped forward long before now. Nor were there any Solars in Ortense—surely his master would have warned him. Had one of the rebels summoned reinforcements? They had not struck him as having any such resources, but he could have been wrong. If so, they would have to be dealt with more quickly than he'd realized, before they were able to summon more.

Finally the light faded, and the blessed darkness returned as it did. The Sower felt his mind clear as the dark enveloped him again, soothing him and restoring his skin. As he regained his strength, he was able to think more clearly about the fight. The man was definitely familiar—in fact, the Sower thought he might be one of those mercenaries he had hired. Yes, yes he was. He had not met the man, only the one called Rangol, but this one had been in the group. In fact—the Sower frowned as he thought back—several of them had protested against killing Mariburn's soldiers who had surrendered. This man had been one of them. Yes!

But if he was one of the mercenaries, what was he doing here? They had all died at Anaka. Or should have.

Perhaps he had been separated from the rest of his group somehow. If he had been outside the town at the time, he would not have fallen prey to the tree. And finding his friends dead would certainly explain his anger.

But a Solar? Surely the man had not been a Solar before. So why now?

The Sower forced himself to his feet and walked slowly, painfully to the palace door. He had no time to waste. He would raise more soldiers and send them after this Solar. They would find him, and report back, and then the Sower would send one of his seeds after the man. Not even a Solar could hope to stand against that! But he had to move now, before the man had a chance to recover and regroup and possibly win allies. The Sower grimaced as he thought about that. If the Solar and the rebels ever found one another, they would pose an actual threat to his rule, and that could not be allowed.

Iuro had watched from a nearby doorway as the white-haired woman crept up the steps and peered through the door. He had desperately wanted to join her, to see for himself what happened when that warrior met Belamis, but Rydec, who had accompanied him, had held him back. And Rydec was right. Personal curiosity was less important than their cause, and getting himself killed would help no one except Belamis.

They could see nothing but the door from where they watched, but that had been enough to see the sudden flare of light within. Right after the light appeared, the woman had turned and fled. And behind her had come the warrior, astride a gleaming horse whose mane and tail looked like fire. The man had been clutching a wound at his side, but he was still conscious and still strong enough to control that magnificent steed as it raced across the courtyard and vanished from view. Again Iuro had wanted to move, to go after the man and offer aid, but his friends had restrained him. And again they had been right. Because a moment later, who should appear at the palace door but the usurper himself.

Belamis! Iuro had thought of launching himself at the man right now, while the wretch was still shaken and perhaps weakened by the warrior's attack. But he knew better. Whatever Belamis had been, the courtier-turned-king had shown that he had dark powers now, and Iuro knew he did not stand a chance against them. He was sorry to see that the fiend had survived, but at least the warrior had destroyed the man's unholy guards, and had escaped himself. Belamis had disappeared back into the palace after a moment, shutting the door behind him, and Iuro had followed his example, turning and leading Rydec back toward the Red Bill and the rest of their allies.

CHAPTER FIFTEEN

Iuro turned and surveyed the long, low room. Most of the men here were fellow courtiers and nobles, men he had known his whole life. Over the past week, since Belamis had summoned his obscene protectors and the nobles had fled the palace, several different inns and taverns had hosted various members of the court. Slowly the groups began to settle into patterns, with each group settling on one location. This tavern by the pier, the Red Bill, had become Iuro's favorite, and his closer friends with him. There were other nobles who he did not particularly like, and a few who did not like him either, and these had moved on to other taverns, so that all of the faces he saw now were men he considered loyal to him and to his goals. The only other people here at this hour were the tavern owner, his wife, and their two sons. Iuro's father had helped them establish their business here, many years before. He knew he could trust them. That was why he did not hesitate to speak his mind now.

"My friends," he said, walking back to his table but leaning against the chair rather than sitting back down, "I believe the time has finally come." He spoke loudly enough to be heard over the sound of the water-wheel out back. "For weeks, ever since my cousin's death, we have groused about the state of our kingdom, and about our new ruler. We have complained, yet we have done nothing. Why?"

"He's a demon!" one of the other nobles said, and several others nodded, Iuro among them.

"A demon? Yes, perhaps. He is not human, that I believe. No human would do the things he has done, or consort with the powers he has displayed. No real man would hide behind walking corpses, or drape the throne with the vestiges of the dead." He shuddered slightly, thinking again about the skulls of his cousins, hanging upon the throne's arms. "We were frightened. There is no shame in that. He has unnatural powers, and allies that cannot die because they are already dead." He banged his fist upon the top of the chair. "But I have just seen those same unstoppable soldiers, those same corpse warriors, mowed down! I have seen a man destroy them as easily as they destroyed our last few fighters, and storm the palace itself!"

"What happened?" A noble asked. "Did he kill Belamis?" None of them ever referred to the usurper as "the sower of decay and distrust" except in his presence.

"No," Iuro admitted, and several groaned. "I know, I know, I hoped so as well. But he did not. He was wounded, though still well enough to leave under his own power, atop a horse the likes of which I have never seen. I suspect he was not fully prepared for the usurper's full power, and had to retreat for a time. But he will be back. And when he does return, I say we march with him!"

Several people stirred, and Iuro glanced around, gauging their reaction. He saw many of them nodding, but others still seemed unsure. He needed to rally them all.

"Think about it, my friends. We have only three choices. We can accept the rule of this so-called Sower." A few called out harsh comments, and others laughed. "We can submit to his disgusting practices and unwholesome plans," more insults were hurled toward their absent ruler, "and accept that our home is now fit only for a graveyard or a slaughterhouse. Our second choice is to flee. We can run, as Trellan did. Pack up our belongings and our families and leave our homes." No one shouted anything. They had all respected Trellan, and were sorry he had gone. Iuro had tried to talk the older noble into staying, particularly since he valued Trellan's advice, but he would not be stopped. "We can find new lives elsewhere, and leave behind our obligations to the land and our people." He paused and tugged absently on the front of his tunic. "Or we can stay and take back our kingdom. We can rally the people, and crush these foul creatures and their master, and make Ortense a place of peace and safety again. We can fulfill our responsibility as nobles, to protect the land and its people against foul treatment, and rid this land of the horror that has infested it!"

"You're talking rebellion," a noble pointed out, and Iuro spun toward him.

"Yes, Marus. Yes I am. The man who sits on the throne now is not fit to rule this land. He has brought only terror and pain, and if allowed to continue, he will drive Ortense to ruin. We must rebel against him. We must rise up and resist his rule. We must overthrow him, and place a proper man on the throne again."

"A man like you?" One of his friends called from the back, and several of the others laughed. Iuro himself smiled.

"Perhaps, Pons. I am a cousin to our late king Mariburn, and I have the royal blood. So do many of you. But we can worry about that later. I say that any man in this room would be a vast improvement over the creature that holds the throne now. Do you agree?" He heard many mutters of agreement. "Do you agree?" This time everyone nodded or said yes. "Do you agree?" he demanded again, and this time they all shouted their agreement. "Good! Then our choice is clear. We rebel!"

"So, how do we do that?" Pons asked, and it was a serious question. Iuro finally dropped into his chair, and the others gathered around the table as well as he thought.

"We need to rally the people," he said finally. "It is not enough for us to rebel. The peasants and merchants and craftsmen and everyone else must rebel as well. Would you agree, Wil?"

The tavern keeper looked up from behind the long polished bar, surprised to be asked. But he nodded. "Aye, lord. If you want to drive out those horrors, you'll need every man you can get." He gulped. "I'm with you, and my boys."

Iuro smiled. "Thank you, Wil. That means a great deal to me." He looked around at the other nobles. "We will each speak to the men we know, and sound them out. We will have to do so quietly, or else Belamis will hear of it. Speak to people, and ask them if they are willing to fight to rescue our city from this monster. If they are, tell them to prepare. Ready what weapons they can, warn their people to stay alert, and wait for our signal to strike."

"We can post messages in the square," Saerian suggested, and a few of the others laughed, but Iuro did not.

"No, you're right," he agreed, which made the young noble turn red. "We'll have to do so carefully, so that Belamis will not suspect, but people do still put up notices there. A few more will not be noticed. We'll just mark them so that people know the messages are about the rebellion." He glanced around, looking for something. He needed a mark, and he knew that it would have to be more than a mere letter or shape. If this rebellion were to succeed, it would require a symbol that the people could unite behind. It needed to have real meaning.

Seeing nothing in the tavern, Iuro glanced toward the door, and his mind flashed back to the fight he had just witnessed and to the warrior with his blazing light around him. "A flame," he said, still staring in that direction. "We shall have a flame, to burn away the rot Belamis has brought, and cleanse our land. Yes." He looked around at his friends and allies again, and raised his voice. "A crimson flame will be our symbol, for we mean to burn out these horrors and restore Ortense to its former glory. Let everyone who agrees to participate know that the messages will be marked with the sign of a flame."

"What about the warrior?" Pons asked. "Do you think we can get him to join our cause?"

"I hope so," Iuro replied. "We will most likely need him." He thought again about the man he had seen. "But we will need to find him first."

"Hold still!"

"Ow! Damn it!"

"Well, hold still, then!"

Gren tried to sit up and Arianna pushed him back down again, eliciting a grunt and another curse as he slammed into the straw-covered ground. They were in a small stable a short ways outside the city's far wall, and she was trying to dress the wound in his side.

"Where did you learn to tend wounds, a kennel?" Gren demanded, pushing her hands away.

"Who said I learned?" she shot back, straightening and brushing off her pants. "Fine, do it yourself!" She was almost shouting at him, using anger to conceal her concern. The wound in his side was unlike anything she'd see before. The flesh actually looked as if it had rotted away, and around the edges it was weathered like old leather and brittle like ancient parchment.

"Fine, I will!" Gren sat up with a groan, one hand pressed firmly to his side. He reached for the bucket of water by his side, and the stack of rags she'd torn from a shirt. "At least I've done this before." He'd already unbuckled his armor with her help, and now he peeled off his shirt, careful to use his other arm to lift it from that side so that he didn't stretch the wound any farther. Then he took the rag, dipped it in the water, and brushed away the dried blood so he could see the damage more clearly.

"Oh." Arianna felt both fascination and nausea when she saw the blood and muscle beneath the skin. Part of her wanted to turn away in disgust from such unnatural damage, but another part wanted to study the wound, and the inner workings now exposed because of it. She decided that asking to touch the naked muscle tissue would be inconsiderate, and contented herself with watching closely as Gren worked.

"Nasty," Gren admitted now that he could see the damage clearly. "I've seen wounds like this, but usually only when someone has left them untended for days or weeks." Fortunately he'd bandaged himself before, and had tended to several of the other Daggers' wounds over the years. He lit a small fire and set within it a spare horseshoe he'd dug out of his saddlebags—Arianna had retrieved his horse and led it here after they'd chosen this spot to rest and recover. Then he drew his dagger, checked the edge, and calmly cut away the injured portions. It did not hurt, which was not a good sign. By the time he had finished trimming, the horseshoe had turned red-hot, and Gren lifted it carefully. "You may not want to watch this part," he warned Arianna, but she didn't move, even when he pressed the horseshoe into the wound itself. A short grunt escaped him as the hot metal seared away the rest of the damage. Then he wiped the wound clean again, and finally bandaged it.

"Don't suppose you have some way to heal this, do you?" Gren asked her, setting the now-bloody rag aside and reaching for a clean one. But she shook her head.

"There are healing spells," she admitted, "but I don't know any. That is more of a Zenith gift, anyway."

"Zenith?" Arianna rolled her eyes at his ignorance. She turned back around, and focused on his face so that she wouldn't have to see the wound directly.

"The Zenith caste," she explained. "The priests of the Unconquered Sun. You are one of those." Gren thought back to the memories of his former self, the tall thin man preaching to the multitudes, and nodded. "I am from the Twilight caste, the scholars. Different castes, different functions, different abilities."

Gren was impressed. How did such a young woman know so very much? Sometimes he felt like he was the child and she the adult, especially when she got that lecturing tone in her voice. "So you think I can heal this?"

She shrugged. "Perhaps. Not every Zenith can, but many could. I do know of a body-mending meditation, which aids the body in healing. I can teach it to you if you've got the patience and aptitude for it."

He thought about that, then eyed the wound. "Well, might as well give it a try," he decided.

Arianna settled onto the ground across from him, sitting cross-legged. She looked relaxed, and Gren tried to match her posture and positioning, which only made her laugh. "How you sit does not matter," she told him. "Just close your eyes." She waited until he had. "Now feel the Essence around you. Feel the energy." He tried to summon the rush of energy he'd felt several times before, most recently when he had charged up the hill toward the gate and its guard. He wasn't angry anymore, though, and after a moment he still didn't feel the same boiling sensation he'd come to associate with the power.

Need to go about this a different way, he thought. *This isn't battle. I don't need rage. I need—peace, I guess.* He let his mind drift, and found himself reliving the sermon of his past self again. The words floated through his mind, and he felt the great peace and calm and confidence of that man. And he felt the warmth of the sun on his face and hands, even there in the dark stable under an overcast sky.

As Arianna watched, Essence swirled about Gren, sloughing away the taint, and a golden, glowing disk appeared on his forehead. "Good," she encouraged him. "Now let the energy flow through your body. Feel the speed at which your body moves, how it heals itself? Like a heartbeat, but you can feel it throbbing in energy instead of blood? Infuse it with the energy around you, and increase its pace." She saw his Essence building, and then smooth out as a warn glow suffused him, and then faded. "That's it." She waited and laughed again. "You can open your eyes now."

Gren did so, and glanced down at his side. He felt better, less fatigued and no longer numb or cold, but was disappointed to see that the wound was still there. The flesh around the edges looked healthier, and even within the wound he could see signs of recovery, but he was a long way from whole.

"It is not an instant result," Arianna pointed out, reading his expression. "But it will speed your recovery a great deal."

"Huh." Gren prodded the spot with one finger, then wrapped it. "Yeah, that helps. Could have used it during my wilder years."

Arianna studied the collection of scars on his arms, chest, and back. "What you could have used, apparently, was full body armor."

That got a grin from him, and from that she could see that he was no longer in as much pain. "Wouldn't have hurt, that's for sure." He wiped the rest of the blood away, then tossed the rags aside, pulled another shirt out of his pack, and tugged it on, careful not to upset the wrappings. "All right, what've we learned?" he asked, leaning back and shoving hay and rags into a makeshift pillow for his head. "Besides the fact that the Sower is definitely the one who did all this. And that he clearly has dark magic."

Arianna sat down as well, her back against a post, but she was soon up again and pacing as she talked. "We know that his guards are dead men brought back to serve him," she pointed out. "We know that he thrives in the dark and cold." And the pieces finally came together for her. "Oh dear."

"What?"

She shook her head. "I just remembered what it was that Swan told me that sounded so familiar before." She glanced over at Gren, and he was surprised to see her lower lip shake as if she were near tears. "The Sower of Decay and Distrust is an Abyssal."

"A what?"

"A deathknight. A creature of the Abyss, and of the Underworld." She could see that he still didn't understand. "He comes from the world of the dead, and has made a pact with a Deathlord, trading his allegiance, and his mortal name, for power." She remembered what Swan had said about the Bodhisattva Anointed by Dark Water, the Deathlord who dwelled in the Skullstone Archipelago out West, near where Swan himself had grown up.

"All right, so he's an Abyssal. What does that mean?"

"It means he is also Exalted, though in a very different way from us." She frowned. "I do not know what caste he is from, or even if they have castes, but he is clearly a formidable necromancer."

Gren grunted, sat up, and unsheathed his sword, checking for nicks and scratches. "So do we have anything that'll hurt him more than the standard steel and wood?"

"Your anima did an impressive job on the guards," Arianna said, coming over to sit beside him, back to a different wall. "It's possible that, if you had been able to reach him, your sword could have cut him as easily as any other Exalt... We need more information, though." She sat watching the whetstone scrape alone the sword's edge. It was a surprisingly soothing motion. "We still do not know enough about him. Or about how he created those trees."

Gren frowned but continued his task. "Yeah, about those things—I've been meaning to mention something. Only I don't really want to." Arianna waited for him to continue. "In Hadovas, the first time I saw people who'd been killed by the trees, I didn't know what had happened. Just that something had swept through there and wiped out the whole village before anyone could react, or run away. And that it had been horrible for them." He pushed images of Rangol and Enjy away, concentrating on the stone in his hand and the blade across his knees. "But there was something I thought of. Something I'd heard could be this nasty and this deadly and this fast."

Arianna nodded. She knew what he meant, because she had thought the same thing. "Contagion."

"Yeah. The big one."

They didn't need to say any more about it. The Great Contagion had swept across the Realm centuries before, and had almost extinguished humanity forever. No one had ever seen a disease like it, and almost everyone who contracted it had died—quickly, and in great pain. Fortunately, the Contagion had played itself out, because it had killed so quickly that people in one town or city did not have time to infect another location. And so it had disappeared as quickly as it had arrived, leaving the Realm littered with corpses.

"The Contagion has never reappeared," Arianna pointed out, and Gren nodded.

"I know, but that doesn't mean it can't. And this sure looked like it. Who's to say it wasn't caused by trees, too?"

She frowned and shut her eyes, trying to remember some of the things she had read back in the tower, what seemed like a lifetime ago. "Some scholars argued that the Great Contagion was Creation's way of thinning the population, to avoid overcrowding. Others thought that it had been contracted from Wyld-tainted travelers from near the Elemental Poles, who were immune to the illness themselves because they were all infected already. But some scholars claimed that the Contagion had been deliberate, and was loosed upon the Realm from beyond its borders. Possibly beyond the edges of the world."

"Yeah, I remember hearing an old man say one time that the Fairies sent it," Gren commented. "Said they wanted this world to add to their own lands, and so they had to get rid of us humans first."

"That could be," Arianna admitted. "The Fair Folk do have powerful magics, and many of them would like to cover all Creation for their own. But this kingdom is tainted in shadow, not madness. I do not think the Fair Folk are at work here. Belamis—the Sower—is the source of the darkness here in Ortense, and he is the cause of the trees and the death they bring."

Gren considered that. "So is he creating the trees, or just using something he found? And are the trees really bringing back the Great Contagion? If so, how can we stop that, just the two of us?" He remembered again the words of the Unconquered Sun. *You are needed here, to right a great wrong and prevent a great evil.* The wrong was probably Belamis taking control of this kingdom—something he had helped cause. Was the great evil the Great Contagion? If so, did the Unconquered Sun really expect two Exalted, one of them completely inexperienced, to stand against the worst disease in history?

"I don't know," Arianna said. "That's why we need more information. We have to find out how Belamis is doing this, and anything we can about where this power comes from. The more we learn about it, the more likely we'll find some way to stop it." She glanced over at Gren, who was now oiling the blade. "I will have to go and speak with him."

That made him put down the oilcloth and give her his full attention. "What? What are you going to do, walk up and ask him how he does it?"

She flashed back upon the arrogant students she had known in her youth, all so full of answers and so desperate to impart what they thought was superior knowledge, and she couldn't stop herself from scowling. "He might even answer me. Tyrants and madmen love an audience."

"What if he attacks you, too?"

"I have to risk it. He won't let you get near him again—not after what you did."

Gren actually looked a little abashed, and he dropped his gaze. "Yeah, sorry about that. Bad tactics. But I—those bodies—I knew he'd done it, but when I saw those bodies, and that guard, I—"

She nodded. "If I had watched my friends die, I might have attacked him as well." She doubted she would have become a rage-driven killing machine the way Gren had, though. It had been impressive but scary, the way he had carved his way through guards without any real pause.

"Yeah, maybe." Gren had a hard time picturing her enraged. She was always so cool about everything. "But I guess he'd recognize me if I showed up again, eh?"

She stood again. "Definitely. But I could go in alone." She thought about it for a moment, searching for an excuse to approach the new king. That led to thoughts about the king himself, and to his strange appearance. Which led to an idea. "Languages," she said, turning to face Gren again. "I will tell him that I am an expert in ancient languages. His skull was covered in tattoos, and they are all from an ancient tongue that all but disappeared long ago, even before the Scarlet Empress rose. I doubt anyone else here in Ortense could read them. That will give me a reason to meet him, and something for us to discuss. Hopefully he will see me as a fellow scholar, rather than a threat."

Gren scowled. "I don't like it, but I doubt I can stop you. When're you gonna talk to him?"

"Tomorrow," Arianna decided after a moment. "We cannot give him time to kill anyone else, and by tomorrow he still may not have all his guards replaced. But I will need to be well-rested and clean before I can present myself."

"How long do you think you'll be in there?" Gren asked her, but she shook her head.

"There's no way to say. If he dislikes me, I may have to exit quickly, but if he welcomes me as a savant, I could be in there for hours. Days even. Why?"

He shrugged. "It'd be good to know when to expect you back. And that way, if you don't come back around that time, I'll know something is wrong." He smiled a small, dangerous smile. "And if you need help getting back out, I'll finish what I started today." He actually had his doubts—the Sower had defeated him without difficulty, and could probably do so again. But Gren was determined not to let that happen a second time, and he didn't want Arianna to know that he had any qualms. He would do his best to help her, no matter what.

"Thank you," she told him, and meant it. "But I can handle myself, and I do not want to do anything that will make him defensive. So unless I send a message to you, asking you specifically for help, do not worry about me. Just check back here every day at noon, and if I can I will meet you here." She sat back down again, and stretched out in the hay, pushing it around to form a nice little depression around her. "For now, good night."

Gren watched her drift off to sleep, half-annoyed that she was so determined to approach the Sower on her own, half-amused at the way she turned into a small child when she slept, curling up in a ball to shut out the world beyond. He sat there for several more minutes, just watching her sleep, before finally sheathing his sword again and lying back once more. He hoped it would go as smoothly as Arianna suggested, but one thing life had taught him so far was certainly true: Plans never go as well as you hope.

The Sower stood in one corner of the chamber, watching the tree. It swayed to a nonexistent wind, its leaves rustling and moving in every direction at once, and the seeds rocked beneath the branches but stayed firmly attached. He could see the darkness coiling and uncoiling about the massive trunk, its feelers searching the nearby air for anyone or anything to grasp, and he stayed well out of their reach. The tree was hungry.

So was he, but not for flesh. He was hungry for more power. Ruling Ortense was not enough. Once, this kingdom had been the sum of his ambition. Now it was barely a start. This tiny little land, with its scattered villages and crude peasants and cowardly nobles, was nothing to him, only a base from which his might could spread. Soon, very soon, he would have the power to breach the borders and claim the neighboring lands as well, and then the ones beyond them and someday on to the edges of the Realm. Soon all the lands would shudder beneath his gaze and recoil from the sound of his name. And that of his master.

At the thought of his master, the Sower felt a hint of panic. All evening he had debated what to tell his master about the morning's attack. What could he say? The attack had failed, and so maybe it was not that important. But the man was an Exalt, here in Ortense, and that was something his master would want to know. He had wounded the warrior, and perhaps the man was so weakened he would be unable to make a second attempt. But he had been strong enough to escape, which made him strong indeed. All day the Sower had considered the matter. He was loath to bother his master, but he did not want to risk being punished for not keeping him informed. That was the same conclusion he'd come to after taking the initiative to steal the tome, after all. So he should tell him.

With a low sigh, the Sower turned away from the looming tree and faced the corner. He chanted softly, the words spilling from his pale lips, and as each word dripped away it left a glistening black streak in its wake, which floated free of his mouth and drifted to the corner. The streaks pressed themselves against the stone there, coating the blocks, and soon the entire corner had become a wet, black darkness even in this unlit chamber, even against the living black of the tree. The corner seemed to fall in upon itself, and then the blocks had vanished, leaving behind a blank space that burned the eyes with its depth and etched its shape upon the retina. And within that darkness something shifted, a shape that stole light from its surroundings, pulling the night into itself and defying the brain to make sense of it.

"Speak, my ambitious servant." The voice flowed out along the blocks, spreading across the walls and floor until the entire chamber reverberated with it. The Sower could feel the sounds vibrating through his feet and up his bones into his head.

"Master," the Sower responded quickly. It did not do to keep his master waiting, even though the Deathlord could and often did respond with glacial slowness. "An Exalted, a Solar, attacked me this very day, here in the palace. He slaughtered my guards." Even to his ears that sounded like the whine of a spoiled child, and the Sower cursed himself for revealing his concern.

The voice either did not notice or did not care. "How did you kill this Solar? Did you use the tome?"

"I did not, Master, as you counseled discretion." The Sower shivered in frustration, rage, and shame. "The Solar escaped me. He is wounded, however, and cannot have gone far. I will find him before long." Of that he was fairly certain.

"Has the Solar's presence upset your revenge or your progress?"

"No, Master."

"Proceed, then." The voice grew sly and dangerous, and the Sower squirmed. "But be vigilant and diligent, Sower of Decay and Distrust, for time grows short. Be ready to receive the fruit and cast the spells as soon as the tree is ready again."

He bowed his head. "I understand, master."

His master did not speak again, and a moment later the corner had become merely dark and shadowy again. The dark streaks slid off the bricks and puddled on the floor, now just a pool of some dark liquid, like oil or juice or ale. And the Sower felt a sense of relief. Mentioning the Exalted had been the right choice after all—his master had not been angry with his failure. His master clearly still expected results—and soon, judging by his light admonition—but was willing to forgive small setbacks. It seemed that the goodwill the Sower had garnered with his daring theft had not yet run out.

Turned away from the corner, he found himself staring at the massive tome set upon the pedestal. It was closed and clasped, yet still the power poured from it, swirling about the binding, covers, and pages. The Sower stepped over to the book, and examined it more closely than usual.

Dried blood caked portions of the cover, some of it so old and so strange that it might have been mere decoration if not for the lack of any pattern in the design. Slipping the clasp, the Sower opened the book to its first page and studied the various pictures and the few words he recognized. If only his master had taught him more of the language! He was sure that each page contained new spells, each one addressed to "the mortal king." But the pages actually appeared to contain not one, but two, variants of Old Realm that he did not know, and the diagrams were too confusing to offer any real help. He had to find some way to translate the rest of the pages. Otherwise he would never be able to tap the tome's real power. Of course, *that* was likely why his master had taught him so little of the language in the first place. Goodwill or no, his master's trust went only so far.

No, the first thing he needed to do, the Sower decided, was find out who that armored stranger was. He would post a reward for anyone who helps him find out more about the mysterious warrior. His name would be the most useful and deadly weapon, but he would not turn down aid from any corner, and any stray information might lead him directly to his foe. Once he had located the warrior, the Sower would summon such an army of corpses that no dead would remain undisturbed within the kingdom's borders, and so powerful that any who fell before them would instantly rise again as one of them. He would crush the stranger and make his master proud. Then, once the great work he had begun in Ortense was finished, he would have more time to discreetly study the book.

The Sower rested both hands on the edges of his illicit prize and smiled. Yes, the tome was the center of his power, in more ways than one. And the sooner he learned how to tap that full power, the sooner his influence could spread as he had always wanted it to.

Soon, very soon. The world would fear his name, and the name of his master, the Walker in Darkness.

CHAPTER SIXTEEN

The next morning, Arianna woke, washed as best she could using several of the clean rags and a fresh bucket of water, then combed and braided her hair and walked back into the city toward the palace. Gren stayed in the stables, safely out of sight, and Arianna left her pack and her daggers with him. She hated having to leave her books behind—it felt as if she were forgetting a part of herself—but she could not risk having those books fall into the Sower's hands. If nothing else, they might reveal her nature as an Exalt and ruin any chance of his speaking to her. But he might be able to take the knowledge contained in her texts and pervert that into something terrible, and she could not bear to be responsible for such a thing.

Gren was not happy either. He hated to be idle and to let others take risks for him, yet here he was, sitting on his butt in a barn while a young woman went unarmed toward the most dangerous man he had ever faced. It wasn't right. He knew it had to be done, but that didn't make it feel any better. At least if he were still incapacitated he could tell himself that he was staying behind because he was not up to full strength, but thanks to his own Exalted gifts, that was not the case. His wound was not completely gone, and his side was stiff, but it was far better than it had been, and would not slow him down much. So here he was, in good fighting form, sending a girl off to do his work.

Arianna sympathized. She was not particularly excited about approaching the Sower alone, especially after seeing him get the better of Gren the day before. She was no match for Gren in combat, she knew that, which meant that she would be no match for the Sower either. But hopefully it would not come to that. It was a warm, sunny morning, and she took that as a sign that the Unconquered Sun was watching over her. She just hoped that would be enough.

Yesterday, when she had followed Gren to the palace, she had been busy worrying about what he was doing and checking to make sure she had not been noticed. As a result, she had barely glanced at the palace itself. She did so today. It was a large, solid building with a row of columns across the front and tall, graceful windows along the side wings. The exterior wall was made of heavy stone blocks that managed to look small because of the building's size, and they were fitted together beautifully, with no visible mortar. This was a well-constructed palace, far better built than the other buildings she had seen here, and she guessed that it was from an earlier age. Given how smooth the stone was, it might even date back to the First Age, though she doubted it had been a palace then. More likely it had been the summer residence of a Solar or Dragon-Blood, a modest home by their standards. But compared to the other structures here it was magnificent, and fit for a king.

The other thing she noticed was less pleasant, and that was the decoration. Apparently the Sower had decided that the plain, clean walls of the palace were not to his taste, and so he had added his own decorative touches. A row of heads marched across the front of the building, impaled on iron spikes more than ten feet off the ground. From their appearance, she guessed that they had been there less than a month, and they were all men old enough to fight. Most likely members of the army that had fought against them. Fought against Gren and his friends, she reminded herself, but she was sure that even the one Gren had described as bloodthirsty would never have done this.

Fortunately for her, the Sower apparently had not replaced his guards yet, and the front steps were empty. She knocked on the large bronze double doors, then pulled the left door open and stepped inside. She brazenly strolled down the same main hallway down which she had crept during Gren's assault, making her way to the throne room to speak to the usurper king. It had been pleasantly warm outside, but it was so cold in the throne room that she began shivering immediately. Part of the problem was that thick curtains covered all the windows, keeping the room dark and cold. The other problem was that the room had no lights save a few small candles guttering in the far corners. But those two factors alone were not enough to account for the drop in temperature. She had noticed the conditions yesterday, when she'd shivered just from standing by the doorway. Apparently, Abyssals simply preferred the dark and sepulchral cold.

Arianna entered the throne room and strode down the center, heading directly for the low dais at the far end and the large carved-stone throne upon it. What looked at first like a bundle of rags and sticks set atop the throne soon resolved itself into a tall, painfully thin man sitting absolutely still, hands folded before his face. The Sower.

The Sower watched the woman approach. He had been sitting here, pondering his next move, when he had heard her footsteps preceding her up the main hallway. Her tread was light but not hesitant, and now she just walked in. He would have to reinvigorate a host of new guards as soon as possible, he reminded himself.

At first glance he thought her a teenager, with her thin figure, light step, and long white hair, but then he saw the light scar across her face and the hard calculating aspect in her eyes. She was either older than she looked or older than her years. But who was she? She was utterly unfamiliar to him, and he knew he would have remembered meeting her before. That made two strangers in as many days, and he was not sure if that was a good sign or a bad one.

He considered frightening her away, but while her fear would be enjoyable it would not last. And he was amused and curious. So he waited there for her to approach.

Arianna had not had a good look at the Sower yesterday, and now she mentally compared the man before her with the description Gren had provided. Tall, skinny almost to emaciation, long fingers with wicked-looking yellowed nails, pale skin, piercing pale blue eyes, and tattoos all over his shaved scalp. He was wearing long, dark black and red robes and a gem-encrusted gold crown perched slightly askew atop his head. And when she stopped finally in front of the dais, he still had not moved.

"Greetings to you, Sower of Decay and Distrust," she began, performing a graceful curtsey. "My name is Adrianna d'Mattelaine." It was close enough to her real name that she would answer if someone shouted for her.

The Sower watched the girl approach from under half-lowered eyelids. She introduced herself, and he was pleased to notice that she had called him by his proper title, rather than using his former name the way many of the courtiers did. "Yes, my dear," he said softly. "What brings you to this humble chamber that aspires to be my court?"

"I am a scholar, Your Majesty," the girl told him. "I had heard that this land was now ruled by someone more… refined." She glanced at the skulls capping the arms of his throne, long enough for him to notice the look. "There are few here who can provide me with worthy conversation. I had hoped you might be different."

The Sower laughed, a low, throaty chuckle. That was a new one, and he thought he'd seen everything by now. People always surprised him.

"Of course, my dear." He gestured toward her. "Approach."

"Thank you, Your Majesty." She reminded herself that she had faced demons and the Wyld Hunt and survived both. She forced herself to step forward, and then onto the dais. They were mere feet apart.

This close, the Sower could see that she was not quite a girl any longer, though her skin was still young and tender and the white hair still soft as only a youth's can be. But her courage impressed him.

"And what shall we discuss, then, scholar?"

Arianna considered the man before her. He seemed to radiate cold. No, that was not quite right, she realized. It was not that he projected cold—it was that he absorbed heat. Her own warmth seemed to leave her as she approached, and her fingertips and toes had turned numb by the time she stopped. His eyes stabbed into her, and for an instant she thought he was going to attack her the way he had struck Gren. Finally he lowered his head, breaking their eye contact, and as Arianna caught her breath she noticed again the glyphs on his head.

At this range she could see them clearly even in the dim light. They were not tattoos, as she had thought yesterday, but scars, and she would have thought they were burned into his skin if not for the crisp edges and the bluish tinge. Perhaps some sort of cold burn? A brand, but ice instead of fire? She was not sure. But the sigils themselves fascinated her, and she forgot her repulsion as she studied them.

"What interesting marks," she murmured, only realizing she'd spoken when his eyes widened. "An Old Realm dialect, unless I am mistaken?"

"Very good," he complimented, bowing his head slightly so that she had a better view. "Do you recognize the dialect?"

She stepped still closer, intent now, and studied them more closely. "D'rai'ic, it called itself, yes?" He could feel a faint tingle as her fingers almost touched them, the proximity of her flesh sending a surprisingly pleasant shiver down his spine, and he bit back a laugh. Ah, the pleasures he had given up! A woman such as this, he could almost remember them, almost miss them.

"Yes," he said, careful to keep his head still so that she could continue her examination. "I had not thought anyone alive could recognize that language." And, unexpectedly, he felt a jolt of excitement. If she could read the dialect, perhaps she could decipher more of the tome! His fervent wish last night that he had some way to decipher the book might be coming true! The Sower had never thought of Fate itself as an entity, but now he could not help but wonder if it were, and if it had somehow answered his plea and sent this woman to aid him in his quest.

"I study ancient languages," she told him, still almost brushing her fingers across the marks. "This is the first time I have seen this one outside of old tombs and a few decaying scrolls, however. This glyph, I believe, refers to potency. And this one speaks to control. These here are the signs for 'night' and 'black' and 'ice.' So together they create an invocation of sorts, designed to grant you control over the darkness and the cold. Or perhaps protection from them."

He smiled. She was close. "Yes, my dear. Quite right. Your skill is most impressive."

Arianna fought to keep her breathing calm and her hands steady. She had read the glyphs easily enough—the tower had possessed two books written in that long-dead dialect, and the Exalt whose power she had inherited remembered it as well. But she had lied to him about her interpretation, deliberately erring in the translation. It was not a protective invocation but a mark of domination, labeling him as the master of darkness and of cold, specifically the light-destroying dark of the Void and the life-stealing cold of the tomb. And the glyphs, all together, defined him as a creature of those same forces.

But her reading had impressed him, nonetheless. And now, as he raised his head, she saw a faint smile on his face. It was not a pleasant smile, though she suspected he meant it to be. And she did her best to smile back in return.

"Come, my dear," he told her then, standing and extending one long-fingered hand toward her. "I have something to show you. Something I believe might interest you even more than these meager decorations of mine."

Something deep within Arianna screamed at her, warned her not to accompany him, but she knew it was the only chance she had to learn more. So, with a faint, tightly controlled shudder, she extended her own numb hand, and rested her fingers in his grip. Then she allowed him to lead her out of the throne room and down the hall.

The Sower could feel her hand in his, and feel the faint tremors as she shook from the contact. A small part of him rejoiced, knowing that he had not, in fact, lost his effect on others and feeding off the fear she fought to hide but could not fully banish. But the rest of him was busy as he led her down the hall and toward his private chamber. If she could read the tome! The spells within it would be unlocked for his use, and he could master the book's secrets fully. What power might be his then! The incantations with which his master had helped him parse from it thus far would be the merest inkling of his power! He could crush this land, this world, with a mere thought. Why, his power would rival, if not surpass, that of his own master!

He quickly tamped that thought down. Who knew what the Walker in Darkness could read in him, even from this distance? And he could only imagine the price of disobedience. But still the thought persisted. He had accepted the bargain his master had offered him, because it had been the better of two bad choices—death or this chance for power and revenge. But with the tome at his full disposal, he would have the power to renegotiate their arrangement, and perhaps to cancel his subservience altogether. And—this thought leapt into his mind and caused his steps to falter, he was so taken with it—he could retrieve the rest of the tomes! If he had the power to stand against the Walker, surely the Mistress would be no match for him. He could stride back into the Mound of Forsaken Seeds with impunity, and collect the rest of the set for himself. Then, with the entire series at his disposal, he could master the full power of the Well of Udr and the forces it contained. Even the Underworld would be his!

His grip tightened, and only a small gasp from his companion reminded him to loosen it. Suddenly this woman was more than a mere curiosity and momentary entertainment. She was the potential key to his success. He would have to treat her very carefully indeed.

"How came you by your knowledge, my dear?" the Sower asked her suddenly as they walked. It was the first he had said since they had left the modest throne room, and it surprised her from her study of the smooth, undecorated stone walls. "Surely it is not easy to locate examples of these long-dead languages, let alone study their meaning?"

"No, it is not," she replied carefully, wishing her mind did not feel as frozen as her hands and feet. "In my own land of Aujerre, there is but one place where these languages are known. And only the finest scholars are allowed to enter its halls and examine its texts."

"Yours must be an enlightened land," he commented, "to allow a young lady to study there. I doubt Ortense would so readily accommodate the notion of woman scholars."

That brought a frown to her face, as she recalled her own upbringing, and she decided that the truth would work best here. "Indeed, my lord, my own land has many of these same prejudices. I must confess, I was only granted access to the libraries because my family worked the grounds. I myself was trained in the kitchen, but I gleaned other knowledge from the scholars there, learning anything anyone would teach me. And finally some of the tutors recognized my skills, and I was allowed to join the other students openly and devote myself to my studies." This last part was mere wish-fulfillment, and she pushed back the bitterness as she remembered sneaking into the tower libraries each night to study after the scholars had all gone to bed. But the Sower nodded, seemingly accepting all of her story.

"Well, however you came by your skills, my dear, they are most impressive," he told her, and she could tell he was trying to be soothing and charming. His voice had become low and soft, though still it held a grating like a file over hard wood or soft metal, a rasp that set her teeth on edge. "I only hope that you can enlighten me on a particular matter which, I confess, is beyond my own skill to interpret."

Now that sounded interesting, and Arianna forgot all about the cold as she pondered his meaning. He had said he wanted to show her something, and she'd assumed that he had wanted to brag about some piece of antiquity he possessed. She had hoped for a moment that he might somehow be drawing power from some artifact of a previous age, and that this was what he meant to display. But if this was something that he could not decipher himself, he could not already be tapping it for anything. What could he have here that was even older than the D'rai'ican dialect, and important enough for him to keep when he could not read it himself?

At last they turned a corner and stopped in front of a small recessed doorway, which held a plain, heavy wooden door bound in thick, black iron. Various sigils had been carved into the stone around the door. The chisel marks were still sharp, as if they had been cut just yesterday.

The Sower turned back toward his guest. "Do you know anything about the mystic arts, my dear?"

She shook her head. "Some of the scholars studied them, but I was not allowed to participate."

"Ah. That is a shame." He hoped it did not mean that she would be unable to decipher the tomes after all. "Well, those marks are arcane in nature. They form a protective ward about the room. This doorway is the only access point, and the walls themselves cannot be breached by spell or by force—which may be the only reason the room survived at all. They also protect the door, shielding it from harm. It is the most secure room in the palace."

Arianna nodded, trying to act surprised. In truth, she wanted the freedom to study the ward marks, but did not dare reveal her interest. She had almost gasped when she had noticed them. She recognized components of the spell, having studied a similar but less powerful incantation in one of her books. But this was the work of a Solar! She had thought the palace might date back to that age—if she was correct, this would have been the sanctum of the resident Solar, and a room blessed by the Unconquered Sun. She was surprised that an Abyssal was able to use it at all, much less select it to hold whatever treasure he was about to reveal.

She waited patiently, pretending ignorance, as he released her hand, took a step forward, and whispered an incantation. It was the spell marked on the doorframe, and by reciting it and adding the appropriate end phrase, he released the mystic lock barring the door. There was a faint click. Then, with a small push, he swung the door open and gestured for her to enter before him. Arianna's cold and fear had been completely subsumed now, overwhelmed by her curiosity. She had never seen, in this lifetime, a place from the age of her former self, and she was eager to examine it as much as possible. She stepped through quickly, careful not to trip over the raised base of the doorway. And then she stopped just inside, stunned by what she saw.

The chamber was far larger than she had expected, at least twenty feet to a side. She guessed, judging from the walk they'd taken to get here and the glimpses she'd had of the palace exterior, that this was the exact center of the building. Just past the door were two wide steps, and they encircled the square room, so that its floor was at least two feet lower than the doorway had suggested. The walls, made from the same rough stone as the floor here and the walls outside, rose up all around, tapering in as they did, and finally ending in a wide square that stood open to the sky. Rays of sunlight shone in, reflecting intermittently off specks of crystal in the floor and walls.

But the room was not empty, and her eyes had deliberately avoided the two objects present while she admired the room itself. It would have been a perfect place to worship the Unconquered Sun, and easily large enough to accommodate a dozen men at once, though she doubted the room had been used in such a way. More likely it had been the owner's private chamber, where he could closet himself in solitary meditation. As she moved left to allow the Sower to enter and shut the door behind him, she forced herself to look at the room's contents, hoping the warmth of the sun would shield her from the chill she had felt as she had glanced past them.

The first was an enormous tree in the center of the room. She could see paving stones piled in a far corner, obviously pulled from the floor so that the tree would have space to grow. And it needed that space. Its trunk had to be at least ten feet around, and its thick branches scraped against the walls and the floor, and even reached up to ring the high open roof. And, though the tree was clearly not natural or normal, she had seen its like before. For it was *almost* a match for the trees that had appeared in Hadovas, Anaka, and the other towns. Almost, but not quite. This tree was larger, and thicker, and its bark was darker and glistened so that it appeared coated in some black liquid. Its leaves were wider and more pointed, and had more red in them, as if this abomination of a plant had been steeped in blood. And its fruits hung more heavily, and darkness swirled within them. Even on such a warm sunny day, she could feel the chill emanating from the tree, and see how the light dimmed around it. And this time she knew that was the case—this tree spawned the dark and the cold, creating them as a normal tree might create sap and fruit.

The second object was, at first glance, far less frightening. It was a simple stone pedestal, carved from the same stone as the walls and the floor. Standing perhaps five feet tall, it tapered gracefully from its base, then broadened back out into an inclined ledge perfect for a book or a parchment. It stood near one corner, but she could see that the bottom had been chipped away crudely, and knew that it had been moved from its original location. Most likely it had sat at the center of the room, where the tree now perverted the space.

But as she glanced at the pedestal again, she saw that it was not empty. Atop it was a wide, heavy book, easily as long as a man's arm and as thick as a man's thigh. The tome was bound in black leather, and clasped in a mottled green metal that looked vaguely familiar, though she could not be sure. A thick strap, the same leather as the cover, held it tightly fastened, and it had no other markings she could see. But if the tree stood in dimness, this book cast near-darkness about it, as if it had a circle of night shielding it from the sun. She knew immediately that this was the item the Sower wanted to show her, and that it was potent indeed. She was also sure, utterly sure, that it had created the tree, which in turn had created all the other trees. This was the source of his power.

"Please," the Sower said, closing the door behind him and gesturing toward the pedestal. He walked behind her as she slowly approached it, and the waves of fear rolling off her were delicious. He had worried, when she had professed ignorance of magic, that she would be no help to him, but he could see now that she knew more than she had admitted. Otherwise he doubted the tome's appearance would have affected her so.

And yet—there was something strange. As she neared the tome, the darkness seemed almost to recede from her, though grudgingly. The closer she came to the pedestal, the more it resisted, and the less ground it gave, until finally, as she stopped right before it, the darkness closed in around her with an almost audible sound. He felt the release of a tension he had not realized was there, and took comfort in the darkness himself. Perhaps he had merely imagined it. Her white hair did seem close to luminous in the reflected sunlight of the chamber, and that might have been why the darkness had seemed weaker around her. He shook the thought away and turned his concentration back to the tome itself, and to her.

"This is the object I wished to show you," he told her, reaching out one hand to caress its surface. He muttered the opening incantation under his breath, and then loosened and removed the restraining strap. "I do not know its age or origins, and I would welcome any insight you might have."

And then he flipped it open to the first page.

Arianna had to bite her lip to keep from invoking the Unconquered Sun for protection from this evil. As she neared the book, she had felt its malevolence reaching toward her, striving to envelop her. She had resisted, and the sun had warmed her still, but with each step closer she could feel its protection ebbing, until finally it could not hold out and she was trapped. It was as if a thick blanket of cold had been laid tightly about her. Her lungs had grown heavy, as if filled with liquid, and each breath hurt. Her eyes blurred, and she felt herself grow dizzy and slightly unsteady, resting a hand on the pedestal for support. Almost she had touched the tome instead, but her fingers had recoiled of their own, refusing contact with it. She had never been so cold, and knew that for the first time since her Exaltation the Unconquered Sun was not protecting her.

This book! She had never thought she could dislike a tome for itself. Certainly she had read texts she had disagreed with, and even some whose writing she had found laughable, but always she had admired the books themselves, from the most cheaply made paperbound volumes to the handsomest works of leather and gold and gems. But this was a travesty of a book, evil itself bound in manuscript form, and she wanted nothing more than to destroy it. But she suspected that was far beyond her power.

She listened intently as the Sower uttered a spell to open the tome, and a chill raced up her spine at the words. It was similar to the D'rai'ican dialect, but the sounds were longer, more drawn-out. And the syntax was wrong. This was an older tongue, which reeked of dark and cold and death, and things beyond death. It was a language meant for ill.

And then he had removed the restraining strap and turned aside the front cover, revealing the first page of the interior. And she could not prevent the gasp that stole from her lips, or the low moan that followed it.

"Is it not beautiful?" the Sower said, enjoying the low cry that escaped as she looked upon the interior for the first time. "Whoever created it, their skill was breathtaking. As I think you'll agree." He stepped to the side, and guided her gently but firmly forward. "You must take a closer look. Please." He watched as she moved, her eyes slightly glassy, and saw that her hand reached out to trace the marks on the page but then stopped and withdrew. Her breath was coming in short gasps, producing bursts of steam that were quickly swallowed by the shadows around them, and she could not take her eyes from the page and its contents.

"Please," he asked, and he regretted but could not prevent the clear longing he heard in his own voice. "Please, tell me what you make of it."

Arianna wanted to look away, but could not. The page was crafted from some skin, but she could not name the animal. Surely nothing would have flesh that smooth and heavy and pale, so pale it must never have seen the light of day? And the ink was a black that sucked in the light, creating an image on the page as much by stealing the light as by any real mark upon the materials, yet it also seemed to have been almost carved, the edges were so deeply inset and so crisply angled. Were these tablets instead of pages? But she could see how they bent from the book's weight, in a manner that only cloth, paper, or leather could manage. Perhaps the words had been carved into the leather, and then sprinkled with ink to fill the depressions? She suddenly knew that this was very close to the truth, but that it had not been ink that had darkened those cuts, and she would have shuddered again if she had not been so cold she could not move. Whatever creature had produced this leather, those words had been carved while it was still alive, and its own lifeblood had welled up to forever stain the marks into its flesh.

The words themselves threatened to crawl in her vision, and she tried desperately to see them only as marks, not as language. But it was no use. Her mind and eye had been trained to make sense of symbols, to organize them into readable text, and nothing she screamed inside her head could stop her reflexes from taking over. The sigils resolved themselves into letters, the letters into words, the words into sentences, and she prayed that the Unconquered Sun would strike her blind before the meaning could penetrate.

She had been right about the language. It was old, older even than D'rai'ican, which was one of the earliest recorded dialects of Old Realm. This she had seen referred to as High D'rai'ican, and it had been the formal dialect used in an ancient court long forgotten. The other dialect was the common variant, a bastardized version. But it was not the language here that horrified her, though the only texts she had seen written in it were of necromancy and other dark arts. Rather, it was the subject of the tome that made her mind recoil in a desperate scrabble to retain some sanity. This text was dark incarnate, every letter a piece of malevolence burned into the world, and its very presence made Creation groan in protest.

She forced herself to shut her eyes, trying to block the image of those letters that had seared themselves into her brain. And then, using every scrap of will she possessed, she turned and opened her eyes again, looking directly at the Sower.

"I am sorry," she told him through frozen lips and chattering teeth. "It bears some surface resemblance to D'rai'ican, but the structure is too different. I cannot read it."

The Sower felt the disappointment wash over him, replacing his excitement with bitterness. So close! She had seemed his best chance to translate the tome fully, and now it was for naught! He was a fool with a fool's hopes. But then his eyes narrowed. If she could not read it, then why had she reacted so strongly to the words? He had watched her response, seen the way her eyes had widened and then strained to look away. He knew the power of the tome, but even though it compelled the viewer, the mere sight of the marks could not cause such an extreme reaction. Only someone who could discern their meaning, all or any part, would have felt the full impact of its power. She was lying.

He smiled, and gave no indication of his thoughts as he stepped up again, forcing her to either brush her nose against his chest or look back at the book again. She responded instinctively, and turned her head away, shuddering out a breath as the tome trapped her sight once more. "Are you sure?" he asked, forcing a polite, almost disinterested tone. "Some of the words seem almost the same, don't you think?"

Arianna cursed inwardly at his trick. Something about the Sower's voice had changed now. When he had asked the first time he had sounded almost desperate. Now he sounded like he barely cared. She felt, with a stabbing certainty, that her answer had not fooled him at all.

And it had been at least a partial lie. She could not read the text fluently—she had only seen the language twice before—but she could make out many of the words. She could puzzle out the meaning of the first few lines:

"Within this work is contained the keys to the darkness. We have inscribed them here that the mortal kings may tap our power, and use it to increase their own reign upon the earth. And with it our dominion too shall grow, spreading the chill across all Creation."

Some of the words were only approximations. "Darkness," for example, was the closest she could come to a definition of the one character, but it was more than that. There was, within that one sigil, a hatred for life and light and warmth, a yearning for the still silence of death and beyond, and a call to obliterate color and joy and change, leaving only a frozen waste. "Chill" was much the same, though that sigil held also a hint of slow, malicious motion, as if cold were a living creature that preyed upon the world and vented its hatred through rage and destruction. She could only guess what the pages beyond might contain, and how much havoc the Sower could wreak if he had full access to them. Clearly he had tapped at least one of the spells herein, if he had created the tree, but that was probably just a tiny fragment of the power this book offered. Power he must never be allowed to possess.

"Similar," she admitted finally, again pulling her eyes free from the tome and this time taking a step back so that she could turn to face him. "But not the same, no. This one here," her finger stabbed at one mark, stopping inches from touching it, "looks like the character for 'king,' but the word next to it should be 'lawful' or 'rightful,' and it does not match. Not at all. Which means that first word might not be 'king' after all." She shook her head.

"This is the problem of encountering a language no one knows," she continued. "Without something we can translate for certain, some sort of key, we cannot be sure we have any of the words correct. And there is also the question of syntax. Some languages place the subject at the end of the sentence, others at the start. Which is this? Without more information, we cannot be sure."

"Well, I do appreciate your examining it," the Sower told her, stepping forward and closing the tome. Arianna felt the darkness ebb immediately, and she almost wept. Even though the area around the pedestal was still cold and dim, she could feel faint warmth returning to her, and her eyesight cleared slightly. The Unconquered Sun still could not reach her, but it was closer.

"I had higher hopes, of course, based on what you said before," the Abyssal was saying as he took her elbow and guided her back across the room and toward the door. She allowed herself to be led without protest, and rejoiced silently as they stepped beyond the limits of the book's power. The sunlight all but dazzled her, and her body flushed with the sudden return of warmth, fingers and toes and nose tingling as they regained feeling.

"I am so sorry I could not be of more help," she told him as they reached the door and stepped back through it. "It is a fascinating tome, certainly. Wherever did you discover it?"

He waved his hand idly as he pulled the door shut with the other. "Oh, it was passed down to me by a distant relative. He had been a collector of books, and I gather he bought this one from an old antiquities dealer, but could never read it. For obvious reasons."

"I doubt there are many who could," Arianna admitted, feeling like herself again now that they had left the room behind. She bemoaned the corruption of such a chamber, designed to worship the Unconquered Sun and now holding two items that were its very antithesis, but there was little she could do about that now. Her only concern at the moment was to leave as quickly as possible, and to share with Gren what she had learned.

But the Sower seemed to have a different objective. As he talked on about this uncle and his collection, he led her back through the palace, but by a different hall than the one they had taken before. When they reached a wide staircase she started to protest, but he appeared not to notice, taking her hand and leading her up the steps without pausing in his conversation. At last he stopped, before a nicely gilded paneled door, and opened it with a key from a ring he pulled from beneath his robes.

"I am sure you must be tired, my dear," he told her, pushing open the door and gesturing her in. "Please, I insist that you stay here as my guest. Once you have rested, perhaps we can examine the book again together. I am sure that, with your knowledge, we can make great headway toward deciphering its meaning. And just think what a coup that will be for you, being the first to translate a language thought lost long ago! Why, you should be able to enter any library freely after that!" And he stepped back out of the door, which she realized then he had never left, and pulled the door shut behind him. Arianna was left in a tastefully decorated bedroom, and even as she stepped back toward the door she heard the click of the lock. She was trapped.

CHAPTER SEVENTEEN

"We found him, my lord."

"Where?"

"Lassner's stable. Just outside the walls."

"Are you certain?"

"Most certain, my lord."

"Excellent."

"What should we do, then?"

"Go get him, of course."

"Where is she?" Gren paced in the stable, slamming his fist into the heavy support beam at one end and then, when he'd reached it, doing the same with the beam on the other side. He had been doing this for several minutes already, and the thick wood was showing signs of distress, which might have pleased him if he'd been paying more attention. But he wasn't. He was too focused upon wondering where his companion was. The sun was beginning to set, and still no sign of Arianna. She had been gone the entire day. What could have kept her this long? When she'd left that morning, she'd mentioned to watch for her at noon each day as if her going to the palace might stretch that long, but Gren had thought she was simply being careful. She had only gone to speak with him, for Empress' sake! And, while they both knew she wasn't the type to engage the Sower in direct combat, she should be able to turn and run. So where was she?

"I shouldn't have let her go alone," he muttered to himself, pounding the nearest beam again and receiving a cascade of dust from the ceiling as a result. He knew he was kidding himself. It had not been his choice for her to go at all, and he couldn't have stopped her even if he'd wanted to. And, much as he hated the thought of Arianna doing all the work, they'd both known that they'd needed to know more about the Sower before they could do anything to stop him. And thanks to his own outburst the previous day, she was the only one who could get close.

"Me and my damn temper," Gren raged, punching the beam again. He'd let his anger cloud his judgment, which wasn't like him. He'd had good reason, certainly, but this was more like something Scamp would have done, or Lirat, or Milch. He'd always been the one to keep them under control when they lost their tempers. But of course there had been no one to control him when he'd let loose, and he'd been gone before Arianna could even try. And now, as a result, here he was alone in this barn, and that poor little girl was facing a monster on her own.

Poor little girl. He snorted at that one. No, Arianna could take care of herself. But the Sower had shown himself to be a lot more dangerous than they'd realized. And what if he'd managed to create more of those unliving soldiers already? Could she overpower them without Gren there to back her up?

Just then he heard a faint creak, and he spun on his heel, his hand going reflexively to his sword hilt. Someone was at the barn door.

"Arianna?" he called out, but there was no answer. He cursed softly. She would have replied, which meant either it wasn't her or she wasn't able to call back.

The door swung open, revealing the night sky beyond. Night already! Squinting, Gren could make out three figures in the entry, and he tensed as they approached. Shaped like men, but they moved slowly, awkwardly. All three carried drawn blades, he could see that now as the light of his lantern reflected off the metal, but none were in very good shape. And none were held effectively. As if the owner had no real experience with those weapons—or no longer remembered his old skill.

"Scum!" Gren bellowed, sweeping his own blade free. "I'll carve you into pieces!" With his other hand he raised the lantern, using its light to reveal his foes.

And then he froze, surprise overcoming his anger, as the three figures moved closer.

Arianna had tried the door as soon as the Sower's steps had faded away. It was locked, as she'd thought. And, beneath its gilt, the door was solid. Not as heavily built as the door to that chamber he'd shown her, but still strong enough to withstand some punishment.

The lock itself was simple, however, and the door showed no sign of spells. She could escape this room easily enough. The question was, should she?

She sat down on the armchair by the window and thought about that. Clearly the Sower did not believe her claims of ignorance. He knew, or at least suspected, that she could decipher that book. The book. At the mere thought of it, she wrapped her arms around herself for warmth. He wanted her to help him read that abomination, and he would not accept no for an answer. So what were her options?

She could escape. But then he'd know she knew something, and he'd know that she had power of her own. He would probably send his dead guards to hunt her down, and she and Gren would either have to run or reveal their true strength.

She could stay here, pretend to help, and lie to him. But he'd seen through her lies today—he would probably see through any additional ones. She simply had no skill for deception. She thought fondly of Swan and his gift for diplomacy. He could have told the Sower that the tome was a collection of old bread recipes and made that sound believable. But she had not those talents, so if she stayed, the

Sower would know she was lying and would try to force her to tell the truth.

Her third option was to stay and actually translate the book. The thought of examining those pages made her skin crawl, but it did have some merit. The more she knew about the book, its origins, and the spells contained within, the more likely she could counter them. Perhaps there was a spell for removing the tree, and for blocking its effects. But why would the book tell people how to defeat its own creations? That made no sense. And if she did translate any of the book in earnest, she would have to share that information with the Sower. And that would only make him more powerful.

No, she could not risk a second encounter with that book. It had all but overwhelmed her today, and she was not sure she could withstand its malevolence again—which meant she had to get out of here.

Now the only question was how.

Whatever method she chose, she would want to make sure it was the right one. No charging down the hall for her—that was more Gren's style. The one thing she did have at the moment was time and a quiet place to think. She decided to take advantage of it. She leaned back in the chair, settling fully into its thick cushions, and closed her eyes. Moments later, worn out from her recent experiences, she was sound asleep.

The Sower sat on his throne, idly watching his servants shambling across the throne room. He had raised more zombies and more Servitors, using the last of the former city guards, and ringed the palace with them once again, but would they be enough to withstand a second attack from that warrior, if he struck again? And what of those timid courtiers who had approached him this afternoon? Were they up to the task he had given them, or would they lose their nerve?

And what of his unwilling guest? He leaned back, stroking the skulls on the armrests as he remembered the morning's encounter. Who was this young lady who could read D'rai'ican so easily, when most people could not even write their own names in their native tongue? Why had she really sought him out? And how much had she gleaned from that first page of the tome?

Because he was sure she had been able to read something there. Her expression had revealed that much. Whether she could understand it fully he did not know, especially since he could not. But she had grasped more than she had told him, that much was certain. She claimed she could not read the book at all, and he understood her resistance. The tome was not for the faint of heart, or for those who believed in life and warmth and color. It was a text of darkness and pain and cold, well-suited to one of his ilk but not so much for a young woman so clearly full of life. He was sure the very sight of it had terrified her. And perhaps that was why she had lied, because she had been frightened.

Unfortunately for her, her comfort was not his concern. He wanted—needed—to know what the tome contained, needed to unravel all of its secrets. And she was the key to that. If she could read more of it than he could—even if she could not translate everything—she could help him decipher more than he had on his own. Perhaps enough to master a few of the other incantations. And, if the ones he had learned thus far were any indication of the others' potency, just a few more would be enough to make his mastery of this land complete, and guarantee that it fell to his master's will.

She would help him.

He would not give her a choice in the matter.

And if she lost her life in the process? That would be a shame, but it was a price he was fully prepared to pay.

Iuro gritted his teeth. He hated this part, the waiting.

He glanced around him, studying the others who milled about in the tavern's main room. Several of the other nobles were clearly as impatient as he was. They paced, talking too loudly, studying their clothes, adjusting their sleeves and collars with too much care. A handful of the others, mostly the older men, sat more quietly and talked more softly. They were more patient, and the waiting did not wear on them in the same way.

Wil was polishing cups behind the bar, and his older son, Johan, had just hauled a string of wine jugs up from where they had hung cooling in the river below. The younger son, Tomas, was nowhere to be seen. Judging from the sounds he had heard, Iuro guessed that the boy and Wil's wife Sarah were in the kitchen preparing dinner. The family was keeping busy, but then this was just another day for them. They did not have the same concerns he did.

He took another sip of his rice wine, then set it down. Much more and he would be too fuzzy to think clearly. And he would need his thoughts tonight, if things went well. He hoped they did. He had wanted to go himself, though that would not have been wise. What if violence occurred? Better to send the others in his stead, for now. At least, if things went sour, he would still be alive to lead this rebellion, though he hated the thought of others dying in his stead.

Accept it, he told himself. If you intend to lead, you must learn to accept it. People will die for you. And you, in return, must live for them.

He glanced at the door, then at Pons, who stood beside it. Pons saw his look and shook his head. Nothing yet. Where were they? Iuro eyed his cup, lifted it, set it back down, then lifted it again and took a quick gulp. Had something gone wrong?

"W-we mean you no harm."

Gren lowered his sword and stepped back a pace. The lantern had revealed the trio to be men, all three of them. Older men in fine clothing, and very much alive. The one on the right's hand was shaking so badly his sword was waving before him, and the one of the left's knees were all but knocking together. All three were sweating. They were definitely alive, and definitely not warriors. Nobles, judging from the clothes. But what would nobles be doing in a barn?

"Who are you, and what do you want?" he demanded, and the two on the sides took a quick step back. The one in the center held his ground, however, and it was he who spoke. He was a tidy man, slender but not underfed, with neat waves of silvery hair and a trim silver beard. The sword in his hand was handsome indeed, and worth quite a few dinars, but he was clearly not comfortable doing more than wearing it.

"Are you the warrior who attacked the palace the previous morning?"

Gren considered lying. After all, he didn't know these men or what they wanted. But what would be the point? There couldn't be that many men in this city who matched his description. So he nodded and sheathed his blade. Even if things turned ugly he would not need it against these three.

"I am."

The man smiled and sheathed his own sword, with a great deal more fumbling than Gren. His companions followed suit.

"I have come to fetch you," the man said then, and something in his tone indicated that this was a great honor to Gren, to have such a man come for him personally. He was not impressed.

"Fetch me where? Who sent you?"

The man shook his head and beckoned Gren closer with one hand. "Come with us, please. All will be explained soon, and there is not much time." But Gren straightened and folded his arms across his chest.

"I'm not going anywhere until I get some answers. Who sent you?"

The speaker sighed. "Please." Then, seeing that Gren still was not moving, "All right. We are—" he said and glanced around, though the stables held no one but the four of them. "We are with the rebellion."

"The rebellion? What rebellion?" Gren knew about the rebellion, of course. After all, after putting the Sower on the throne in the first place, the Daggers had been kept on to put down any rebellions. But he was tired and irritable and didn't much care for these men's attitude, so he decided to play dumb. Besides, it gave him time to study them.

The noble looked irritated, which amused Gren. "The one that will remove that tyrant from the throne and rid our land of this evil. And our leader wishes to speak with you. Now please, hurry. Before his guards find you as well."

Gren considered. So there *was* still a rebellion—he and Rangol had both thought the rebels had folded too easily and too quickly. This rebellion could be a very good thing for him and Arianna. It could make an excellent distraction while they dealt with the Sower and the trees. Of course, it could also make him more paranoid, and cause him to tighten his security, which would be a bad thing. But it was worth talking to these rebels, and finding out their plans.

"All right," he said finally. "Let's go." He started to gather up the rest of the gear, and moved toward his horse, but the man waved that aside.

"Don't worry about all that. We'll send people back for it. We have to get you out of here right away." That didn't seem right to Gren, but then he wasn't used to the idea of other people fetching his belongings for him. Still, it was this man's town, so he was calling the shots. Gren shrugged, quickly pulled his armor on, grabbed Arianna's pack because he knew she'd never forgive him if he left behind either her daggers or her precious books, and followed the three men to the door. The one with the knocking knees pushed it open—

—and they found themselves facing their own reflections.

At least, it might as well have been, Gren thought. Three more men stood on the other side of the door, one of them in the act of reaching for the handle. They also wore fine clothes, and they also looked scared. These three had swords as well, though they were still sheathed.

The middle man of the newcomers was stockier than his counterpart, and had thinner hair that was still more brown than gray. His face was doughy, and his beard was a fringe that ran all the way around his wide chin. But his eyes were sharp as they glanced at Gren and then at the three men with him, finally settling on the one who was their spokesman.

"Armand," the newcomer said, nodding his head, and Gren saw at once that he did not like the man he addressed.

"Rydec," Armand replied with an equally short nod. Clearly the feeling was mutual.

"Won't you introduce me to your friend?" Rydec asked, looking at Gren again. "I do not believe we've met."

"I would," Armand said, "but we are in something of a hurry. Perhaps some other time."

"I really must insist, Armand."

Armand laughed. "Oh, must you?" he turned to Gren. "I warned you that his men would be here soon. And here they are."

"What? Whose men?" Gren shook his head. "You mean the Sower's? His guards are all corpses!"

"His guards, yes." It was Rydec who replied. "But a handful of courtiers have decided that serving an evil king is better than not being at court, apparently. They meant to bring you to him as a prize, proof of their new loyalty."

"Precisely," Armand said, stepping in front of Gren and reaching for his sword. "But we will not allow you to take him."

Gren almost laughed. This guy was going to defend him against that guy? Neither of them looked like they could handle a drunken legionnaire, let alone him. Wylds, he could probably take all six of them if he had to. But he didn't really want to. He wished Arianna were here—this was all getting too confusing for him.

"So you're saying that these guys," gesturing toward Rydec, "are working for the Sower?"

"Yes," Armand said.

"And you"—looking at Rydec— "are saying that *they're* the ones working for him?"

"Exactly."

"And whoever isn't working for him is with the rebels?"

"Definitely." The two nobles all but spoke in chorus, and Gren shook his head again. Being a mercenary had been so much simpler.

"So which one of you is lying?"

"He is!" Armand cried, stabbing a finger toward Rydec. "No, he is." Rydec was calmer, but just as determined.

Okay, that didn't work, Gren thought.

He tried to puzzle it through. Obviously both trios had come looking for him. Armand had gotten here first, but that didn't mean anything. He and his companions had approached with their swords drawn, but Gren couldn't blame them for that. He'd have had his own blade in hand, if the situation had been reversed. Rydec and his friends didn't have their swords out, but that could just mean they were more confident they'd convince him to go peacefully. Armand had told him not to grab all of his gear, which could be because he would be dead soon and wouldn't need it. But it could also be because he had others coming to retrieve it and bring it back to safety. The two men both looked noble, and they knew each other, so it wasn't a case of a stranger trying to trick everyone like in those old folktales. Wylds, he was the only stranger, it seemed.

And he was the one being tricked. Because he couldn't figure out which one was lying.

Then he remembered how he had met Arianna, and how he had known that her words were true.

"Unconquered Sun," Gren called out, his voice ringing through the stables, "shed your light upon us, and grant us the gift to hear truths as they are spoken!"

In an instant, he heard a faint ringing in his ears. It faded quickly, and he found his hearing sharper than ever—every sound was perfectly clear.

"All right." He turned toward Armand. "Who do you work for?"

"The rebellion," the noble answered a touch irritably. "I've already told you that."

Gren ignored that. He was still listening to Armand's answer, and the echoes that whispered beneath his words. Then he glanced at Rydec. "And who do you work for?"

"The rebellion," Rydec responded. "And unlike this traitor, I really do." And Gren heard the echoes there as well. And now he knew the truth.

In a single motion, Gren stepped back, drew his sword, and swung. The blade leapt down and out, slicing cloth, skin, and bone without pause—

—and Armand's lower half crumpled to the ground. His upper torso and head followed a second later.

"Gods!" Rydec stepped back, his face turning pale. Two of the others began heaving, one on each side. Rydec's other friend had the presence of mind to draw his sword, but Armand's remaining ally tried to run. Gren removed his head in an instant, then stabbed the third man through the heart as he straightened from retching. As quickly as that, all three were dead on the floor, the hay turning slick from their blood.

"Grab that gear," Gren ordered, and the man with the sword hurried to obey, rushing over and picking up the items Gren had started to leave behind.

"Did you have to kill them?" Rydec demanded, and Gren nodded but didn't look up. He had kneeled beside Armand, and now he laid one hand on each half and whispered a blessing. After all, even a man like that deserved a chance to move forward. Perhaps in his next life he would make better choices. Rydec stepped back, cursing, when the white light flared about the corpse, and stared as the light faded to reveal the two small mounds of ash.

Gren rose to his feet and stepped over to the next body. "If I hadn't," he answered Rydec finally, "they'd have run back to the Sower and told him what happened. Does he know you're a rebel?"

Rydec looked surprised and shook his head. "No, not yet."

"And do you have family he could hurt?"

The noble's face was still pale, and his eyes widened. Then he nodded. "I see your point."

He watched Gren bless and incinerate the other two bodies without another word.

When they had finished, and Gren had spread fresh hay on the floor to cover the bloodstains, he collected his horse, took his gear back from the third noble, and turned toward Rydec.

"All right," he said. "You were coming to get me. Well, now you got me. Let's go."

Arianna woke with a start, and for one panicked second, she had no idea where she was. Her hands dove for her daggers, and her panic increased when they came up empty. But then she recognized the bed on the other side of the room, and the chair she was sitting in, and relaxed, forcing herself to breathe slowly. She was still at the palace. She must have fallen asleep.

A glance out the window confirmed that. It was already dark outside. She had slept for several hours at least. What must Gren be thinking? She was half-surprised he hadn't gone on another rampage, and a tiny bit offended. Was she not worth it? But that was a silly thought, and she pushed it aside, rising from the chair and stretching stiff muscles. She had slept the night before, but seeing the book and facing its evil had drained her. Clearly she had needed to recover.

Unfortunately, the Sower was likely to be far more comfortable at night than during the day. That meant that he would probably be back soon to seek her aid again. She had to be out of here before he arrived.

She eyed the window, but dismissed that idea immediately. It was far too narrow even for her, and even if she did manage to climb through where would she go? She was on the second floor, or possibly the third, and that meant at least thirty feet up. She could jump the distance, but it would attract attention, and that was the one thing she needed to avoid.

No, her best option was to spring the lock on the door, sneak down the hall, dart down the stairs, and then find a back entrance and slip out. All of which she was sure she could do. It helped that she'd seen no courtiers this morning or last, and no servants either. No living ones, at least. Which meant fewer people to encounter.

What still concerned her was disappearing so quickly. Right now the Sower knew she had a gift for languages, but she did not think he knew she was Exalted. She would prefer to keep that secret, which meant not doing anything extraordinary. Springing a lock was possible, but sneaking through the palace unseen? She wasn't so sure.

Still, it had to be done. She moved toward the door, fingers trailing along the bed as she passed it, and stopped. In fact, why not give herself a little more time to escape? A small smile crossed her lips. This was very mundane, but it might fool him the first time, and that would be enough. She grabbed the items she needed and quickly set to work.

A few minutes later, she used one of her hairpins to spring the lock, and slid the door open. It creaked, but not much, and the thick stone muffled the sound. A quick glance revealed a quiet hallway. Nothing moved. Arianna opened the door wider, then waited another moment. Still nothing. Finally she stepped out into the hall. When it stayed quiet and still, she straightened and pulled the door shut behind her. So far so good. Watching her step as best she could in the dark hallway, she crept along, thankful that her soft-soled boots made little noise on the stone floor. Before long she had found the stairs, and was descending as quickly as she dared.

She chose a hallway that angled toward what she thought was the back of the building, and after many twists and turns came to the kitchen. Perfect. It was unoccupied, and looked as if it had not been used for weeks or even months. What use did a creature like the Sower have for food, after all? But the kitchen had a plain wooden door in the far wall, and Arianna pulled it open a crack and peeked out.

Beyond was a small courtyard with a hen house and several small pens to one side, and a well to the other. Beyond them was a gate, which led out into the city proper. She watched for several minutes, but did not see or hear anyone approaching. Finally she eased out of the door, gently closing it behind her. Then she waited several more minutes. She had thought to tie up her hair before leaving the room, which was a good thing—otherwise the white braid would have stood out in the darkness. Instead it was swallowed up by a dark scarf.

When the yard and the area beyond had been silent for several minutes, Arianna decided it was time. She straightened up, took a deep breath, and walked across the courtyard, moving quickly but not running. She tried to look as if she belonged there. She reached the gate and opened it easily, then stepped through and shut it behind her. A moment later and she was between two buildings on the other side of the street, and could finally breathe again. She was out of the palace. She had escaped.

With a small sigh, she looked around. She was on the far side of the palace, near the back. That meant the barn was in the other direction, almost diagonal from her. It was going to be a long walk, but that was fine. And she had rested before she left. Resisting the urge to whistle but almost giddy at having left that heavy malevolence behind so easily, Arianna turned and made her way quietly between houses and shops, angling toward her destination. She started to run.

She hoped Gren would not be too angry at her for taking so long.

Iuro started as the back door slammed open and four men stepped into the tavern's main room. The first three he knew, of course, though they looked shaken. But the fourth man— Iuro had only seen him from across the street before, and then only briefly. Up close the man was even larger than he'd realized, tall and broad and powerfully built. His armor was scratched and dented, signs of long, heavy use, but it was well maintained and clearly solid. The sword at the man's side was massive, and its handle and guard were simple but well constructed. He glanced up at the stranger's face, and found the man watching him just as closely.

"I take it you're the boss," the warrior said in a deep rumble. "Fine. Let's talk."

Gren had allowed the three nobles to lead him around the city wall to the river, across a narrow rope bridge from the bank to the pier, and then up a ladder alongside a small waterwheel, into the back room of what looked suspiciously like a tavern. As soon as they'd entered he knew he'd been right—only a tavern could smell quite like that. He breathed deeply, and smiled. Many of his best times had been in just such a place. But the men had not stopped, and so he had followed them through the kitchen and into the main room.

It was a nice tavern, he saw, wide and comfortable, with a low beamed ceiling and walls made of real wood rather than the usual rice paper, and woven grass screens for the windows that were currently closed for the night. Paper lanterns hung from the beams and from small wooden arms on both sides of the windows, and either side of the long bar provided ample light. It was much cleaner than most of the places he had frequented. But then, the men standing and sitting around the room were clearly wealthier than his usual drinking partners. Everyone stopped to stare at them as they entered, and he mentally sized up each man in turn. Most of them would be useless in a fight, but a handful looked like they knew how to handle themselves. One of those was the man waiting for them at a table in back.

Reasonably tall and on the slender side, the man was younger than many of his companions, though the touches of silver at his temples and the lines around his eyes and mouth said he was no youth. Neat black hair, a short beard, and gray eyes that studied Gren carefully. The man's clothes were well-made but not too fancy, Gren noted with approval—no silly frills at the collar or cuffs, and only a hint of embroidery to denote rank. His sword was elegant and expensive, but looked like it might have actually seen some use, and the way the man's hand rested near it confirmed that it was no mere ornament. Other than a heavy ring on one finger and a brooch on his cloak, the man had no jewelry.

"Have a seat," he told Gren, waving at the empty chairs across from his own. "And a drink. Then we can talk."

Iuro waited until the warrior was seated and served before sitting again himself. He was glad he had not drunk more earlier, and the shock of the man's entrance had chased away any clouds on his thinking, so he was able to face the fighter with a clear mind. And that was good. He'd seen the way the man had looked about when entering the room. It was the way a cat measured mice, or a soldier studied peasants. If this meeting went poorly, the warrior was fully prepared to fight his way out, and Iuro knew that all of them combined would not be able to stop him. Hopefully it would not come to that.

"I am Iuro," he said, foregoing his usual titles. What good were they now anyway?

"Gren," the warrior nodded, extending a massive hand. "Grendis Lam."

"Gren." Iuro took the proffered hand, shook it firmly, and then leaned back. Gren's handshake had been strong, but not overly so—he had not tried to crush him. That was a good sign. It suggested that he was a reasonable man. He started to say something, then noticed that Rydec was still standing near the table, and glancing nervously at the newcomer.

"Rydec, is there a problem?"

The older noble flinched. "Just—Armand is dead."

"Dead? How?"

Rydec jerked his head toward Gren in reply. "Lucas and Phalen as well."

Watching the man's face, Gren was afraid that there might be a problem. He did not seem happy to hear about the three deceased nobles. But all he said to Gren was "explain." And so he did.

"Armand and his two buddies showed up and told me they were from the rebellion, and that their leader wanted to see me. Then these three arrived with the same story. Armand was lying." He shrugged. "It wasn't safe to leave them alive."

Iuro stared at him for a moment, and Gren started pondering where he should place himself once he'd kicked back from the table and drawn his sword. But then the noble nodded.

"I cannot say I am sorry to see Armand gone," he admitted. "He was a fawning little man, always prancing around trying to ingratiate himself. Lucas was much the same. Shame about Phalen, though. He was weak, but a decent man." He placed his hands flat on the table. "You were right, though. Once they'd found you, and seen you with Rydec, it was not safe to leave them alive."

Gren nodded. Here, at least, was a man who recognized hard facts. That was a good thing. Too many rich men, particularly lords, seemed to think that the world was all rosy and happy. Iuro apparently knew better.

"Okay, so what do you want?" Might as well ask up front.

Iuro smiled in response. "I'd have thought that was obvious, Grendis Lam. We want you on our side."

The Sower ground his teeth in frustration. The one living servant he had bullied back into service had come back down, saying that the young lady was fast asleep and did not respond to his questions. He had left the tray of food and drink sitting on the small table, closed the curtains, and then shut the door quietly behind him.

It was understandable, to be sure. She had faced something far beyond her understanding this morning, and would have been drained by the encounter—not to mention that he suspected the tome actually fed off the lives of those around it. So she needed sleep. And if he wanted her mind to be clear and focused, he had to allow her that rest. But it was unfortunate that it came now, during the night, when he was at his most alert and most powerful. Her resistance to help him would have crumbled quickly if he could have spoken to her under the cover of night.

Perhaps he could wake her and speak to her briefly, and then let her return to her slumber? No, that would not do. What if she could not get back to sleep? Or what if she only half-woke, and tomorrow treated their conversation as a half-remembered dream? He would have to wait until she was fully recovered before he approached her.

His fingers dug into the chair skulls and he bared his teeth. Mortals were so flimsy, and required so much maintenance. He was pleased that he no longer had such concerns.

Arianna entered the stables quietly, letting her eyes adjust to the darkness before she moved farther than just inside the door.

"Gren?" she called softly. There was no reply.

As her eyes adapted, she saw that the stables were empty. Where had he gone? She knew he had not gone to the palace, because she certainly would have heard that. Had he simply gotten tired of being cooped up, and taken a walk? She moved quietly to the side where they had made their camp the day before, and saw that nothing was left. Her pack was missing, as was his, which suggested this was not just a brief outing. He did not expect to be back right away. She paced around the stables, wondering where Gren was and what he was doing. And then her boot slid on a patch of something wet.

Kneeling, she saw a small puddle beneath fresh hay—the hay had absorbed most of it but had missed a spot. Her fingers dipped into the puddle, and she brought them to her face. It was dark, whatever it was, and it smelled salty, coppery. Blood.

Quickly she glanced around her, studying the floor more closely. Had there been a fight? She found several other patches of blood, also covered, but all small and all here near the door. Had Gren been attacked? If so, by whom? Had they killed him, or carried him off?

Or had he been the victor, but decided the stables were no longer safe?

She rose and padded about the area in an ever-widening circle. And when her boot raised a puff of pale dust, she immediately dropped down to examine the spot. Her fingers found a small pile of ash, and she saw again Gren disposing of corpses in Anaka.

It was a man. Or at least, the remains of one. That had to be Gren's work.

She spotted three more piles of ash. Four men, all dead, and no sign of Gren.

Well, she admitted, leaning against one of the support beams, if I had just been attacked by four men I would not want to stay here either. Obviously these men had found him, which meant others could as well. He would need some place new to hide.

And so would she. At least until tomorrow. Hopefully Gren would return here at noon, looking for her. Then she could find out exactly what had happened, and tell him what she had learned. And they could decide what to do next.

She started toward the door, then stopped. No one in their right mind would stay in a place where three men had already died and their blood still stained the ground. Which made this the perfect hiding place. She glanced around again, and then quickly climbed the ladder up to the hay loft. Then she burrowed into the loose hay, fashioning a rough bed, and curled up again. Despite having slept most of the day, she was still tired, and she knew she would fall asleep soon. *I wish I had my books*, she thought drowsily, letting her eyes close. *I hope Gren's careful not to damage them.* And then she was asleep again, nestled in among the hay.

The Sower rose with the dawn and strode quickly down the hall, up the stairs, and down the second hall, stopping outside her door. He was carrying a tray of bread, cheese, fruit, water, and juice, and a part of him hoped she appreciated the honor he was showing her by actually delivering this food personally. When his knock got no answer, he unlocked the door and pushed it open.

"Adrianna?" He called her erroneous name and stepped inside, enjoying the fact that the room was still dark. The curtains blocked the sun's first rays, though it was already growing quite warm as the heat penetrated the heavy cloth.

"Are you awake?" He set the tray down on the chair, since last night's tray was still on the table. She had not touched any of the other food, he noticed. Must have slept through the night. Good, then she should be well rested. She still did not respond, and so he moved toward the window. Gritting his teeth, he pulled the curtains back, allowing the sunlight to fill the room. It stabbed into his eyes and he turned away quickly, glancing back at the bed again. Still no response.

"It is morning," he informed her, his patience beginning to wear. "You have slept the night through. I have brought you food, and then, once you have eaten, I would appreciate your insights once more."

Still no reply. Now he was becoming irritated, and he strode over to the bed. "Wake up!" he shouted. She did not move. Furious now, he grabbed the covers and tore them away—

—to reveal several large pillows bunched together.

"What?" the Sower roared, flinging the pillows from him, and spun about, but a quick glance was enough to show him that the room was empty. The woman was gone.

He turned back toward the door, but it had been locked when he had approached it just moments ago. And the servant had locked it behind him as well last night. The window was too small for anyone but a child to pass through, and fully three stories up. Where had she gone? And when? How long had he been sitting patiently in his throne room, waiting, while only a stack of pillows enjoyed his hospitality?

He marched back out of the room, slamming the door open so hard it cracked. Then he was taking the stairs two steps at a time, his blood seething. How dare she? He had welcomed her, made her a guest, and this was how she repaid him? Running off like a thief in the night?

At the thought of thieves, a sudden panic stabbed through him, and he leapt the rest of the way down the stairs, then ran to the chamber door. It was still closed and locked, its spells still in place, but he hurriedly opened it nonetheless. It was only when he saw the tome still resting on its pedestal that he allowed himself to relax again. She had not taken it. No, she had simply been frightened and run away rather than face him, or the tome, again.

The fear was something he appreciated, and he admired her resolve. But she had left without permission, and that was unacceptable. Locking the chamber once more and returning to his throne room, the Sower glanced about.

Those whining little courtiers had not yet returned, but he did not need them. He summoned two of his guards, and gave them their orders instead.

"Find the woman who was here. Tall, young, long white hair. Find her and bring her to me. Alive and unharmed." His eyes narrowed. "Make that alive and mostly intact. Now go." The guard shuffled off to obey, and he leaned back in his throne. She could not have breached the walls, which meant she was still in Ortense. And he would find her. Then she would help him with the tome, as planned. Only now it would involve less pleasantry and more pain.

Arianna woke suddenly to the sound of creaking. Her hands reached for her daggers, and their absence woke her fully. Brushing hay from her face, she peered about. The hay loft had no doors of its own, but the slabs of wood that made up the wall were loose enough that light shone between them, telling her it was day again. And the creak had been the sound of the stable door opening.

Doing her best to move silently, she extricated herself from the nest she'd created last night and stood, absently removing bits of hay from her clothes and hair. Peering over the side of the loft, she saw the stables below looked quiet and empty. From here she could not make out the bloodstains at all. It was peaceful.

I know what I heard, she told herself. That had been the door. It was slightly ajar now, and she knew she had closed it last night before climbing the ladder. But perhaps it's just the wind. Gren would announce himself when he opened the door. Wouldn't he?

Not if he doesn't know I'm here, she realized. Not if he's worried that those four bodies down there might have friends waiting for him.

And not if it wasn't him at all, but really were those corpses' friends.

Carefully she threaded her way through the hay bales until she had reached the ladder. Climbing down would leave her exposed until she reached the barn floor, and anyone else in the stables would know she was there. Staying up in the loft meant she could hide, but it also meant she had no way out. She was cornered if she stayed, exposed if she went. Which was better?

Which would Gren choose?

Well, that was an easy one, at least. So, with a small sigh, she swung onto the ladder and began to climb down. She didn't bother being quiet, but worked on taking each rung as quickly as possible instead, and leapt the last three to the ground. When she landed, she wasn't alone.

As she watched, cursing the absence of her blades, a large shadowy shape detached itself from the nearby support beam, and stepped toward her. It seemed to grow larger and larger even as it moved toward the sunlight—

—and then Gren's face was grinning down at her.

"Morning," he said. "Hungry? I've got a few friends waiting on us for breakfast."

CHAPTER EIGHTEEN

She stalked forward, and the daylight parted before her, swiveling away to leave her in shadow. She smiled but did not slow down.

Her mistress had been most clear about the urgency of this mission. "Return it to me with all due haste," she had intoned. "Allow none who have touched it to live. And with it shall be the thief's eyes, hands, and heart."

And so the Shoat of the Mire pursued the thief out of the Underworld and into the land of the living.

She did not understand all the nuances of her mistress's plan. When the theft had been discovered, she had dispatched the Shoat immediately. And the Shoat had caught up to the intruders while they were still within the Marshes. There had been two of them, one short and slight, the other tall and lean. The short one had been trained to stealth and infiltration, while the tall one was skilled in necromancy. Only the necromancer had taken one of the tomes, but each had to be caught and punished for daring to profane the Mound of Forsaken Seeds with their skulking and spying.

She had found only one of them, but he had been impressive. He had been short, though well taller than her, and fast on his feet; wiry but strong. He had drawn a pair of long, thin daggers from sheaths on his forearms, and moved toward her at a crouch, the blades angled back toward his elbows. His first, testing strikes had been lightning-fast, the moves of a viper.

She had allowed his feints to go without reply. Then, when he had committed to a quick slash from the right hand, she had trapped his wrist, snapped it, and twisted so that the dagger spun free. With her free hand she had caught it, and jabbed it through his left elbow. He had dropped the second blade, clutched at his arm, and screamed.

His screaming would go on for a long time, the Shoat had decided, then it would be time then to find the other one—the necromancer, who had had the temerity to steal from her mistress. Yet a call from her mistress had brought her up short.

"Leave the other one," the Deathlord had commanded inside her mind without explanation. "Arrangements have been made. But finish the other one, and make it slow. Then return with his head."

The Shoat had obeyed. She had tortured the little man, stripping bits of flesh from his body with his own dagger, slashing small wounds elsewhere, and then stuffing the bits into those wounds. It had taken hours, and though she could not see the necromancer, she could feel him watching the entire process. He was somewhere nearby, and she could have tracked him down, but her mistress had commanded otherwise. Finally the Shoat had killed the short one, removed his head, and hoisted it in one hand. Then she had walked away, returning to the Mound with her trophies.

Time had passed, but finally her mistress had turned to her. "It is time now," she told the Shoat. "Seek out the thief. Retrieve my tome. Bring me his eyes as well, and his hands and his heart."

The Shoat was not completely sure why she had been forced to wait before pursuing the tall one—the *actual* thief—but she knew that it was part of her mistress' larger plan. She was content not to understand, as that was not her place.

Now, she studied the watery ground ahead of her, watching for his tracks. Not that she needed them. She could see the Essence around her, and a thick band of oily corruption floated before her, wending its way to some unknown destination. The Shoat had walked the boundary before, and never had she seen a path like this. Someone or something had brought the darkness out of the Underworld and into Creation, and was spreading it farther. The line between the two was blurring. And it was all in the living world, where the world was growing darker and more infested with shadow as the taint spread throughout the Essence there.

The tome was making its presence felt.

She continued walking, hands twitching slightly. She had not killed yet today. And the day before had been only an old fisherman and his wife. Hardly a challenge. She hoped that, wherever the tall one had gone, he would put up a fight.

She hoped he had friends who got in her way.

Briefly the Shoat considered stopping at the next human habitation and amusing herself. But she set the thought aside. Her mistress had instructed her to make haste, and it was unwise to leave the Dowager of the Irreverent Vulgate in Unrent Veils waiting. Unwise and unhealthy, even for one such as the Shoat.

There would be time for entertainment later.

The Sower sat up and looked around. What had just happened? He had felt something—not in his own flesh, but something else. Something had changed.

He studied his cramped throne room. All looked in order, and his guards still stood at their posts. No, wait. They were swaying slightly, as if blown by a strong wind. Or tugged by a tide.

And that was what he had felt as well: a tugging. Something had pulled at him just now. Something in the shadows.

But not something here in the palace. It was farther than that. Yet he had felt it clearly. And so had all the shadows around him. They had all answered, leaning toward whatever it was.

Something had entered Ortense. Something the shadows loved. Something they obeyed. And that filled him with unaccustomed fear. For what could they love more than he, their creator and supporter?

What had the power to supplant him in shadow?

"Okay, tell me again why you're here in this tavern," Arianna said, spooning several dumplings into her bowl from the large steaming dish in the center of the table, and then selecting one and popping it into her mouth. She had forgotten to eat anything yesterday, and was starving now.

"Why not?" Gren replied, shrugging as he reached for the platter of fried quail eggs. "They came to see me and wanted me to come here." Iuro was currently discussing something in the back room with the owner, Wil, and none of the other nobles seemed that keen on sitting right near them. As a result, Gren and Arianna had an entire back corner to themselves.

"They could have been lying."

"They weren't." He explained again how he had parsed the truth from the lies.

Arianna nodded, remembering how Gren had done the same to her when they had first met. "But even if they're not evil, they are rebels."

"Yeah, and good for them," Gren said around a mouthful of egg and dumpling. "Somebody needs to get rid of the Sower, and we've both come up empty so far. Why shouldn't they try? Iuro knows what he's doing."

Arianna glanced over at their host. "He does seem capable," she admitted, "but that was not my concern. We need to get to that tome and either destroy it or remove it to some place where it can be destroyed. That's our only interest right now. How these people choose their ruler, and how much they obey him, is not our problem."

"I know that," Gren said, taking a deep drink from the glazed cup before him and then slamming it back onto the table. "But anything that distracts the Sower from us is a good thing. We'll need to keep him and his dead guards occupied, and the easiest way I can see to do that is to give them another threat to face. Then we can get in there and do what needs to be done and get back out again. And hopefully that will declaw the Sower as well, in which case we can simply leave him to them."

"And if that doesn't work? If we get caught sneaking back in? Or seen breaking back out? What if capturing the tome does nothing but anger him further?"

"Then I will face him one on one," Gren rumbled, causing several people to look over at them. "If he wins, he gets to destroy me and most of the people here, but has to leave you alone. If I win I gain possession of the tome and its secrets."

Arianna was horrified. "He'll never agree to that!" *And even if he does*, she thought, *he'd be lying!*

"Probably not," he admitted, shaking his head. "Though you never know. But we have to do something. And I think we're better off working with this rebellion than without it."

She studied his face. Something about the way he wouldn't meet her eyes told her there was more going on. "We could just let them make their own plans, and trust that it will help by keeping the Sower busy. Why do you really want to work with them?"

"Ah, well," Gren rubbed the back of his neck with one hand and actually turned a little red. "It's just... I feel responsible for all this, that's all." When she didn't say anything, he continued, though he kept his voice down so that no one else could hear. "We put him on the throne, the Daggers and I. None of this would have happened if not for us. This is—if we help Iuro and the others, I can set things right. That's all."

Arianna studied him carefully. "All right," she told him, "we'll do what we can to help them. But our first priority is still that tome."

"Right." He took another swallow of rice wine. "So what did you find out about it, then?" She had told him what had happened to her, but not what she had learned.

"It is old," she said. "Very old. It is written in an ancient dialect of Old Realm, now long dead, from a court once renowned for its dark sorcery. And it contains spells no mortal should ever possess."

"The tree?"

"Yes, the tree is almost certainly the result of one of them. The book and the tree are in the same room, and feel similar to me. But the tree, for all its power, is the lesser of the two. The book is very large and very thick, and the Sower said that he could only read a tiny portion of it. I am afraid to think how many other incantations are hidden within those pages, or what they could do. That is why we must take it away from him and destroy it, no matter the cost."

"What do you think he plans to do with it?"

"I don't know." She hesitated, then continued. "I had a thought, though. I do not know if this is true but—I told you when we first met that this land was covered in tainted Essence, like a dark shadow."

"I remember."

"The taint is strongest here, and centered around that book. Even on a sunny day, its shadows covered the chamber. And they are barely held in check. I think—" she paused again. "I mentioned that the Sower came from the world of the dead. That is a literal truth. Do you understand that it is a separate world from this one?" Gren shrugged a little then shook his head. "It is. The Underworld mirrors our own, but it is a world of death, darkness, and despair. In some places, the two are very close, and easy to bridge. But in many places the two lands are separate." She absently shredded a steamed bun, her eyes seeing distant possibilities. "It may be that the shadows are thickening in order bring the lands closer together. Corrupting this land's Essence, making this kingdom a place of shadow, so that the Abyssals may enter it freely."

Gren frowned. "Those trees were spreading shadow, and they were close to the border. And if more of the shadows are spreading from here—"

"The entire kingdom would be engulfed," Arianna finished for him. "Yes. And once that happened and they could cross at will, they could marshal their strength and the push outward, into the neighboring kingdoms. And on from there."

"We have to get that book."

"I know. The only question is, how?"

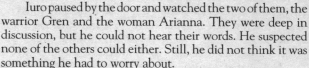

Iuro paused by the door and watched the two of them, the warrior Gren and the woman Arianna. They were deep in discussion, but he could not hear their words. He suspected none of the others could either. Still, he did not think it was something he had to worry about.

He and Gren had spent half the night talking and drinking. As a result his head ached dully behind the eyes this morning, and his mouth felt dry and rough, but he felt he had grasped the warrior's character. Gren was direct and honest and had more scruples than he had expected, particularly once he had learned that the man had been a hired sword. Iuro had recognized him then as one of the band who had put Belamis on the throne, and Gren had not denied it, though he claimed to have changed since. Certainly his actions supported that. And Iuro found that he trusted him.

The woman was harder to read. Gren had left before dawn to look for her in the stables and had insisted on going alone. He had returned with Arianna beside him, and at first Iuro had thought she might be the warrior's daughter. But she was older than she had looked at first glance, and they did not act like father and child. Nor did they seem like lovers. More like… partners, which was hard to fathom. Even harder after what Gren had said about her last night. A female scholar? Iuro had never met such a woman, but he had accepted Gren's word for it. And, upon seeing her, it was clear that the warrior was right. Everything about her resonated with intelligence, knowledge, and learning.

And now they were discussing what to do next. Iuro was sure of it. He hoped they decided to stay and aid the rebellion. Gren had seemed inclined toward that, last night, and they could certainly use his strength. And he suspected that Arianna had her own gifts to offer. Was she a Solar as well? Strange to be looking to so-called "Anathema" for help, but if Gren was any example, the Immaculate Order had long been exaggerating their crimes. Gren might be something more than human, but he was no monster. And from what

Rydec had said about Gren praying over Armand and his cronies, the warrior was a far better man than most, Anathema or not. But they were not from Ortense, so they had no vested interest in seeing Belamis ousted and someone ruling in his place. And, without knowing why they were here, Iuro could not be sure that their goals coincided with his own.

He saw that they were both leaning back slightly and that Gren had returned his attention to the food on the table. They had apparently finished their conversation, which made this a good time for him to speak to them. Iuro took the clean cup Johan offered him, and made his way toward the table, making no effort to hide his approach.

"Have you thought it over, then?" he asked as he sat down at the table and poured himself juice from one of the pitchers arrayed there. Both of them turned to face him as he added a steamed bun, some fruit, some fish, some eggs, and a few dumplings to the plate in front of him as well.

"Why should we?" Arianna demanded, though not harshly. It was not the first time this morning that she'd asked him that. In fact this was the third. But he answered her again.

"Why should you not? Belamis is a tyrant who mistreats the people, the city, the land, and the kingdom. He has no right to the throne, save force, and even if he did have a legitimate claim his behavior and actions would disqualify him. He is a cruel man who cares nothing for Ortense, and only seeks power for its own ends. The kingdom is dying beneath him, and he does not care." He took a quick sip of juice to cover the shudder that passed through him. "He seems to enjoy it, in fact. More fodder for his unholy army."

"And you want us to help you take the throne from him. So that you can rule in his stead?"

He shrugged. "I would make a decent king, I think. And I am of the royal line. But if the other lords want Rydec or Pons or some other on the throne, I will bow to that. Any of us would be better than Belamis by far."

Arianna thought about it, glanced at Gren, then nodded. "We will help you."

"Excellent!" Iuro slapped the table. "That is excellent!"

"Understand, however," she continued, "that our goal is to remove his power, not to usurp him."

He shrugged again. "One and the same."

"No, they are not, and you must understand the difference." She leaned forward and he found he could not look away from her eyes. "You want him off the throne and out of this kingdom. But if he were removed and ousted, that would be enough for you. We want him powerless to harm another. We do not care if he stays on the throne, as long as he can no longer slaughter whole towns and summon unliving soldiers and practice other foul arts. And if it becomes a choice between defanging him and removing him, we will take the first path. You will choose the second. Thus our goals are not the same, and our choices may become different."

He frowned. "I see. Thank you for explaining that." After a moment, he nodded. "Yes, I understand. My first concern is Ortense. Yours is Belamis himself. But as long as our goals coincide, we can work together. If they diverge, I will not fault you for pursuing your own goal."

"Fair enough," Gren reached across the table, and Iuro clasped his hand. He could not prevent the smile that spread across his face, particularly when Arianna extended her own hand as well. Suddenly, with these two at their side if not enlisted in their cause, the chance of success seemed so much greater, actually within their grasp. It was as if the sun had shone in, bathing them all in its warmth, and he felt the joy flow through him. Everyone else felt it as well, and a wave of relaxation passed through the room, as some of the tension and anxiety faded. For the first time since Belamis's return, it seemed that everything might be all right.

CHAPTER NINETEEN

The Shoat stepped into the town and glanced about. It was quiet—a quiet she knew well. Nothing living walked this road or dwelled in these buildings. This was a place only of death.

Yet where were the bodies? Where was the blood? She saw only wood and paper, rotted food—and ash. Small mounds of ash scattered everywhere. She frowned. That was not what she had expected. The buildings were unharmed, the wooden walkways unscorched. Fire had not ravaged this town. Yet ash littered the ground where she had expected corpses. Strange.

But she forgot the ash when she saw the tree. It stood in the center of the town, long since withered, its branches curled in upon themselves, its leaves shriveled to brittle gray slivers. She smiled. This was something she could appreciate.

Stepping closer, the Shoat studied the tree carefully. It had clearly spent its energy, and all its branches were bare of fruit. A hint of shadow still swirled about it, but the sun had washed away much of that, as had whatever flames had burned away the bodies. Still, a touch of shadow was all she needed.

Stopping a pace away from the trunk and half-turning away, she drew her blade, spun it around, and stabbed in a single fluid motion. The tip passed through the tough bark without pause, and then she withdrew it, leaving a small but deep cut at the tree's center. Re-sheathing her blade, the Shoat extended one hand toward the wound and beckoned.

Nothing happened. Perhaps the tree was too far gone. Not taking her eyes from the fresh gap in the bark, the Shoat held out her right arm, palm up. Her left hand rose, forefinger hooked, and that nail slashed quickly across her bare wrist. A thin cut appeared, then widened, but no blood emerged. Instead black smoke gusted from the wound, a few thin ribbons of it. She blew upon them, and they drifted toward the tree and twined themselves about its trunk. One touched the opening she had carved, and was sucked in with a faint pop. The tree's aura darkened, and its bark glistened in places, though only dully. It would be enough.

She beckoned again, using her right hand still. The cut was already closing.

Slowly, a tiny tendril of shadow wafted from the tree's interior, passing through that opening and drifting toward her. It resembled the smoke that had been pulled into the wound, but darker and flecked with red. The tendril touched her forefinger and curled about it, then spiraled down until it was wrapped around her arm, a dark bracelet nestled against her pale skin.

Holding that arm out before her, the Shoat stepped away from the tree and turned her back to it. Then she gave a short command. The tendril's tip rose from her wrist and swayed slightly. It continued to waver for a moment, then stilled, pointing off toward the south. When she moved her arm to the side, the tip turned so that it continued to point in the same direction.

The Shoat smiled. Now she had a guide. The tree's last spark would lead her back to its creator, and to the tome that had summoned it. And then her mistress would be pleased.

Chapter Twenty

Over the next several days, signs began to appear around the city. They bore messages like "Peace and Security" and "Live without Fear." None of them had more than a few words on them, because even though most of the people of Ortense could read, not everyone could read well. The signs had been

Iuro's idea, a way to reach out to the people and let them know what was going on, but it had been Arianna's suggestion to keep them short and simple. Each sign was hand-lettered, often in elegant script, but none were signed. They did, however, share a mark. At the bottom of each page was a small flame, drawn in carnelian-colored ink.

People began to discuss the signs, though quietly so the Sower's guards wouldn't overhear. Each sign reminded them of things they had lost, things they had enjoyed when Mariburn had been king: happiness, peace, comfort, safety, freedom. None of the signs said anything about a rebellion, or encouraged the people to rebel, but the message was clear enough: If people wanted those boons again, the carnelian flame would provide them. They had only to wait until it told them what to do.

Ortense had grown sullen over the past month. Most of the people had taken to staying indoors whenever possible. Errands were conducted quickly, and no one stayed to talk. Neighbors and friends no longer visited one another, and no one went out at night. But now that began to change. The signs appeared on the walls of butcher shops and bakeries, on poles outside the central market, stuck to the side of a craftsman's booth. And wherever they appeared, people stopped to read them, and to talk about them. They began lingering in the shops again, and discussing current events with their neighbors. They began visiting each other's homes, both to complain about the Sower's rule and to discuss what the signs meant and who had created them. Though people still shied away from the Sower's guards, they also began to walk the streets more, and to hurry less. Slowly they were regaining their courage, and their fear was shifting to anger.

The Sower felt the change, and those courtiers desperate to win his favor confirmed it. The fear was tapering off. No one opposed him directly, but a ripple of resistance had surfaced. People no longer believed as strongly that they had to obey him. The city's Essence was still tainted, but the corruption was no longer spreading.

He tried to counteract this new strength. He ordered his soldiers to cut people down in the streets for the slightest crimes, in the hopes that this would frighten the residents back behind their doors. Instead, they began to travel in small groups, and actually resisted the guards. One such group managed to destroy a guard with a torch, and suddenly every group carried several torches, and waved them at any guard who approached. One group even took to marching past the palace each day, as if daring the guards to attack. The Sower considered it, but the group was thirty men strong, and he worried that it might be a way to distract him and occupy his forces while others struck elsewhere. So he let them walk unmolested, not realizing that this only bolstered the other inhabitants' morale.

Iuro was thrilled. He started organizing the other nobles to go out into the city carrying small scraps of parchment with the carnelian flame drawn upon them. Everywhere they went, they showed those images, and the people welcomed them. They returned with fresh food, drink, information—and pledges of aid.

"The miller and his three sons are getting ready to fight," Mykel told him.

"The baker and all five of his daughters are already ready," Donal added. When the others laughed, he shook his head. "You have no idea how hard those girls can hit."

"The craftsmen are starting to stockpile torches," Pons reported.

"The same with the fishermen and the rice farmers," Rydec confirmed.

Everything was coming together. The people had been tired of Belamis' rule from the start, but now they were no longer willing to put up with his cruelties. They were ready to fight back. Just as importantly, everyone in the city was starting to speak to one another, and to plan together. Soon the entire city would be working together as a single unit. Maybe even as a rebellion.

Gren was also keeping busy. He had removed his armor and wrapped himself in a large green hooded cloak. It was hardly a perfect disguise, but it did enable him to move about freely, and he had taken to walking the town with several of the local groups. He had not been with the residents who had destroyed that first guard, but he was with the second group to accomplish that, and the third. Although he had been here before with the Daggers, he found that no one seemed to remember him clearly. They knew Scamp and Lirat and Milch, who had been the more aggressive ones, and a few remembered Rangol, who had been their spokesman, but Gren and Hud and Dyson and even Enjy had faded into the background. That was a good thing now, because no one had any grudges against him. In fact, he found most of the people to be very welcoming. A few had heard of his fight in the palace, and several of the younger men did their best to copy his walk, his mannerisms, his speech, and even his appearance. Most of them were too young to grow proper beards, but they stopped shaving and started cutting their hair so short it curled. The older citizens were polite, friendly, and oddly grateful. Gren had not realized at first that Iuro and the others had been deliberately spreading the stories about the fight. When he did find out, he confronted Iuro about it.

"You're telling people about me," he said, walking in and dropping into a chair. Iuro glanced up from the documents spread out before him and raised an eyebrow.

"What do you mean? I have told no one your name," he replied.

"Maybe not, but it seems like everyone knows about the fight in the palace. And today, Neils the baker told me that he wished he'd seen it himself. So I asked him how he knew about it, if he hadn't been there. Know what he said?" Gren leaned forward. "He said Marus told him. So I asked Marus about it." In the back, Marus, a middle-aged noble with thinning black hair, met Iuro's glance and shrugged apologetically. "He told me you said to tell everybody." Now Gren was resting both arms on the table, and his face was only a foot from Iuro's. "Why?"

Iuro laughed but did not back away. "You know why, Gren. Think about it. You understand tactics. Why would I tell everyone what you did that day?"

Gren frowned. He'd only been thinking about the Sower's guards finding him, and about how embarrassed he got each time people thanked him for something he hadn't thought they'd known he'd done. Now he considered it the way Iuro suggested.

"Exactly," Iuro said, seeing realization bloom on Gren's face. "These people—all of us, really—were terrified of Belamis. And of his soldiers. They were not alive, and could not be killed. They were invincible. Until you arrived. Now everyone knows that they can be destroyed. That gives people hope. Dravyn and his sons never would have fought that guard if they hadn't known that it was possible to destroy it. You gave them hope, Gren. And they need that. We all do."

Gren coughed, uncomfortably aware that he was blushing. "Yeah, well—next time just warn me before you start making me famous, okay?"

"Done."

Despite his embarrassment, Gren was having a fine time. For the first time in his adult life he was protecting people instead of attacking them, and staying in one place instead of wandering around, and it felt good. Arianna, on the other hand, was not happy. And each day was worse than the last one.

She had argued that, if Gren could wander the streets safely with only a hooded cloak for concealment, so could she. But both Gren and Iuro had disagreed.

"You don't move like a man," Gren had told her bluntly. "And that hair of yours is hard to miss... unless you want to chop it off?"

She had clutched her braid protectively, which had made him laugh. But she was serious.

"Why must I stay here?" she demanded. "I am tired of being cooped up. The Sower had me prisoner, and now you're doing the same thing!"

"It's not the same," Iuro argued. "That was so that Belamis could use you. This is for your own protection. And, perhaps, for ours." When both Arianna and Gren glanced at him, he shrugged. "You told us that only you can decipher the source of his power. And thus you will be instrumental in removing it. We cannot afford to lose you. And, if he finds you, the Sower will do anything to get you back. We cannot take that risk."

She had known he was right. She could read the tome, at least in part, and even the Sower could not. That made her one of the rebellion's greatest assets. And even her spells couldn't protect her if the Sower realized she was a threat, discovered she was still within the city, and allowed one of his deadly trees to cover Ortense itself. She had to stay out of sight.

But she hated it.

She had spent her whole life before Exaltation within or right around the tower. A tiny area had circumscribed her days and nights, and she had chafed against it. But at least her mind had roamed free, fed on the books of the library. Here she had only the few texts in her pack, two of which she had not yet deciphered and one of which she had already read thrice over. And at the tower she had had tasks, chores. Not all of them had been pleasant, but they had given her purpose, and structured her days. Here she was simply a guest. She sat in on Iuro's strategy sessions, and offered suggestions, but she was not needed. She offered to help Sarah, the tavern keeper's wife, with the food, and was told that she was a guest and should not trouble herself. So she was forced to sit and watch while Gren went out each day, Iuro made plans, Sarah cooked, Tomas swept, Wil served and cleaned—while everyone else did something useful. Everyone but her.

The third day of her friendly captivity, she was watching one of the nobles, a man named Gerard, write out the latest sign. He was a heavyset man, surprisingly muscular for a courtier, and his hands were better suited to the axe or the sword than to the quill. When he accidentally ran one long curving line across two vertical ones, changing the whole sense of the character he was trying to write, she stomped over and swept the quill from his hand.

"Give me that!" she demanded, and shoved him out of her way. More startled than injured, he nonetheless fell out of the chair, and Arianna quickly took his place. She flipped the parchment over and wrote the whole thing over with a smooth, clean hand. "There!" Setting the quill aside, she blew on the ink to dry it, and took up the signet Wil had carved, dipped it in the red ink, and stamped the carnelian flame on the bottom of the sheet. "That's better." It was only when she stood up and lifted the parchment to bring it to Iuro that she realized everyone in the room was watching her. And that many of them were smiling.

After that at least she had something to do. Each day she composed new signs, and discussed with Iuro and a few of the others where to place them. But she was not allowed to deliver them herself.

Still, it was better than doing nothing.

The Shoat paused. From this vantage, she could see the city on the hill, and the shadow around her wrist was pointed straight toward it. Even without that sign she would have known this for her destination, however. She could see the darkness curling about it, and the gates and walls were wreathed in shadow.

As she stood there, studying the city and judging the best place to enter, her thoughts were disturbed by a slow sound. A paddle. And it was growing closer. Glancing to the side, she saw a small boat approaching. A single figure sat cross-legged in it, paddle dipping from side to side, its body swaying.

The Shoat smiled. A local. At last.

"Ho there!" The man called out, flicking his paddle to swing the boat up against the bridge beside her and grasping the bridge support to hold steady. "Well now, where did ye come from, eh? And where are ye going?"

"Down there," she replied, stepping closer but gesturing toward the city. The man chuckled. He was older but still fit, and he had the weathered skin and deep tan of someone who worked outdoors all day. His boat, she saw, was filled with various plants.

"To the city, eh? So am I. Ye can hop in, if ye like. Just don't bruise the herbs none."

She did not follow his directions, but stood, head tilted slightly, studying him.

"Well," he asked after a moment's silence, "did ye want a ride or didn't ye? It's near dark and I've not got much time."

"I have," she replied, still studying him. Then she smiled. "You have nice eyes." They were clear and green, and friendly.

"Why, thank ye." He grinned at her. "Yers are mighty fine as well."

"Give them to me," the Shoat continued, ignoring his reply. And then, before he could react, her hand was on his arm and had yanked him from his boat.

They had grown darker.

The Sower paced before the pedestal, stopped to glance at his surroundings, and then began pacing again. Yes, definitely darker. The shadows had thickened since yesterday, here and throughout the palace. And he should have rejoiced, because with their renewal his power was also restored. There was only one problem.

He had not caused this.

Someone or something had given the shadows fresh strength. Someone tied to them as intimately as he was—more, because they had done this from a distance. Someone from the Underworld, with its necrotic Essence billowing thick around him.

His mind leapt back to his journey into the marshes, and to the fate of his former partner, the Herald of Pain and Lamentation. And he shuddered. His path since his reawakening had been one of pain and death and suffering, but even that had not prepared him for the sights he had seen then. For what she had done to him.

The Shoat of the Mire. The very name caused his hands to tremble, and he looked about quickly to make sure he had not somehow summoned her. She had pursued them then—could she be after him now?

No, he thought. Surely not. The Dowager had many servants. True, he had never heard of another *deathknight* serving the Dowager, but surely she had others. He clung to that belief. This was another of her vassals, but not that one. The thought calmed him. He was more willing to face a hulking warrior than her—two or three of them, even, with hooked, serrated blades and spiked armor.

Someone was definitely coming. And, since his master had not informed him of it, he could only assume that the newcomer was from some other Deathlord. It had to be the Dowager. The tome was hers. She had sent someone to retrieve it, and to deal with him in the process. That must have been what the Walker in Darkness had meant by his warning that time had grown short. Presumably, his own Deathlord master had stalled the Dowager for as long as possible (just as he had originally done to give the Sower and the Herald a chance to sneak into her citadel), hoping to give the Sower a chance to fortify his position.

The Sower smiled, the first time he had done that in days. The Dowager had miscalculated. Her servant's approach was only helping to taint the local Essence further, granting him strength again. When her deathknight did arrive, it would find the Sower of Decay and Distrust ready and waiting.

And once he grew strong enough, he could use the tree again. He glanced admiringly at it. For several days it had been weak from repeated use, its branches drooping, fruits dimming to a dull gray. But now it was lustrous and strong again, bark glistening in the starlight, fruits swaying invitingly. Soon he would be able to release more of those fruits, and the darkness would swell yet more, until it washed over Ortense completely, and spilled beyond its borders.

Soon Creation itself would break beneath the weight, shadows pressing against it from both sides. And all of Ortense would become a shadowland. But this land belonged to the Sower, by the grace of the Walker in Darkness. The Dowager would be displaced, her land overlaid with this new kingdom. All would belong to the Walker, and he would reward his servant appropriately.

The Sower's smile grew wider, baring his teeth. Yes, soon. Soon the Dowager's deathknight would reach him and receive a most unpleasant reception...

Even if it was *her*.

CHAPTER TWENTY-ONE

"Did you hear?" Tomas was practically bursting as he slid onto the bench. Gren was busy checking the edge of his blade, and didn't bother to put down the sword and whetstone.

"Hear what?" The tavern keeper's younger son had been awestruck by Gren since he'd first arrived, following him whenever possible. He was a good lad, though, and didn't get in the way. Gren remembered from his own youth that children often found things out before adults, so having a boy who wanted to impress him wasn't a bad thing.

"They found another body," Tomas said, taking a plum from the basket on the table and tossing it from hand to hand as he spoke.

This Gren hadn't heard, so now he did set the sword aside. "Where?"

"Near the edge of the market," Tomas told him, taking a bite between words. "It was Old Man Kabar." He swallowed. "They said his eyes were missing."

"Damn." Gren stood, slamming his sword into its sheath, and reached for his cloak. "Tell Iuro and Arianna where I've gone." Then he was striding toward the door.

This was the third body in five days, and, if Tomas was right, it would look like the previous two. Limbs broken in several places, chest torn open, heart and liver removed. But the worst part was the eyes. Whoever was doing this was removing them intact. And though the other organs were always found near the body, the eyes stayed missing. The killer was taking trophies.

The first body had been an herbalist outside of town. A rice farmer had seen the boat drifting along the river, and had retraced its path to the body, which lay on a footbridge that crossed the river a short ways outside the city. The second body had been a woman who'd gone to the river just beyond the walls to do some washing. Now the third was near the market, which meant inside the walls. The killer was getting closer.

At first Gren and Arianna had thought the deaths were the Sower's work. Certainly they were terrible, the sort of horror no normal person would commit. But he wouldn't be outside the walls at all, only within, and probably close to the palace itself. These were starting from farther away and working their way nearer.

Yet, given the grisly nature of each death, and the way the area's Essence was reacting to it, they couldn't avoid a certain grim suspicion of who was responsible: another Abyssal.

"Why would it want to do this?" Gren had wondered out loud after they'd heard about the first body. "Why bother? That old man with his plants wasn't a threat or even an obstacle."

"It makes a sort of sense," Arianna had said. "I can see the tainted Essence, the shadows, around this kingdom, I have told you that before. And they are thickest here, near the Sower and that book. But, of the last week, they had stabilized." She'd nodded at him, and at Iuro as well. "Your doing, as the people take heart. They're standing up for themselves, not letting themselves be killed. Essence reacts to death and horror, so with resistance and hope the taint weakens. Which weakens the Sower in turn."

"So we've been hurting him?" Iuro had asked, and a grin had split his face at her nod.

"Yes. Which may be why he has not countered recent events. He is hoarding what strength he has." She sighed. "But now this... People are afraid again."

"And that helps the Sower?" Gren had asked her.

"Even so," she'd said. "His strength comes from the tainted Essence, and anything that bolsters it restores him."

"So this other Abyssal is helping him get his strength back."

She had frowned. "Perhaps. But this one may only mean to increase its own strength, and the Sower's restoral is merely a coincidence."

"Regardless," Gren had pointed out, "this is bad."

"Yes."

"And we should stop the killer, whoever it is."

"Yes."

Since then they'd told everyone to watch for any strange deaths, and to send word to them immediately. Gren had been one of the first to reach the second body, and now he was heading toward the third. But even if the residents did not cluster around the corpse themselves, they heard the stories, and Arianna was right. They were scared, and it was getting worse. The groups that wandered the streets openly had grown smaller, and went out less frequently. People were talking more quietly, and not visiting as often or for as long. Ortense was reverting to where it had been before. And he wasn't sure they could do anything about it.

Despite the renewed fear, a large crowd had gathered around the body by the time he reached it. They moved back to let him through and stayed a cart's length from both him and the corpse, but they did not leave. Gren crouched to inspect the body, but he already knew what he would find. It was the same killer, without a doubt. The expression on the old man's face was terrible, every bit as bad as the looks he'd seen on the trees' victims, and made worse by the gaping holes where his eyes had been. His chest was a twisted mess of bone, flesh, skin, and congealed blood, and his limbs were bent at unnatural angles and in too many places.

Staring down at this man whom Gren had met twice before, he wished there were something he could have done to take away his pain—and that there was someone he could vent his rage upon. He also wished he could destroy the fear he could hear in the crowd, in their hushed whispers and chattering teeth and shaking knees. The fact that he couldn't help them only enraged him further.

And then he had a burst of inspiration, as if the sun had shone its light upon him and illuminated the path he must follow.

Standing, Gren turned to face the crowd. He had heard several half-shouts of "Who did this?" and "Why!" Now he answered them.

"You want to know who did this?"

No one shouted back, but several murmured that they did, and he knew the others agreed. They were just too scared to speak. Hopefully that was about to change.

"I'll tell you who," he shouted, letting his anger lend his voice volume. He wanted to be sure they all heard him. "It's a creature called an Abyssal. A monstrous warrior of darkness and shadow." He heard moans from the crowd, and saw faces pale. They had suspected that the deaths were not natural. "And you want to know why? This monster isn't after us. It's after him!" He swung one hand and pointed—directly at the palace looming in the center of the city.

"What?" One of the residents, a heavyset middle-aged man Gren recognized as the baker, pushed his way to the front. "But he's a creature of darkness, hisself!"

"Yes, he is," Gren agreed. "The Sower's powers come from darkness. But they aren't his by right. He stole them." A gasp ran through his audience. "That's right, stole them. Why're you surprised? Didn't he steal the throne? Well, he stole these powers, too. Now this Abyssal's here to get them back."

"What's that got to do with us?" the miller's son demanded. "Why kill us?"

"Because the Abyssal thinks the Sower cares what happens to us," Gren replied. "It thinks hurting us will hurt him."

He heard several replies to that, but an old woodworker summed it up. "He don't care none! Why should he? We ain't nothing to him!"

The crowd muttered agreement. And Gren could feel the shift in the air. They weren't as frightened now. They were getting mad.

"Kabar was a damn fool, and stubborn as an ox, and pigheaded to boot," the woodworker continued, "but he was a friend of mine! We worked the market together going on fifty years now! And that thing killed him, just to piss off some tyrant who don't even care? To hell with him! To hell with them both!"

This time the crowd roared its approval, and Gren nodded.

"You're right," he shouted to them. "It's not fair! It's not right! We're stuck between these two monsters, and we're the ones who get hurt! There's only one thing we can do!" He paused, and the crowd fell silent, waiting. Gren felt a strange thrill shoot through him, seeing all these people hanging on his every word, and it was strangely familiar. Then he realized—it was the same feeling he'd had when entering the memories of his past self. It was the exultation of leading the people, of molding them into a single unit. It was the sudden knowledge that they were listening to him, and more—that they were waiting for him to tell them what to do. It was the sudden powerful pride in being their guide.

"We fight!" he shouted finally. "We show them we won't put up with this! We take the throne from the Sower, and punish him for what he has done to us! And we teach this Abyssal what happens when we are wronged! We'll show both of them that such travesties, such horrors, will not be tolerated! Their cruelty, their evil, will reap only a bitter reward!"

The people shouted and cheered, and Gren knew that if he turned and charged the palace this instant, every one of them would follow behind him, ready to die for the cause. His heart filled with pride, not for himself but for these simple fishermen and merchants and craftsmen who had overcome their fear and were willing to risk everything to make this a better place.

"We're with you." The baker spoke quietly, but his voice cut through the noise, and the others nodded and shouted their agreement. "Tell us what to do, and when to do it."

Gren looked at them. He hated to lose this moment, but he knew that Iuro wasn't ready. Soon, but not yet. "Be ready," he told them instead. "It'll be soon. Watch for the signs from the carnelian flame, and be ready to move. And don't lose that anger," he cautioned them. "Remember, this is our home, not theirs. They have no right to be here. It's okay to be afraid, but don't let that control you. Be angry about it instead."

He turned back toward Zabar's remains and knelt beside him. "Rest in peace, my friend," he said, placing one hand upon the corpse's face, covering the empty eye sockets. "May the Unconquered Sun fill your soul with warmth and guide it to its next place in the Great Cycle." He felt the now-familiar surge, and the white light flared about the corpse, and then there was nothing but a small pile of ash that blew away in the morning breeze. The people gathered there stepped back, and he heard many gasps as he stood again. From the way they stared he knew that his golden mark of Exaltation was visible again. But he did not flinch away, or move to hide it. Instead he stood and faced them.

"Yes, I am a Solar Exalt," he told them proudly. "Reborn from the First Age. The Unconquered Sun has granted me these gifts to right wrongs, to reward the just, and to punish the guilty. And I tell you now that the Sower has earned my wrath, and that he will pay for his crimes. I will see justice done upon him." And he turned and made his way back toward the Red Bill.

The crowd parted around him. As he walked away he heard murmuring behind him, but it did not sound like the hate he had heard in Hud and the others when they had discovered he was Anathema. This sounded, instead, like sober consideration, mixed with some pride. There was anger in those voices as well, but he did not think it was aimed at him. He only hoped it would last.

The Sower ground his teeth, spitting curses between them. He had felt the Essence flow in his favor just before dawn, and had heard about the first two bodies the locals had uncovered. He'd known immediately that their discovery was responsible for the surges of strength he had felt recently. Those deaths had done quickly what his tactics would have accomplished more slowly, and brought the fear back. Now, with this recent spike, he had felt fully confident... for perhaps three hours.

And then, just now, just past dawn, that had changed. Something had shifted, and suddenly the shadows were even thinner than before. The sunlight was shining down upon this city, and cutting through the darkness, dissipating it, bathing every building and street with its light and warmth. The taint was being held at bay in the city's Essence by a clean, warm surge of life that filled him with disgust. His power was the most fragile it had been since his return to Creation, and his guards were sluggish, their strength tied to his own. What if the rebels struck now?

If only he had a name to use! He could cast a seed from the tree and destroy the rebellion utterly. But the spell required a name and a living victim, and he didn't have one to give it. True, he could aim for any noble in Ortense itself, but even at full power no single seed would have been strong enough to slaughter everyone in the capital city. The tree was not yet back to full power—its seeds would probably only cover one city block. Without knowing which block, his attack would be useless, and it would drain both his and the tree's energy. He needed to know who he was fighting! But all he knew was this red flame he had seen on the signs his guards and withering toadies had torn down and brought back.

Nor had they had any luck in locating the giant warrior, or the white-haired girl, Adrianna. Where had they gone? He was sure one or the other of them was still here in Ortense, most likely hidden either in or near the city, but there were too many places to search each one, and his guards were not that attentive to detail. Were either of them working with the rebels? He had no way of knowing.

"That was brilliant!" Iuro slapped Gren on the back enthusiastically as he tossed his cloak onto a hook and pulled out a chair. "Mykel was there in the crowd, and he told me what you said. And how they reacted. Fantastic!"

Gren shrugged modestly. "I just didn't want them to be scared anymore," he said, pouring himself some water and draining it quickly.

Iuro watched him, trying to read his ally. He had wanted the warrior initially for his strength and his sword, but he was starting to realize that the big man was a lot more than a mere fighter. Over the past week he had learned more about Gren and had come to trust him. He'd seen the way the former mercenary had organized patrols to wander the town, and more importantly, he'd noticed how people reacted to him. They felt safe around Gren. So did he, actually. It wasn't just his size and strength, it was his direct way of looking at things, and his calm. And from what Mykel had said, the people had been ready to follow the warrior into battle this morning. They would need that soon.

Arianna, meanwhile, was also looking at Gren. "You are a true Zenith," she murmured to him, and Iuro didn't know what that meant but he could tell it was a compliment. "A warrior-priest," she added for his benefit. "A leader of the people."

Gren shrugged again, though he had reddened slightly. "I'm just doing my part."

"Well, your part is about to get a lot bigger," Iuro told him. "The people are obviously ready to fight. So are we. And now's the time, while the Sower's off balance."

"When?" Gren asked, sitting forward.

"Late this afternoon," Iuro said, but Arianna was already shaking her head.

"He's strongest at night," she reminded him. "And we are strongest in daylight. If you wait until afternoon and his troops slow us enough, it will be dusk before we reach the palace, and his strength will be growing while ours wanes."

Iuro was impressed. She always seemed so quiet, just a girl who liked to read, and then she would say something, offering insight like a flash of sunlight on an otherwise cloudy day. "All right, when should we strike, then?"

She frowned. "It is too late to gather everyone before afternoon today," she said finally. "So we should strike at dawn tomorrow. That way we have the entire day, and the Sower will only grow weaker as the sun climbs in the sky."

He glanced at Gren, who nodded, and then at the other nobles around the table, who also nodded. "Done," he said, pounding one fist upon the table. "Pons, Saerian, ready the men. Mykel, Rydec, Paer, ready the people. Arianna, we will need a new sign to warn them. Wil, please check our supplies." He glanced around. "All right, then. We will eat well tonight, and sleep as well as we can. Tomorrow we fight."

Arianna glanced over at Gren as the nobles moved off to their assigned tasks. "Are you ready?"

"Absolutely," he replied, and his knuckles whitened as he gripped the back of a chair so tightly it creaked. "You?"

She nodded, though her stomach fluttered at the thought of the battle to come. "Just remember, the book is our first priority."

"I know," Gren replied, but the deep furrows in his brow said he didn't believe it. "But dealing with that thing is your job. The Sower is mine."

Arianna saw that there wasn't any point in arguing with him, so she took out parchment and ink and quills instead, and started writing out a new sign for the rebels to post. She just hoped that Gren's rage wouldn't get the better of his judgment tomorrow.

Gren stood there, watching everyone else talking and arguing and making plans. But his mind was focused on one thing and one thing only. Tomorrow he would face the Sower again. The last time he had been unprepared, reckless. This time he would be careful. His anger would propel him, but he'd control it, turn it cold and deadly. The Sower would pay. For the villages, for the trees. For Gren's friends. He would pay.

CHAPTER TWENTY-TWO

Early the next morning, Gren and Arianna rose, washed their faces and hands, and readied themselves. Gren had cleaned his armor the night before, and now he buckled on the system of interlocking lacquered plates, tightening straps and pins until everything was secure. His sword was at his side, and he checked it and his dagger, then pulled on the layered, metal-studded greaves and bracers. Next, his lacquered helmet, with its layered bands that splayed in back to protect the neck and its demonic faceplate, and finally his banded gloves. For Arianna, it was like watching a man transform. When she had first met him, he had been wearing his armor, but more casually, with his gauntlets tucked into his belt, the helmet loosened on his head, and the faceplate removed. On the way here he had hung the helmet from his belt, and loosened the armor itself. Once they had joined Iuro, Gren had set the armor aside altogether, wearing a tunic and loose pants and that heavy cloak. He had seemed to relax more with each change, becoming less the hardened mercenary and more a normal man. But now he reversed the process, and suddenly he was every inch the warrior again. Nor was it just the armor. He carried himself differently, stood more erect… he loomed. She knew it was necessary for battle, this mindset, but it still gave her a shiver as she watched her companion disappear and this fierce military man take his place.

"Ready?" he said at last, his voice flat and toneless. She nodded and followed him downstairs.

Iuro and the others were already awake as well, and wearing their own gear. Many of the nobles had armor, though it was as pretty and as unused as their swords. A few had breastplates or armored jackets with scenes and emblems etched in gold or detailed with bright gems, and Arianna had to resist the urge to go over and inspect them. Some of this armor might be centuries old, heirlooms passed down through the generations. Each piece would have its own history, and some were made of materials or in styles no longer used today. To see them here, in this room of lords who had surely inherited these treasures but not the skills to use them fully, she almost laughed.

Iuro turned toward them, and she saw that his breastplate gleamed gold and winked with gems as well. He saw her glance and smiled.

"Yes, it is an heirloom of my family," he told her and Gren, who was also gazing admiringly at the armor. "They say it was worn by Andalar Ortense Visone, the first of our line, who swept back the beasts and the Wyld and claimed this land for our people. My cousin Mariburn wore it when he was king, and when Belamis killed him one of our family's servants managed to smuggle the armor away and bring it to me. But enough of that." He glanced at Gren, and frowned, though something in his eyes suggested he was not truly displeased. "My friend, your armor is missing something."

"What?" Gren did an automatic inventory. "No, it's complete."

But Iuro shook his head. "No, definitely missing something. Perhaps... this." His hands had been behind his back, and now he brought them around to reveal what they held— a battle standard. But not just any standard.

She heard Gren suck in his breath beside her, and realized that she had gasped as well. So had several of the nobles.

What Iuro held was a long silk banner, of the kind meant to mount upon a pole and attach to a man's armored back. The banner was a golden yellow, and from the way it glittered she suspected it had metal thread woven through it. Emblazoned upon it was the carnelian flame, the symbol of the rebellion, but far larger.

Iuro smiled. "I had Dalia, the weaver, fashion this for me, and old Hrain the armorsmith fit it to the pole. It is the standard of our cause." He extended it to Gren. "And now it is yours."

"Mine?" Gren looked startled, though one hand had reached for it automatically. "No, I can't. You are the heart of the rebellion. You're the leader. You should wear it."

But Iuro shook his head. "You are wrong, my friend. I am the head of the rebellion, yes, but I am not its heart. You are. You have given us hope, and sparked the fire of this rebellion. You are the flame, and this standard belongs to you." He held it up again, and this time Gren accepted it.

"Allow me." Arianna took the standard from him and, slipping around behind him, fitted the pole to the proper groove along his back. The standard waved proudly above his head, the flame catching the light, and each noble glanced at it and seemed to draw strength from the sight.

Gren waited until she was done, then turned back to Iuro. "Thank you," he told the noble quietly, not trusting himself to say anything more. "Thank you."

"Thank you, my friend." Iuro turned toward the door. "It is time." Pons opened it and held it for him, and he stepped outside. People were already gathering in the marketplace when they reached it, answering the summons Arianna had penned for him yesterday, and he both rejoiced and sorrowed to see them. It was heartening that so many of the city's citizens had rallied to their cause and were willing to join the fight. But he knew that many of them would not live to see the end of this day, and he mourned their loss already.

Nonetheless he walked forward, head high, and behind him he could feel Arianna, and Gren beside her. Empress! When the big warrior had faced him, the Carnelian Flame waving behind him, Iuro had felt a powerful impulse to kneel before him, or to run away. He had seen Gren fight before, and had been awed then, but now—! Iuro was just glad the man was on his side.

Or, at least, that their goals aligned. He glanced back at Gren, and then at Arianna. She had told him from the start that their objective was to remove the source of Belamis' power, not to dethrone him. And he had agreed to that, because their interests coincided—a powerless Belamis would be easier to defeat. Since then, he'd felt that Gren's interests had shifted. The big man had made friends among the people settled in. Mykel had told him how Gren had told the crowd yesterday, "We're the ones who get hurt… This is our home," he'd said, and Iuro knew that he had meant it. Gren was one of them now.

But Arianna was another matter. She had never lost her focus. If it came down to a question of killing Belamis or destroying his power, he knew which one she'd choose. He didn't blame her for that, but he wasn't sure it was the right choice. And he was no longer sure which path Gren would follow.

But he pushed all of that from his mind as he reached the far edge of the crowd, stationed just within the wooden posts that formed the boundary of the marketplace square, and they parted for him. The other nobles assembled around him, Gren and Arianna as well, and Iuro looked over them all. This was his army. These were the men and women he was about to lead into battle. He hoped he was doing the right thing.

"People of Ortense!" he shouted. "Today we fight for our freedom!" He heard as much as saw the ripple of agreement. "Today we take back our kingdom! Today we rid ourselves of that monster who sits on the throne, and make this land safe again!" Several people were shouting now, things like "yeah!" and "he's gotta pay!" and Iuro could feel the energy building. "Belamis sits there while we bleed and die!" he shouted. "And he laughs! He enjoys our suffering! Well, today he will be the one suffering! We will take the throne from him, and destroy those abominations that guard him, and we will be free to live in peace once more!"

Now the crowd was stamping and writhing like a single great beast, champing at the bit, and Iuro drew his sword. "To victory!" he shouted. "For Ortense!"

"For Ortense!" the crowd thundered back. And, when he turned and began marching toward the palace, hundreds of men and women marched beside him.

Sitting in his throne room, the Sower heard a great rushing sound in the streets beyond. Then one of his tame courtiers ran into the room, skidding across the slick floor and nearly colliding with the dais.

"Rebels, sire!" the man gasped. "They are coming here!"

"At last!" The Sower stood and gestured to his guards. "Gather my troops. Fill the courtyard. Kill everyone who approaches." He stepped off the dais, then glanced back at the courtier, who still knelt by its edge. "Kill that one as well," he ordered. The man's screams followed him as he left the throne room and moved toward the nearest stairway.

Finally, the Sower thought, climbing to the second floor and entering one of the rooms that faced the courtyard. He had grown tired of waiting, always waiting, and every day in this disgustingly life-filled land was a torment. Now his army could finish off the rebellion, once and for all. And, when they fell, the rest of the people would be devastated. But when the dead rebels rose again, and joined his other soldiers, the taint would multiply, and the shadows would fill the land.

He stepped to the window, pushed it open, and stepped out onto the balcony, where he could watch the coming carnage. Soon it would all be over, and the land would be his.

As the mob neared the palace, they saw the Sower's guards. The walking corpses had multiplied over the past week, and now more than four hundred of them stood between the rebellion and the front steps. Seeing them, with their milky eyes and lolling mouths and blackened teeth, their skin gray and marbled, their remaining hair and flesh rotting, the people slowed. But Iuro signaled, and the nobles moved among the crowd, dividing the men and women into smaller groups. And assigning each group to a single target. As each group focused upon their particular warrior, they forgot much of their fear. Four hundred zombies were a heart-stopping nightmare—one squad of zombie was horrifying but manageable. The people advanced again, though more warily now.

Gren had walked quickly, not running but staying at the front edge, and now he raised one arm. Instantly the crowd fell quiet, and Gren paced before them, the war banner fluttering at his back.

"Belamis!" He shouted toward the palace. "You who call yourself the Sower!"

From his balcony, the Sower cursed. Damn! *He* was with them! And more than that, judging from the banner he bore. Then he noticed another figure, and his curses grew more fervent. It was the woman, Adrianna! She was one of them as well! And she had seen the tome!

"Come forth and face your punishment!" Gren bellowed, but the Sower stayed where he was, and the shadows from the window curtains concealed him from their sight.

"You have been judged," Gren continued, "and found wanting! You have committed crimes against the people of Ortense, and against Creation itself! Your very presence is a blight upon the earth, and an insult to the Unconquered Sun!" He drew his sword, and his anima flared as it swept free, the light gleaming about him and reflecting off his blade.

"These creatures," Gren gestured toward the zombies, "are an affront to nature, and evidence of your foul corruption! We shall return them to their rightful place within the ground, freeing the souls to move on. And then we shall visit our judgment upon you as well! You have been warned!"

With a great sweep of his blade, Gren stepped forward, closing the distance to the unliving army. His anima grew still brighter, its light so intense no one could look directly at him. The carnelian flame of his banner seemed to dance within that glow, as if it had turned to real flame itself. And the zombies shuddered away from Gren's presence, unable to bear contact with his light.

Then Arianna stepped forward, hands already moving in a complex pattern, a series of strange, hushed words falling from her lips. The Sower cursed again. She *had* lied to him, and more than he'd realized! She was a sorceress! Another Exalt, he realized as he saw the anima flare around her, and glowing kanji form in the air around her hands. And he had given her access to the source of his power!

But the spell she cast now did not come from the tome. As she completed the last gesture, a cloud of tiny forms materialized all around her. They were shaped like butterflies, but glittered like tiny fragments of the night sky, and Gren's light reflected on the gloss of their jet-black wings. Arianna's arms swept forward, and the cloud of obsidian butterflies flowed past her and flooded into the first rank of the Sower's army. Their razor-sharp wings shredded flesh from bone, and the zombies in her path collapsed, limbs separating from torso and head separating from everything else. A clear avenue appeared through the army, and Arianna raced forward, only one goal in mind. The Sower.

Gren led the rebels forward behind her. But, up above, he saw a tall, dark-robed figure step forward on the front balcony, and heard the Sower call out to his unliving servants, "Close the gap! Protect the door!" And the remaining zombies shuffled in, filling the path again.

I must reach the tome! the Sower thought as he fled the balcony and raced for the stairs. *I cannot let her get to it first!*

Then the first group of rebels reached the front-most guard. The guard swung his rusty sword, but one of the men ducked the clumsy swing and struck out, his heavy club connecting with the guard's forearm. The rotted bone snapped, and the sword was knocked loose from the impact. The rest of the group fell upon him then, using axes and swords to cut him apart. In another minute the zombie had collapsed, and the rebel band moved to the next target. The cheers, which had paused for Gren's speech and then begun again when he had cowed the zombies, grew louder.

All across the courtyard, the rebels were attacking. The tactic of surrounding a zombie was working, though in several cases the dead warrior killed the person standing before him before the others could disarm him. Gren desperately wanted to follow Arianna into the palace, but he could not leave until he was sure the rebels were in control. Instead he strode about the battlefield, lending his sword wherever a group needed aid. One warrior had managed to kill a man and wound another, and the remaining members of that band were backing away. Gren lopped off the creature's head with a single backhand stroke, then whirled his blade around and removed the corpse's arms as well.

Gren couldn't stop grinning. The adrenaline was rushing through him, making his blood sing, but it was more than that. With his anima about him, his blade in his hands, the other rebels at his side, he felt invincible. No, that wasn't right. He knew he could still be beaten, still die. But that didn't matter. He felt strong, capable, and more than that he felt happy. He was enjoying himself—not the slaughter, perhaps, though these creatures were unclean and deserved to return to their graves. He was enjoying being alive, being healthy, being able to swing the blade and meet his foes in open battle. Life was good.

Then he heard a cry in a familiar voice. Whirling around, Gren saw Tomas. The boy had apparently joined the crowd, staying in back so that he would not be noticed and sent home. He had a small, sharp kitchen knife in his hand, and had made himself useful darting from foe to foe—though the corpses did not feel pain, a severed tendon still rendered their legs useless. But one of the warriors had stepped back at just the wrong moment, so that Tomas's knife had jabbed it in the flesh of leg instead. And alerted to a foe at its back, the warrior had turned. Now Tomas found himself facing the unliving creature, which caught him by the shirt with one hand. The other swept up, its rusty sword poised to strike.

"Damn!" Gren knew that he could never cover that distance in time. But Tomas would die without his help! In desperation, he hurled his sword. The blade flew across the courtyard, trailing black blood as it passed over the heads of several rebels, its simple guard catching the light. And then it struck, imbedding itself in the zombie's head with such force that the guard shattered the front of its desiccated skull. The creature staggered back, dropping Tomas as it raised its hand to grasp the handle protruding from its forehead, and the boy took the opportunity to dance out of reach.

For an instant, Gren worried about being unarmed in the midst of a fight, and his other hand reached for his dagger. But then another First Age memory surfaced, and he knew what to do.

"To me!" he called, his sword hand stretching toward the zombie, fingers reaching. And, in the zombie's forehead, the sword quivered. It shook. And then it leapt backward, exiting the creature's head with a hail of bone and rotted flesh and crumbled brain matter, and flew back to Gren's waiting hand, trailing golden light. The rebels nearby gasped, but not out of fear. They knew this big, grinning, glowing giant was on their side, and the very thought renewed their courage. The zombie had collapsed, the sword's departure throwing it forward, and now several rebels dismembered it to make sure it would not trouble anyone again.

Satisfied that that creature was well in hand, Gren glanced about. The zombies had not been given clear instructions, or perhaps they could not handle detailed plans, and so they had simply lashed out at the nearest foes. The rebels, on the other hand, had stuck to their strategy and were dispatching the walking corpses quickly. What's more, the dead stayed down. This battle would be long, but the living could win it—he saw that selfsame reassurance in Iuro's eyes, and in the eyes of the other nobles leading the rebel forces. The Sower was not raising the fallen dead to continually replenish his forces, so as long as the courage of the living held, the living could prevail. That meant Gren could finally turn his attention toward his real foe.

"Belamis!" he shouted, deliberately using the Sower's discarded human name instead of his title. "I'm coming for you!"

As the battle continued around him, Gren headed for the door, and for the man he had sworn to kill.

Gren was not the only one after Belamis, nor was he the first to reach the palace.

CHAPTER TWENTY-THREE

As soon as her spell had opened a path, Arianna had run forward, heading straight for the palace door. As she ran, she incanted her second spell, transforming her hands. Her fingers cracked and split, the skin twisting and stretching and in some places bursting as her hands extended into long, gnarled claws. The first digit of each finger was overly long even on those oversized hands, and tapered down to wicked-looking claws that bore the whorls and grain of hard oak. She lashed out with her right hand, carving open the neck of a guard who had stepped within range, and continued on as he dropped by her feet. She was ready.

Several other guards attacked her, but Arianna barely noticed them. Her main concern was Belamis and the book. She burst through the palace doors, decapitating the two guards stationed there before she had even registered their presence. All of the other guards were outside already, dealing with the rebellion, and she could just see Belamis darting down a stairway farther down the hall, on his way toward the chamber. Damn!

She ran after him. She had hoped to catch him off guard, but he'd been watching the battle and had clearly realized his guards were outmatched. Now he was going for the book. She couldn't let him use it—there was no telling what would happen, what horrors he could pull from it. Even if it was just another of those trees, he could kill every one of the rebels and lay waste to the city. Possibly still tug this land into the Underworld. But even if she and Gren survived a second such attack and saved Ortense, Belamis would probably get away and take the book with him. She could not allow that to happen.

She caught up with him as he stepped through the chamber door. He was starting to shut it behind him, and Arianna did not slow down but flung herself feet-first at the closing gap, using her momentum to force it open. Belamis stumbled back, his foot sliding off the step, and he crashed to the floor as Arianna flipped forward and landed lightly on her feet. His tumble gave her enough time to spin and lash out with one foot, kicking the door back against the far wall. She wanted Gren to be able to follow her through, and she knew he was on his way.

Belamis hit the ground hard, and if he had been mortal still it would have knocked the breath from him. As it was, he folded over from the impact but curled into a ball as he struck, then uncoiled like a striking snake, springing back upright and on his feet. When he realized who he was facing, his gaze narrowed and he bared his teeth in an unpleasant smile. "I should have suspected you for a rebel. Instead I thought too highly of you."

"I am only *with* them," she corrected. "My concern has always been you—and that book." She glanced past him, to where the tome still sat upon its pedestal. The Sower laughed. It was a chilling sound.

"Ah yes. You *were* able to read it. I knew you were lying to me! You want it for yourself!" He had not bothered to climb the two steps again, but they were still eye-to-eye as he closed the distance between them.

"No," she corrected him. "I want it destroyed. And you with it."

He sneered at her. "It will take more than a gift with languages," he glanced at her hands, "...and an impressive manicure to destroy us." And then he struck.

She had noticed, when she had entered the room, that the shadows were still thick here. Clearly the presence of the tree and the book were maintaining the darkness despite the battle raging outside. Belamis would still be strong here.

Even so, she was not completely prepared for his attack. One minute he was standing there taunting her, and the next she realized that the dark Essence in this room was coalescing about his right hand. Then he stabbed that hand forward, and a bolt of glittering-black energy shot toward her. It was the same attack that had wounded Gren so seriously.

But the big warrior had been spent when he had faced the Sower, and Arianna was not. She spun on one leg, leaping up as she did, and the bolt passed harmlessly beneath her, striking the wall but dissipating harmlessly against the stones. Arianna was still in the air, and she flipped in a tight circle, one arm lashing out as she rotated. The claws on that hand slashed across, catching the Sower's arm and carving through cloth and flesh before he could back away. Then her feet were beneath her again, and she extended her legs once more, touching down lightly not two feet from her previous position.

"Very well," he told her, retreating a few steps, the darkness of the room wrapping protectively around him. "If that is the way of it." And he spoke again, but the words sent a chill down her spine, for they were not words still remembered by the living. She had read the language of the tome, but she had never heard it spoken before, and each word was crafted from hatred and contempt and the darkest aspects of humanity. The words he cast at her seemed to embody all the worst thoughts and emotions of the world, and they drew the darkness with them as they spun a web around her. Soon her sight dimmed as the shadows formed a cocoon, walling her off within their depths.

And thus it ends, the Sower thought as he watched the dark cocoon constrict around his foe. He turned away, thinking the young woman finished, but a soft hiss stopped him. He spun back, and suddenly the cocoon was carved to ribbons from within. A single jagged claw emerged at the top, followed by several more as a strip of the mystic prison fell away, and Arianna vaulted upward, her skin now casting red-gold reflections from the light about her as if she had wrapped herself in bronze. On her forehead, a mark much like his own Abyssal brand blazed bright enough to make him wince as she landed on her feet. The cocoon collapsed and faded away behind her.

The Sower's eyes widened at her escape, and for the first time he worried that her sorcery might exceed his own. But no matter. The spell had given him the time he needed. And here, within this chamber, his power was still strong enough to cast the necessary incantations. He had planned to target the palace itself, ridding himself of his foes in one fell swoop, but he would deal with this arrogant woman first. His lips curved back in a smile again. She wanted the book for herself, he knew that despite her protestations. Well, let her discover what fruits such study could offer.

As she shook off the last vestiges of the cocoon's darkness, Arianna saw that Belamis had not remained idle. He had moved quickly toward the tree at the center of the room, and now she saw him reach up to one of its thick, twisted branches. A heavy globe hung there, and his long fingers wrapped around it. Then he muttered something and Arianna shivered. Those words! D'rai'ican had been bad enough, but this! He was speaking the language of the tome, and she knew with sudden certainty that only her own Exalted nature had shielded her from certain madness. No human could bear to speak such words, or to stand in their presence, without their mind fleeing forever, such was the power contained within those syllables. Nor was it the dark but human strength of the language itself, but the incantation they formed. This was an evil that had never been meant for this world.

But Belamis spoke the words without fear of reprisal, his Abyssal strength protecting him in the same manner. And he had clearly spoken these words before. The fruit came loose in his grasp, and he lowered his arm so that it was now cupped before his mouth. Then he turned to face her again, and the smile on his lips was horrifying in its malevolent glee.

"Adrianna d'Mattelaine," he whispered. And she watched, unable to move, as the fruit burst open. Its glistening red-laced, black skin split into knife-bladed wings that hung about a sinister, angular black body. The abomination's wings beat rapidly, slicing the air, and he raised his hand to assist its flight—

—but when he lowered his hand it still rested in his palm, and the wings slowed and then stopped moving. He stared at the fruit in confusion, then glanced up at his opponent.

"Idiot," she sneered at him, descending the steps to face him on level ground.

His reply was an inarticulate snarl, and he flung the fruit at her. She lashed out without thinking, catching it in one hand, and clenched that hand into a fist, crushing the deadly fruit between her claws.

That proved to be a mistake. The fruit was shaped entirely from dark Essence, not the Essence of this world tainted but the true Essence of the Underworld and the darkness of Oblivion. The spells cast to birth the tree and retrieve its fruits gave them shape, using sorcery to temporarily bind that necrotic Essence, but when her claws pierced its skin, the fruit collapsed, and all the Essence within it spilled forth as a cloud of dark, noxious gas. The thick, cloying shadow enveloped her much as the Sower's cocoon had, but her claws proved useless against this foe—it lacked substance for her to carve open. And now it was seeping into her lungs, her ears, her very pores, flooding her with its filth, drowning her light in its unholy shadow.

The Shoat watched the battle with interest, particularly when the armored man with the battle standard had stepped forward. A delicious shiver had run through her when he had raised his blade, and again when the light had burst forth around him. A Solar! Here! This was proving more entertaining by the moment.

Alas, her objective came first. She saw the Sower disappear back into the palace, and reluctantly left her perch to follow. Perhaps later she would have a chance to try her hand against this Solar warrior. But that would have to wait.

Without a sound she slipped across the street, weaving her way silently through the courtyard. Caught up in the melee, none of the rebels noticed her, and the guards' sight she had already blocked from her presence. And thus, unseen, did the Shoat of the Mire enter the palace and pursue her quarry.

Gren burst into the palace, stumbling over the bodies that lay there just inside the door. He saw at once that they were more of the Sower's guards, and that what had ripped them apart looked like a beast's claws. Then he remembered a glimpse of Arianna running toward the door, her hands transforming into the grotesque wooden claws she had revealed at Anaka. This was clearly her work. He did not pause, but headed across the throne room and down the hall, following the directions she had given him the night before.

The Sower watched as the woman he still thought of as Adrianna—though he now knew that this was not her name—fought against the dark cloud that had erupted from the shattered seed. He had to admit he was impressed. She moved fluidly, her anima swirling about her, the light it cast glistening from her gleaming metal skin, her elongated hands carving desperately at the shadows enveloping her. The golden mark on her brow, a circle with the bottom half empty like a gaping wound, glowed brightly and burned away the darkness that surrounded her. It matched his own in design, though his mark glistened black like heart-blood, and absorbed light in an eye-dimming black glow.

He wished she were not his enemy. With his knowledge and her power, they would have made a formidable pair. But, alas, that was never to be. Instead he tore his eyes away from her struggle and turned toward the tree again. Another fruit hung within reach. He had hoped to dispatch her before dealing with the rebels outside, but she was too busy to stop him and that would suffice. Once he had released the second seed and it had grown to its full strength, the rebels would be dead and the shadows here would be restored. Even if she escaped the cloud, she would be alone and he would have regained his previous power. She would not stand a chance.

He reached up, fingers extended to grasp the fruit, when a movement caught his eye. Turning, he saw that someone else had entered the room through the still-open door, and he cursed the woman, for she had clearly left it open to allow for reinforcements. Then his eyes registered the newcomer, and they widened. A chill shot through him, and his hand fell limply to his side.

"You!" he gasped through lips that had suddenly turned numb.

Arianna swung again, cursing. The shadows around her were simply too vaporous for her to harm, and already her lungs burned from the traces of taint that she had swallowed with each breath. Finally she admitted that her claws would not be enough to free her. And at the instant she accepted that, she knew what *would* be enough.

"Unconquered Sun," she breathed, choking on the foul stench around her but forcing the words out nonetheless, "grant me light to burn away the darkness of your enemies!" Her anima, which had faded as the taint had crept upon her, flared up again, its light slicing through the cloud just as her claws had cut through the cocoon. The glow burned away the foul Essence around her, boiling it off until it vanished in a puff of oily steam. Finally she was free again, though she'd had to stand at death's threshold and there surrender herself entirely to divine providence.

Taking a deep breath, she wiped the sweat from her metallic brow and looked for her foe. He was standing near the tree again, but her first fear proved unfounded because his hands were empty. In fact, they hung at his side idle, and his face had gone even paler than before, eyes wide and mouth slightly open. Shock? And he was staring in horror, off to her left. Near the door.

At last! Arianna thought as she turned around, a remark to Gren already on her lips. But it died away as she realized that the new arrival was not her friend after all. Instead a tiny woman—no, a girl—had entered the room. She was barely three feet tall, and looked to be around ten years old, with large dark eyes and long, jet-black hair that flowed in a tangled cascade down her back. Too dark, Arianna realized as the girl glanced at her. The pupils and irises were the same deep black, and Arianna could feel herself falling into that gaze even from such brief contact. She also noticed, almost absently, that the girl's skin was chalk-white, and her teeth when she smiled were perfect and white and very sharp. The final clue, however, was the darkness. It had pulled away from Arianna when her anima had flared, but now it wrapped around this girl, draping itself about her like a favorite pet. Where it touched her, it grew stronger.

"You!" she heard Belamis gasp, and she wondered at the terror she could hear in his voice.

The Shoat studied both of them, and smiled. The woman was a Solar as well! Excellent.

But first to business. She turned to the Sower, and bowed mockingly. "My mistress sends her condolences to your master, the Walker in Darkness, at the end of her forbearance," she recited, word-for-word as directed. "She regrets your imminent demise, as your soul will no longer linger upon this plane or any other. For your crime, she sentences you to enduring pain before your final passing. I am to return with you, that she might have the opportunity to punish you herself." Her eyes drifted to the tree. "This will be destroyed," she informed him, "and another will be planted in its place, that this kingdom may enter her Marshes as is proper. The tome itself," her eyes slid to it, "will be returned to her, that the set may again be complete. And what little you were allowed to learn of its secrets will be torn from you before you are allowed to slip away into the final darkness."

She smiled again, and turned to face the woman. "You I have no quarrel with. Unite with me, and we will finish this one that much more quickly. Then I will take the book away from here, out of this world, back to where it belongs."

The Sower's eyes had widened as she spoke, and now his mouth flew open. "No!" he screamed, but he seemed unable to move as the girl and the woman regarded one another.

For a moment Arianna was tempted. This girl-thing must be powerful, if the Sower feared her so much. And the book would no longer be here in Ortense, which was her goal. She even suspected that she could trust the Abyssal to abide by their bargain and walk away after the Sower had been defeated. Except for what else the girl had said about another tree... Arianna shook her head.

"I have no dispute with you," she agreed, eliciting a faint whimper from the Sower, "and you are welcome to him. But that tome must be destroyed."

The girl nodded, and she did not look displeased, which worried Arianna. "Very well," the petite Abyssal replied, and suddenly a long, slender dagger was in her hand, its beautiful blade glinting black even against the shadows. "Know, then, that the Shoat of the Mire is your opponent, and that I will make your death slow and painful, as befits your rank." The girl spared a single sidelong glance toward the Sower. "Your account I shall settle anon."

Suddenly the girl's outline wavered, and for an instant in her place flickered a tiny black star, a miniature human figure who flitted above the ground and whose very form seemed cut from utter darkness. Then the Shoat was herself again, and advanced upon Arianna, whose anima suddenly seemed too weak to battle the darkness that surrounded it.

CHAPTER TWENTY-FOUR

The Sower had watched the exchange with increasing horror. The Shoat. Why did it have to be the Shoat? The girl's very presence terrified him. And she had come to kill him and reclaim the tome, as he'd suspected. But then she offered to ally with the Solar woman against him! He had only been able to breathe again when the white-haired sorceress wrapped in bronze had refused. And then he barely dared to hope when the Shoat had focused her attention upon the woman instead of him. Never mind that she would come after him next. For now, he was unharmed. And perhaps the Solar would be strong enough to defeat her. If not, at least she might be able to wound the Shoat, which would increase his own chance of survival. No matter who won, he would stand a better chance than he had a moment ago. So for now he simply retreated as the Shoat took the fight to her new foe.

The girl's long dagger lashed out at Arianna while she still seemed too far away. But somehow the blade reached her, slipping past her guard and slicing a line across her stomach, through her clothes. The gleaming black edge ignored her bronze skin as if it were silk, and blood seeped from the wound. It was not a fatal blow, or even a serious one, and the girl's malicious smile said that she had known it. This was simply a first cut, a demonstration of how easily she could bypass Arianna's defenses.

And she was right. Arianna swung at the girl in turn, but the tiny Abyssal ducked her blow easily. That ebon dagger flickered toward her again, and Arianna spun backward, arcing to one side to avoid the deadly blade. But not fast enough, as the tip caught her forearm and another thin red line creased her gleaming metal hide.

Arianna tried taking the attack to her diminutive opponent, kicking out against the nearby wall with one leg and using the momentum to propel her in a backward flip over the girl, spinning as she moved and her claws slashed down across the girl's face. But the girl was no longer there—she had dropped down, one leg sliding out so that she fell into a low crouch, and her dagger had snaked up to slice a thin stripe of wood from one of Arianna's claws. She had not even realized, before that instant, that her hands could be harmed in that state, but the wound burned, and what looked like sap seeped out as she completed the turn and landed on her feet again, pivoting and barely turning a thrust from her shoulder so that it cut along her upper arm instead.

I can't match her here, Arianna realized as she swung one hand in a wide arc, hoping to back the girl away. Instead the Shoat ducked easily beneath the blow, and only by throwing herself backward did Arianna keep the girl from severing the hand on its return path as the dagger thrust perfectly upright, waiting for her body's own natural motion to slam flesh against the soulsteel. She let herself fall off the steps then, and turned the plummet into a spinning flip, then flung her other arm out as she dropped. Her claws caught in the wood of a tree branch, and Arianna swung around it, using the forward motion to leap up and land lightly atop the heavy bough. The girl was too small to easily hit, and too fast to target. On the ground, that petiteness was an advantage. Up here, Arianna's height meant she could cover more distance, bridge larger gaps between the branches, and hopefully she could use the tree itself as a shield.

But the girl, seeing her among the branches, simply laughed. For an instant she was again the tiny glittering dark light, and then she had flung herself forward, one hand wrapping itself around a thin branch and the other slashing across with the dagger even as she dropped to the branch below. Arianna danced back, the blade barely missing her foot, and dropped to her belly, the breath knocked out of her by the impact as her claws jabbed down to the girl's perch. But then she was sliding off the branch to one side, using one claw to slow her descent and swing her around, and leaping across that branch to the one beyond it as the Shoat sidestepped her attack and nicked her hand yet again.

For an instant Arianna was in mid-air above the Shoat, one arm extended toward the next branch, and the girl took advantage of the moment to lance upward, turning as she did so that her blade drove up at an angle, following her foe's flight. Arianna's free hand slammed down, knocking the dagger aside, though again she lost skin and blood as a result. But her right foot tapped the next branch, and she spun about, her other foot landing squarely on the thin bough as well. The Shoat had already launched herself, and though Arianna tried to carve her across the face and chest with quick intersecting slashes, the girl twisted aside, using her dagger to block the one hand and leaving nothing but her long streaming hair in the path of the other. Wisps of hair fell away, mingling with the shadows until Arianna could not distinguish them. Then the Shoat was standing on the same bough, and they struck out again, each hoping to make the other lose footing and fall to the hard stones below.

It was Arianna who dropped first, quitting that branch to the Shoat and deliberately stepping off into air to avoid a particularly lethal thrust. One hand snapped up to catch another branch, this one far too small to support her weight, and as she fell she pulled it with her, using its resistance to slow her descent. Then she was on one of the lower boughs, and released the upper branch so that it snapped back toward the approaching Shoat, the sudden onrush of wood and leaf distracting her just enough for Arianna's right claws to connect. She felt a brief spasm of hope as the blood welled up along the girl's shoulder, but that faded when she saw the look in the Shoat's eyes.

Up to this point, she realized, the girl had been toying with her. But now the Shoat was angry.

Belamis had been standing to one side, admiring the martial display. The two of them, the girl and the woman, both moved with unearthly grace, the one a malevolent raven-tressed sprite and the other a shining beauty with flowing white hair. It was a true dance of light and dark, light and death, as they swayed and leapt among the branches, and their speed and poise had held him motionless as he watched the ballet of steel and claws. But a reminder of his duties intruded, and he shook himself from his appreciative trance. He had just started forward again, raised hands clenched, when a bellow split the air, and a massive figure hurtled toward him, golden fire trailing behind it.

Gren had reached the chamber as soon as he could. It was as Arianna had described it, a wide open space with two steps around the edges and a great open roof. In some ways it reminded him of the chamber in his memories, but far grander—that had been a meditation space for one, this was built for many. The tree filled the center of the room, and its resemblance to the other trees they'd dealt with was obvious—or, rather, *their* resemblance to *it*, for despite their power and malevolence, he saw at once that those trees were mere copies of this one, lacking its full power. Off in one corner he spotted the pedestal, and could just make out the large book sitting atop it. Arianna was here, her anima fluttering about her, but she was weaving among the branches of the tree, ducking and dancing and spinning, and she was battling a tiny dark-haired girl with a flashing blade of some strange black metal. But Gren's attention was captured by the tall figure standing nearby. Belamis!

"Enough play." The Shoat's whisper was soft, but Arianna heard it nonetheless, and the glee and anger mixed up in those two words. What had she unleashed?

The Shoat jumped upward, sailing above the tree's highest branches. As she rose, her dagger lashed from side to side, severing leaves from their stems. The oily, red-laced leaves drifted down from their former homes, twirling as they fell point-first to create a shower of small, soot-like objects. So many were cut free at once that Arianna could not make out anything but the sudden deluge, and was forced to raise her hands to protect her face from the surprisingly sharp edges.

Exactly as the Shoat intended.

As she reached the top of her arc, the Shoat doubled over, hands thrust down past her feet. She began to fall again, gliding through the leaves like an arrow through mist, her dagger thrust before her. The leaves cascaded around her, hiding her from view, and her blade flitted between them, never nicking a single leaf, until its glittering tip crested the front of the wave—

—and lanced deep into Arianna's right shoulder.

With a wordless cry, Arianna toppled from her perch, twisting to avoid the Shoat's free hand, which shot out to crush her throat. Unable to connect with her grasping fingers, the Shoat tugged her dagger free again, a spurt of blood following as it exited the fresh wound. The two combatants fell from the tree, toward the hard stone below. Arianna managed to swivel about as she dropped, and landed on her feet, though the impact almost dropped her to her knees. The Shoat landed more lightly a few paces away, the last of the leaves drifting down beside her, and idly licked the blood from her dagger as she slowly, tauntingly closed the gap. Arianna crouched down to conserve her remaining energy and raised her claws before her, but she knew she did not have the strength left to block another blow.

Gren let his rage erupt in a wordless shout as he leapt through the door and over the steps, landing almost on top of his foe. His blade was moving before his feet were planted, right at the necromancer's head, and his anima floated along its length as it cut through the darkness, leaving clean air in its wake.

Belamis ducked the blow, backpedaling frantically, hands raised to shield his head from attack. At first Gren thought he was imagining things, but he looked harder and knew that he had seen aright. The shadows around the Abyssal were weakening against his light, except for right around Belamis' right hand, where the darkness was pooling instead. It swirled there, roiling with something similar to the black after-images left by lightning, and then that hand jabbed toward him, and a bolt of pure darkness crackled toward Gren's head.

But this time Gren was ready for it. He spun to one side, the bolt arcing harmlessly past him and striking the wall beyond, and his sword spun with him, its edge licking out to slice across the sorcerer's upraised hand. Belamis staggered back, face gone bone-white, as blood black as ink fountained from the gaping wound in his palm. He pressed the hand to his chest in shock.

"Hurt, did it?" Gren growled at him, closing the distance again. "That's nothing compared to what I'm going to do to you next, you filth! You killed all those people. You killed the Daggers. You killed my friends! I'm going to make you pay!" He raised his sword again, and he could see in the Abyssal's eyes what they both knew—that this blow would be the end of him.

"Gren!" The voice was Arianna's, but as he'd never heard it before. It was full of pain, but more than that, it held fear and desperation. Glancing over his shoulder, he saw that she had fallen from the tree and was half-crouched on the floor near the pedestal, the girl right beside her. One of Arianna's arms hung useless, drenched in blood, and she was bleeding from a dozen other wounds, including one across the chest and one across the stomach. The girl seemed unharmed save a row of minor scratches on one shoulder. Even as he watched, she sidestepped Arianna's claws and ducked past her, so that now she was standing at the pedestal. And then the hand with the dagger flickered forward, the blade sinking deep into Arianna's leg and crumpling her to one knee, and the girl's free hand darted out to touch the cover of the book.

Instantly the shadows thickened, springing forth from the book and flowing across the room like water. Arianna's anima flickered and vanished under the onslaught, and the tree stirred with renewed vigor, its branches straining against the walls and its leaves blocking the light that filtered through the ceiling. The girl herself was bathed in darkness, and the deep glow of it hurt his eyes, leaving a strange negative image when he blinked to clear them.

"Stop her!" Arianna cried, trying to stand again, her good hand scrabbling against the nearest wall for support. "Don't let her use the book!"

A movement behind him caught his eye, and Gren turned back to see Belamis raising his uninjured hand. A second dark bolt shot toward him, and Gren was too close to move aside—but the blow was not aimed for him. Instead it struck his sword, enveloping the blade in a corona of tainted energy, and before his eyes the gleaming steel corroded, splotches of rust appearing along its length and spreading rapidly, until the blade crumbled away to nothing.

Now it was Belamis's turn to sneer. "Not so tough without your sword, are you?" he taunted the warrior, stepping back to give himself more room. He had torn a strip from his robe and wrapped it around his damaged palm, and now he lifted that hand as well, and more dark lightning danced about it. "Your strength is impressive," he noted almost absently, his eyes glittering with malice. "Give it to me." And then he hurled the ball of energy forward. It exploded when it struck Gren's chest, showering him with jolts of force, and spread across him like water or oil, until he was trapped within pulsating, light-consuming bands. And as more and more of his body came in contact with the energy, he felt his strength being leached out of him.

Belamis wore a look of absolute, uncontrollable hunger, and suddenly Gren knew that his foe's last taunt had been serious. He was siphoning off Gren's strength, and meant to consume it to make himself stronger. Belamis was planning to sate himself on Gren's Essence. And that meant that, even after Gren himself had died, a part of him would live on, forced to do the necromancer's bidding.

"No!" Gren's blood boiled at the thought. Nothing of his would ever serve that fiend! He had to break free!

If only he had a blade!

As if in answer to his thoughts, a single stray beam of sunlight pierced the darkness and fell upon Gren's right hand. Or had the light sprung from between his fingers instead? All he knew for certain was that a shaft of golden radiance suddenly danced above his clenched fist, and as he watched and concentrated it slowly gained definition according to his will. His anima seemed to feed it, channeling strength into the beam before the dark bands could steal it away, and now the shaft extended some four feet above his thumb, and several inches below as well. Just above his hand the glow spread out, while at its very end it began to taper. And now Gren knew the shape.

It was a divine blade.

But not just any sword, for it was created from pure light—a gift from the Unconquered Sun—and the blade still blazed gold against the darkness. With a twist of his wrist he brought the edge in contact with the bands across his chest, and Gren felt the black lightning cringe from the sword's touch. Another ounce of pressure and the blade had severed the bindings as easily as a knife cutting a loose thread, and Gren was free again. His other hand moved forward to grasp the blade's handle as well, and it glowed even more brightly, driving Belamis back as it burned away the nearby shadows.

The Shoat had been stalking toward Arianna, intent upon finishing the wounded Solar, when the radiance appeared behind her. Squinting against the sudden, unwelcome light, she glanced back, and her eyes widened. She had seen the big Solar from outside attack the Sower, but had thought the necromancer could handle him. Evidently she had been wrong. The glowing sword in the warrior's hand was impressive, and she did not entirely blame the Sower for cowering as it approached him. The Shoat smiled. The woman could wait. The warrior was the immediate threat—and he looked like he might even be a worthy opponent.

Gren had not noticed the Shoat's pause. He was still intent on Belamis, and with the glorious solar saber in his hands, the necromancer was easy prey. He did not even try to defend himself; he merely shrank back, hands over his face, as Gren approached. At the sight of the creature who had killed his friends and so many others now whimpering like a caged beast, a growl rose deep in Gren's throat, and red rage threatened to cloud his sight. He raised his sword to cut down his foe—

—and then, as if the sun had burst upon him and shone its light deep within his mind, Gren's thoughts cleared.

He heard Arianna telling Iuro, "We want him powerless to harm another." And he remembered her telling him earlier, "We must take it away from him and destroy it, no matter the cost." And she had just warned him that everyone would die. The book was the key.

His rage vanished in an instant, and he felt calm again, calm as he had not felt since he had seen Rangol die. This was why he was here. This was why the Unconquered Sun had Chosen him, and prepared him, and warned him. He was not here to kill Belamis. That was simple revenge, and would only satisfy his rage. It would not remove the danger. No, he was here to rid Creation of that tome, the source of Belamis's power. He was here to stop this kingdom from sliding into shadow. Rage was not the answer. He was doing this, not to satisfy his anger, but because it was right. Because it was necessary.

His anima flared then, surrounding him with its glow. And it was no longer red at all, but a blinding golden white, so bright the necromancer staggered back as if struck. Both arms were still shielding his eyes, and Gren grabbed him by one wrist, his hand completely wrapping around the Abyssal's arm. And then he tensed, muscles bunching, and flung Belamis across the room, slamming him into the far corner, even as he leapt forward himself. And landed right beside the pedestal, and near this small girl with her very deadly book.

"Now we finish this," he told her, and the smile she gave him said that she felt the same.

CHAPTER TWENTY-FIVE

The Shoat smiled. The Solar woman's blood and fear were delicious, but she was not a fit opponent. The Sower was within reach and would not escape. She had the tome before her, and a mere touch of it had given her strength such as she had never possessed before. And now the Solar warrior was facing her across the pedestal, and she knew that this would be a worthy fight. His strength was phenomenal—he had tossed the Sower across the room as if he were a rag doll. And his blade was fearsome indeed. She would win, of course, but it would not be too easy. And that made it all the better.

"Come, then," she told her new adversary, lifting the tome and holding it against her left side. She would not allow it out of her grasp now that she had recovered it. At the same time, her right hand moved to place the dagger before her, and she imbued it with a rush of Essence, dark tendrils from her own aura wrapping around it and clinging along its length to form a pulsing nimbus that would lend it even more speed in the attack.

The Solar's only response was a tight grin and a sudden overhand blow. It was too strong for her to block directly, so she stabbed upward, the blade of her dagger catching the glowing sword on an angle and deflecting it to one side even as she twisted the other way. Then her blade lashed out, and he barely pulled back in time. The edge raked across his armor, leaving a deep furrow in the heavy metal, but did not penetrate it.

Damn but she's fast! Gren thought as he backed away from the blow. *And strong!* The book was as long as his arm, and almost as wide, but she held it as if it were a paper kite. And that glowing furious blade of hers moved like lightning. She'd actually parried his first stroke, something most grown men couldn't have done, and then come close to cutting through his armor on her return strike. He suspected the glow had added to the dagger somehow, and it left afterimages every time it moved, which stung his eyes and tugged at his concentration. This would not be easy.

He kicked the pedestal hard, sending the heavy stone falling toward her, and jabbed with his blade at the same time, creating barriers on two sides. She didn't try ducking past either of them. Instead she darted forward, pulsating dagger slicing again, and scored another hit, this time across his left forearm. Again the armor held, though only just. And he was the one who backed up, spinning to face her as she jumped over the fallen pedestal and wheeled around him. Her blade hand moved too fast to follow, looking for an opening, her point seeking a spot between the plates of his armor. She was moving so quickly her dagger seemed to flicker about him, leaving strange shadows and more afterimages in the darkness, and he was having a hard time locating the real blade among its shadows.

On her next attack she actually spun around in a circle, dagger weaving high and low as she moved like a maniacal top, and with each stroke her blade left a wisp of black mist behind it. The trails circled around her, confusing Gren's senses further, unfolding like some strange and deadly flower. The sight so distracted him that she almost scored a direct hit across his wrist, which might have severed his hand had the blow connected as intended. Fortunately, he backed up reflexively, and her dagger slid across his sword just above the guard, the two weapons shrieking against one another in what sounded like cries of outrage. Then her own momentum carried her back away, even as he jabbed toward her stomach, and somehow her dagger blocked it from both sides at once and almost drove the tip into the ground.

He knew already that she was faster than he was by far. And her size was an advantage here—she could move in close, too close for him to use his blade effectively, and strike before he could get out of the way. His size made him an easy target, while hers made her hard to hit. His armor had stopped her attacks so far, but it would not hold for long. And her lack of armor mattered not at all if he couldn't hit her.

Plus she had the book. Darkness was still spilling from between its covers, creating a plane of shadow like a tower shield along her left side, and he knew that no normal weapon could penetrate that. His sword probably could, but it was a gamble, and might slow his swing enough for her to punch through under his arm, where only cured leather protected him.

He realized he had to get the book away from her. It was the real threat here. Even if she escaped, the kingdom would be safe as long as the book was destroyed.

But how?

The Shoat watched him, waiting for her chance. The Solar was a powerful opponent, perhaps the greatest she had ever faced. His swings were mighty enough to split stone, but he never over-committed, and he was incredibly fast on his feet for a man his size. Several times he had dodged her blows, or at least enough that she had not cut through. That was impressive enough, given her natural speed and the charms she had enacted to aid her. His armor, though not fancy, was tough, and none of her strikes had drawn blood yet. And that glowing golden sword of his, if it hit her, could do serious damage. It, like him, was surprisingly agile for its size, and turned and blocked more quickly than most short swords could, let alone massive two-handed weapons.

Fortunately, her speed allowed her to stay out of his way. And the book was shielding her unarmed side. She noticed that the Solar stayed away from her left, never swinging toward it, and suddenly she knew she had the advantage. Her anima flared, its purple-tinged black cloud stronger than ever thanks to the book's presence, and formed into a roiling cloud above her head. This she hurled at her foe, and though his sword lashed out and cut through it, even that blade had no effect upon pure Essence. The cloud struck him about the head and shoulders, settling like a dark mantle and dowsing his glow in those areas, and she could tell the scouring erosion had weakened him. Now was the time to make her move.

Gren was surprised when the strange, swirling darkness gathered around him—he had not expected her to use magic like the Sower had. And when it touched him, he felt weak and slightly drowsy. Yet another spell to steal his strength! He threw his own will into his anima, and it blazed forth again, vaporizing the cloud. That was better! But while he had been distracted, the Shoat had moved closer, until now she was standing almost between his feet.

He threw off the cloud, as she'd known he would, but it had merely been a distraction. Spinning into him, the Shoat shoved the book at his chest, letting its darkness push him back for her and tangle his blade high. Then her dagger flashed forward, ebon lightning flickering around it. The darkness parted for it, and it moved cleanly through, finding the gap between the lacquered plates covering his chest and his stomach. She smiled, baring her teeth, as she felt the point enter flesh. At last!

Gren jerked back at the sudden pain in his lower chest, and slammed down with both arms. Her dagger was knocked aside, its tip red with his blood, and she danced back, kart wheeling to one side to avoid his sword as it arced toward the floor. Then she licked her blade and smiled at him, blood gleaming on her lower lip.

"Give me more," she whispered to him.

And he was afraid he might. She had used the book as a real shield, battering aside his attack and then stabbing under its edge. He'd been afraid of that. And now that she knew it would work, she would try it again and again, until she hit a vital spot or simply weakened him with so many cuts he could no longer swing his sword. He had to stop her before then.

But how? He'd never faced a foe like this one before. She was his equal in combat, and his better in speed and agility. His sword was made of sunlight, but hers seemed drawn from darkness, and strange black light danced along it when she struck. Blade to blade, he was not sure he could win, and that book tipped the balance. Its darkness gave her the edge.

Well then, he realized, straightening. *If it's darkness that's helping her, I'll turn to the light. Stop thinking of this as a soldier,* he thought, and his memories whispered their agreement. *You are more than just a fighter.*

You are a child of the Sun.

You are a Zenith

Let your light shine forth, and banish the darkness from your sight.

"Unconquered Sun!" Gren bellowed. "Hear your servant, your child! Grant me your light, that I might banish this evil from the land, and restore your presence to this world!" He lunged forward, his blade dancing about him as he spoke, blocking the Shoat's attacks and lashing out as if it had a mind of its own, and with each clash of soulsteel and golden sunlight, his anima grew brighter.

Arianna, in the act of moving toward the still-stunned Belamis, glanced over at her friend. She had never heard him speak like that, and it was more than just the words themselves, or the fact that he had called upon the Unconquered Sun deliberately. It was the majesty in his voice, the self-assurance. The quiet, dignified power.

And the Unconquered Sun answered his prayer. Gren's anima flared around him again, and then grew brighter and stronger. It dwarfed him now, and more than a mere glow it had a form of its own. She had half-expected a massive bull or a bear, something to match his strength, but what she saw instead took her breath away. It was a lion, its mane pure gold and its fur almost white-blond. It surrounded Gren, and its roar shook the room. The carnelian flame of his war banner danced triumphantly behind its right eye.

Gren shouted again, and the lion's roar echoed and amplified his words. The Shoat's dagger had danced toward him again and his sword had blocked it, but now he batted her smaller blade aside, and used the momentary respite to point his gleaming, glowing sword directly at the base of the tree beside them.

And, with a massive crack like thunder, the darkness above them split apart as streaks of fire fell from the sky.

They rained down upon the tree, balls of flame that struck it like missiles. The lesser tree in Anaka had withstood Gren's flame, but that was mere fire he had summoned forth. This was the Unconquered Sun's own blaze, and nothing could endure that. Where the blazing storm touched, the tree ignited, its leaves shriveling to ash and the unharvested fruits shattering like overripe melons tossed into a raging hearth. And, as the tree curled in upon itself, its bark fading from black to gray to bone-white, the ceiling was cleared. The clouds, already parted by the airborne attack, were washed away, and the sun shone down upon them fully, lending its light to Gren's own.

Belamis, still huddled where he had struck the wall, curled into a protective ball, his face toward the stone, both hands over his eyes. But the crystal flecks within the walls and floor caught the light and reflected it, transforming the room into a prism of colored light, and no matter which way he twisted, one ray or another still stabbed through his clenched lids and deep into his eyes.

The Shoat gasped as well, the darkness about her obliterated by the sudden onslaught. Even the tome's shadows could not withstand that light, and they were sucked back between its covers. Suddenly it felt ten times as heavy, and sagged against her, a dead weight instead of a shield, even as she squinted and tried to see her foe through the blinding glare.

That was what Gren had waited for. Her hand had lifted reflexively, trying to shield her eyes so that she could locate him, and the darkness was no longer protecting her. He stepped forward, sword raised before him, right hand high on the handle and left firmly below it, and feinted to her right. She saw the move, then, as her dagger thrust up to block, his left hand dropped from the handle and punched forward against it, kicking the blade back toward his forearm. His right wrist twisted, bring the blade to that side even further, and then he snapped his wrist forward and slashed hard from that side. Weakened as she was, and sluggish in the light, she could not reposition her dagger in time. He put all his force into the blow, and the glowing edge bit into her left side just below the shoulder. It sheared through her arm, the limb and the tome both falling to the floor, and powered through half her chest as well, finally stopping when it struck the breastbone. With a tug he pulled it free, and a fountain of black blood sprayed after it, but the blade itself was clean, the dark liquid vaporizing upon contact with its golden surface.

A quiet cry escaped the Shoat's lips before she could stop it, as her remaining hand dropped the dagger and groped desperately at her wound, trying in vain to stop the blood that poured forth. She knew the blow had finished her. Never had she seen such a sight, or felt such force! With her last energy, the Shoat bowed to the warrior, then raised her chin. "Strike clean," she whispered, and he nodded. His second blow was perfect and precise, and her eyes had glazed over even before her head had struck the wall and bounced back, rolling to stop just beside the tome itself.

The Sower saw his intended assassin's body collapse, but he barely noticed. He was still reeling from the destruction of the tree, his tree! The shadows had fled, and the warrior had the tome at his feet. The Sower knew that he had lost here. There was little more he could do, beyond escape back to his master. He rose, still squinting against the light, and edged toward the door—

—until a slender, white-haired figure sprang past him, rolled in mid-air, twisted as she straightened, and faced him, her feet now planted firmly on the stones just before the doorway. Arianna's one arm still hung useless at her side, but her other hand was raised, claws at the ready, and she had a grim smile on her lips.

"Going somewhere?" she inquired.

"Stand aside, witch!" the Sower snarled, summoning another Crypt Bolt and hurling it at her, right between her eyes. But she spun to one side, his attack hurtling harmlessly past her, and swept out and across with her claws. He felt the edges slice deep into his flesh, searing his throat—

—and then, for the second time, the darkness and the cold claimed the man who had been called Belamis. And this time, he knew, no voice would come to save him.

Gren heard sounds of struggle by the door, but he did not let that distract him. He had a task to complete. He leaned down and grasped the tome with his free hand, but his wound prevented him from lifting it, so he knelt down instead. The girl's head was next to the book, her sightless eyes staring as he rested his free hand palm-down upon its cover. Even now, with the full power of his anima behind him stripping away the shadows, he could feel the evil of the book. It writhed against him, trying to evade his touch, and he felt a faint hiss and a sizzle as his skin came in contact with it. The touch of the Unconquered Sun was anathema to this thing. And that told him what he had to do.

Allowing his golden sword to dissipate, unraveling into wisps of sunlight that were absorbed back into the surrounding Essence, Gren rested his other hand upon the book as well. He could feel his anima around him, and marveled at its form. Now he concentrated, willing its energy to focus upon this one spot, and the lion of light growled and crouched around him, opening its mouth to grasp the tome between its teeth.

"Unconquered Sun, hear your child!" Gren called, his words ringing through the chamber. "Grant me the strength to burn this abomination from your sight, to strike its evil from this world forever! Let your Unquenchable Conflagration destroy this foul artifact, and wash away its taint!"

Once before, he had summoned the flames deliberately. That had been an act of rage and sorrow, after Rangol's death. This was neither. He was calm now, and in control. He had accepted his fate. He was a Zenith Solar, the voice of the Unconquered Sun itself. And through him its will would be done. He directed that will now, calling forth its flames, and they rushed to do his bidding. His hands grew warm as the power pulsed through them, and a red-gold spark shot from his fingertips to the tome. When it landed on the book's thick cover, it burst into a small flame, which quickly spread until the entire tome was bathed in golden fire.

At first the book resisted, pitting its evil against the light. But it was far from its source, and the sun's rays had burned away its protective shadows and destroyed its defenders and allies. And Gren did not relent. Soon the book's cover had grown hot, and began to darken along the edges. Still he focused, the lion tightening its grip, and the flames grew in intensity, turning white-hot. Now the book was fully ablaze, shrieking as if it were a living thing. Its pages blackened, the ink burned away, and then finally it was consumed in a ball of fire so hot Gren was forced to back away. He watched as the last of the cover twisted and warped, then shriveled, and finally turned to ash. And then the light faded, and his anima with it, leaving the room seeming almost dark though the sunlight still poured down upon them.

"It is done." Arianna limped toward him, and rested her good hand upon his shoulder. Her claws faded, her hands returning to their normal appearance, and he reached up and took her hand in his, smiling through his sudden fatigue.

CHAPTER TWENTY-SIX

Several days later, Iuro asked Gren to meet him in the throne room. People were still cleaning the palace, but Gren found Iuro there, sitting a little uncomfortably upon the throne his cousin had once occupied. The people and the other nobles had unanimously chosen Iuro after the battle had ended. And it was a good choice. Though he'd spent only a week or so with him, Gren knew that Iuro was a good man, smart and considerate, and that he really cared about the kingdom and the people. He would make an excellent king. But he was still getting used to the idea.

"Ah, good," Iuro called out as Gren approached. "I have something for you, my friend." He gestured to Rydec, who grinned and stepped forward. He was carrying a breastplate similar to the one Iuro himself had worn during the battle, its bands of burnished, overlapping metal and wood glinting in the early light. "This is for you," Iuro said as Rydec handed the breastplate to Gren. "Ortense's new Guardian needs appropriate armor, after all." The new king grinned as Gren studied him, mouth open in shock.

"Guardian?" he finally managed.

"It's an ancient title from before the Hundred Kingdoms were in the disarray that defines them now," Iuro explained. "More than just a champion-at-arms, the Guardian protects the people from all dangers, physical and spiritual. I have heard it referred to as Warrior-Priest and the People's Defender as well." He leaned back in the throne, which had been rid of its grisly ornaments. "From what our histories imply, I think the position was once held by one of your kind. By an Exalted." He smiled. "I would like to make that a tradition here in Ortense. We need someone strong but supportive, who will listen to the people's needs, and help them in ways a king cannot." He watched Gren carefully as he spoke. "I would like that someone to be you."

"Me?" Gren tried to laugh off his embarrassment. "I'm just a sword for hire." But they both knew that wasn't true, and Iuro shook his head.

"If you don't want the job, say so," he said. "I certainly cannot force you to take it. But I've seen you with the people, Grendis Lam. I know you like it here. And they like you. So do I. You're a good man, and not just for your fighting skills. I think you would keep the peace, both because people would be afraid to cross you and because they'd know they could tell you the problem and you'd listen and sincerely try to help." Iuro leaned forward. "I'm offering you a real place here, Gren. I think you'd do well at it, and I think it would do well by you."

"I—I'll have to think it over," Gren told him. But he already knew what his answer would be. He'd never thought, before all this, that he might have a real home. He'd never thought beyond being in the Daggers. But now he had a chance to go on protecting people, and to help make Ortense a better place. And Iuro was right—he did like it here. And he felt that he could make a difference.

Besides, he was itching to try on that armor.

Arianna looked up as Gren walked into the inn the next morning. "Very official," she commented.

He grinned in response, and made a show of brushing imaginary dust from his new armor. "You like it?"

"Impressive," she admitted, and it was. He had told her about Iuro's offer, and asked her opinion.

"I think it's a great choice," Arianna had replied. "You fit in here, and the people love you."

And now he stood before her in his golden armor, with a handsome new sword at his side and his green cloak upon his shoulders, the hood thrown back. At his neck was a new clasp, a golden circle with the stylized red flame of the rebellion upon it.

"It's now the royal symbol," Gren said when he saw her glance. "It's sort of my badge of office."

"And what about that?" she asked, gesturing to the crimson dagger hanging at his side.

"My past," he replied. "I'm not going to forget who I was, or what I did. It's part of me, too. But it's not who I am now."

"No, it is not," she agreed, securing the last tie on her pack. She stood up, swinging the pack onto her shoulder, and winced slightly as it strained the muscles of that arm. Even after almost a week of rest and meditation, she was still a bit sore.

"You are a good man, Lam," she told him, stepping closer. "I am glad we had this chance to meet, and I value your friendship." It did not escape him that she had used his more personal name for the first time.

He grinned at her. "And I yours, Arianna. But you make it sound like this is farewell."

"You know I cannot stay," she told him. "You have found a place here, and I rejoice for you, but Ortense is not my home. I am moving on."

"I know," he said, still grinning. "Iuro told me. But I'm going with you." As she opened her mouth to protest, he held up one hand. "No, wait. I'm not leaving the kingdom. But you've got to travel through it to reach the border. I thought I'd accompany you—if you don't mind." The gleam in his eye said he knew her answer already.

"For such a small kingdom, the bridges and rivers are hopelessly muddled," she admitted, "and I could use a guide. But what about your new duties here?"

Gren's grin dimmed a bit as he turned serious. "I've decided that my first task is to check in on all of the villages and towns in the kingdom. I want to make sure there aren't any trees we missed—or bodies that need to be buried."

"It is not the Great Contagion, you know," she told him. "The sickness from the trees." He watched her, head tilted slightly, waiting for her to continue. "They may be distantly related," she added, "but this was not it. This illness was more specific, and more localized, and it was not contagious. The people died too quickly for anyone to spread it."

Gren nodded. He hadn't even realized that before, but she was right. No one who'd been stricken had lived more than a few minutes, let alone, long enough to infect anyone else.

"That girl," Arianna said, thinking back to the fight, "the Abyssal." They both shuddered slightly, remembering the malevolence and destructive glee wrapped in that deceptive little body. "She said something to Belamis about the set being complete again when the book was back with her mistress." They both tried not to think about that too carefully as she continued quickly, "Maybe that's the difference."

"What do you mean?"

"Belamis used this one book to create that tree," Arianna explained, "and its seeds created those other trees. But he had only one book of several, and couldn't read much of it. What if it takes all of the books together to unleash the Great Contagion?"

Gren nodded. "Then it'll never come back, because I destroyed the one he had."

"That's right." She smiled up at him. "That would mean you single-handedly stopped the worst plague ever known from returning. Not bad for a hired sword."

He grinned back at her. "I wouldn't say single-handedly. But thanks." Then he reached for her pack. "Why don't you let me carry that for a while? Does your arm still hurt?"

"Not really," she argued, but she let him take the pack from her, and couldn't stop the sigh of relief as the weight lifted off her shoulder. "All right, a bit."

As they stepped outside, Gren took a deep breath and let it out slowly. The sun was out, and it was a pleasant day. Children were playing, and several of them waved when they saw him. He waved back. A few of the nobles and a handful of craftsmen were over by the palace steps, discussing repairs and restoration, and they waved to him as well, though in a more dignified way. He nodded back politely. Yes, he belonged here. He wasn't Grendis Lam, sword for hire, anymore. Now he was Grendis Lam, Guardian of Ortense. He had a place, and a job that was about helping people instead of hurting them. And he had made a difference. He had rid the land of a great evil, as the Unconquered Sun had required, and righted a great wrong. And maybe he'd even protected the entire world in the process. That was funny, since most of the world would still call him Anathema—including its accepted, self-appointed defenders, the Dragon-Blooded.

Tilting his face up, Gren closed his eyes and let the sun's warmth wash across him. It felt like approval, something he'd never had before. Maybe he was still a monster to the Realm, but the thought didn't bother him. He had found his place in the world, and he knew who he was. And that was enough.

Then he turned and looked over at Arianna, who was watching him with a small smile. "Shall we?"

In response, she raised one hand to her mouth and whistled sharply. In the distance, they could hear the sound of hooves approaching.

EPILOGUE

Deep within his domain among the Spires of Pirron, the Walker in Darkness sighed. He had felt both the destruction of the Sower of Decay and Distrust and the weakening of the shadows that had gathered around him. The Sower was no more, and with him had faded the unexpected opportunity to build a bulwark against the domain of the Dowager of the Irreverent Vulgate in Unrent Veils.

Not that it mattered. He had tested the security of the Dowager's citadel, and found it lacking. His servants had penetrated her domain, infiltrated her citadel at the Mound of Forsaken Seeds, and even stolen from her an artifact of incalculable power. True, that had not been their actual mission—they had been instructed only to scout the defenses and report back—but the Sower had pursued a more aggressive course.

The loss of his servant disturbed him, however. The Sower of Decay and Distrust had been made only recently, but he had shown great initiative and a willingness to improvise, just as the Walker prided in himself. Yet now the Sower was gone, the fourth deathknight the Walker had lost in less than a year. And the *third* he had lost to Children of the Sun—the first being the Witness of Lingering Shadows in the city of Nexus, and the second being the Drinker of Seeping Poison in the city of Mishaka. Although the Exalted portions of their souls returned to him each time their undying forms were struck down, the Walker sorrowed at the loss of every faithful servant. He honored their memories and their sacrifice.

Now the Walker gazed out over the Spires, deep in thought. The Well of Udr contained powers that had not yet been tapped, and the tomes were the keys to it. The Dowager had not yet used those keys to their fullest, but that did not mean she had mastered their secrets. He would find some other way to station an outpost along her borders, the better to guard against her should she rediscover her ambition as a result of the Sower's needling. And, with the proximity his forthcoming (and appropriately disingenuous) display of humility at the "rashness" of his "overzealous" servant would win him, he would find an opportunity to suggest an alliance between them. His superior strategic and tactical mind, coupled with the power of the Well. Slowly he would learn its secrets, until he no longer needed the Dowager's aid.

He laughed, a sound that cut across the darkness and echoed even in the living world. For the moment, it drowned out his thoughts of those knights who had fallen in his service—and who still had yet to fall in the name of his everlasting glory.

About the Author

Aaron Rosenberg is originally from New Jersey and New York. He returned to New York City seven years ago, after stints in New Orleans and Kansas. He has taught college-level English and worked in corporate graphics and book publishing. For the last 10 years, the majority of his writing has been in roleplaying. In that time, Aaron has designed three games (*Asylum*, *Spookshow*, and *Chosen*), co-designed four more (including the original *HKAT!*), and done freelance writing for such companies as White Wolf, West End, Decipher, and Pinnacle. In 2002, he won an Origins Award for *Gamemastering Secrets, 2nd Edition*. He also writes educational books, because being a game writer isn't time-consuming enough, and he writes *Star Trek* books and fantasy novels when he wants to take a break. In his spare time, he runs his own game company (Clockworks, online at www.clockworksgames.com). He lives in New York with his wife, their two-year-old daughter, and their cat, unless they've moved out while he was chained to his desk again.

Acknowlegements

I'd like to thank Carl Bowen for a superb edit; Alex Kolker, Fred Herman, Paul Hudson, Lois Spangler, and Scott Campbell for their feedback on the initial ideas; my family and friends for ongoing moral support; and my wife and daughter, for their love and understanding.